"RACHEL GIBSON IS AN UP-AND-COMING STAR."
Karen Robards

"[GIBSON] AMUSES AT EVERY TURN."
Publishers Weekly (★Starred Review★)

"GIBSON IS FUNNY,
TOUCHING, STEAMY . . . PURRRFECT!"
Elizabeth Lowell

"I can't believe I slept with you," Clare moaned.

Sebastian chuckled. "Last night, you thanked me."

"Last night I was drunk. I never would have had sex with you if I hadn't been drunk. You took advantage of me."

"Is that what you think?"

"It's obvious."

"You didn't complain."

"I don't remember!"

"Now, that's a real shame. You told me I was the best sex you'd ever had in your life."

He smiled and dropped the towel.

By Rachel Gibson

RACHEL GIBSON

I'm In No Mood
For Love

AVON BOOKS
An Imprint of HarperCollins*Publishers*

This is a work of fiction. Names, characters, places, and incidents are products of the author's imagination or are used fictitiously and are not to be construed as real. Any resemblance to actual events, locales, organizations, or persons, living or dead, is entirely coincidental.

AVON BOOKS
An Imprint of HarperCollins*Publishers*
10 East 53rd Street
New York, New York 10022-5299

Copyright © 2006 by Rachel Gibson
Teaser excerpt copyright © 2007 by Rachel Gibson
ISBN-13: 978-0-06-077317-5
ISBN-10: 0-06-077317-0
www.avonromance.com

First Avon Books paperback printing: October 2006

Avon Trademark Reg. U.S. Pat. Off. and in Other Countries, Marca Registrada, Hecho en U.S.A.
HarperCollins® is a registered trademark of HarperCollins Publishers Inc.

Printed in the U.S.A.

10 9 8 7 6 5 4 3 2 1

*I would like to express my heartfelt thanks
to the romance readers who have
faithfully supported me
since the publication of my very first book.
This one is for all of you.*

Acknowledgments

I would like to express my gratitude to those who took the time to answer my questions when writing this book. Journalism teacher at Texas at Arlington and *Time* reporter, Adam Pitluk. Gerri Hershey, contributing editor to *Vanity Fair*, *GQ*, and the *New York Times Magazine*. And a huge thank you to Claudia Cross, at Sterling Lord Literistic, for going above and beyond the call and providing me with names and contacts.

One

The first time Clare Wingate found herself in a strange bed, she'd been twenty-one, the victim of a bad breakup and too many Jell-O shooters. The love of her life had dumped her for a blond art student with an impressive rack, and Clare had spent the night at Humpin' Hannah's, holding down the bar and nursing her broken heart.

The next morning she woke in a bed smelling of patchouli oil and staring up at a poster of Bob Marley, the guy snoring beside her drowning out the pounding in her head. She hadn't known either where she was or the snoring guy's name. She hadn't stuck around long enough to ask.

Instead, she'd grabbed her clothes and bolted. As she'd driven home in the cruel light of morning, she told herself there were worse things in life than random sexual encounters. Bad things like flunking out of college or getting caught in a burning building. Yeah, those were bad. Still, a one-night stand wasn't for her. It had left her feeling disgusted and disturbed. But by the time she reached her apartment, she'd chalked the whole thing up to a learning experience. Something a lot of young women did. Something to learn from, and something that was good to know for the future. Something she vowed would never happen again.

Clare had not been raised to reach for a shot glass and a warm body to make herself feel better. No, she'd been raised to curb her impulses and contain her feelings behind a perfect facade of warm smiles, kind words, and impeccable manners. Wingates did not drink too much, talk too loud, or wear white shoes before Memorial Day. Ever. They did not wear their hearts on the sleeves of their cashmere sweater sets, and they most certainly did not jump into bed with strangers.

Clare may have been raised on restraint, but she'd been born a romantic. In the pit of her soul she believed in love at first sight and instant attraction, and had a bad habit of leaping into relationships before she looked. She seemed destined to suffer repeated heartache, painful breakups, and the occasional drunken one nighter.

Fortunately, by her late twenties she'd learned to put into practice the restraint she'd been taught. For her reward, at the age of thirty-one, destiny blessed her and she met Lonny. The love of her life. The man she'd met at a Degas exhibit, and who swept her off her feet. He was beautiful and romantic and not in the least like the heartbreakers she'd dated in the past. He remembered birthdays and special occasions, and was brilliant when it came to floral arrangements. Clare's mother loved him because he knew how to use a tomato server. Clare loved him because he understood about her work and left her alone when she was under a deadline.

After a year of dating, Lonny moved into Clare's home, and they spent the next year in total sync. He loved her antique furniture, and they both loved pastels and had a passion for texture. They never fought or even argued. There was no emotional drama with Lonny, and when he asked her to marry him, she'd said yes.

Lonny really was the perfect man. Well . . . except for his low sex drive. Sometimes he didn't want sex for months at a time, but really, she told herself, not all men were horn dogs.

Or so she believed, right up to the moment she'd rushed home unexpectedly the day of her friend Lucy's wedding and found him *in flagrante delicto* with the Sears service technician. It had taken her several stunned moments to process what was happening on the floor of her walk-in closet. She'd stood there with her great-grandmother's pearls in hand, too shocked to move, while the man who'd fixed her Maytag the day before rode her fiancé like a cowboy. And none of it seemed quite real until Lonny glanced up and his shocked brown gaze met hers.

"I thought you were sick," she'd said stupidly, and then, without another word, gathered up the hem of her silk and tulle bridesmaid's dress and ran from the house. The drive to the church was a blur, and she'd been forced to spend the rest of the day in a pink puff of a dress, smiling like her life hadn't jumped the rails and sailed off a cliff.

While Lucy read her vows, Clare felt her heart break piece by piece. She'd stood at the front of the church, smiling as she fell apart inside until she was hollow and empty, except for the pain squeezing her chest. At the wedding reception, she pushed the corners of her mouth up and raised a glass to her friend's happiness. She felt it was her duty to make a suitable toast, and she did. She would rather have died than ruin Lucy's day with her own problems. She just had to remember not to get toasted. She told herself that one small glass of champagne wouldn't hurt. It wasn't like knocking back straight shots of whiskey, after all.

Too bad she listened to herself.

Before she opened her eyes the morning after Lucy's wedding, a feeling of déjà vu crept into her pounding head. It was a feeling she hadn't experienced in years. Clare peeked through scratchy eyelids at morning light falling through a wide crack in the heavy curtains and spilling onto the gold and brown quilt weighing her down. Panic tightened her throat, and she quickly sat up, the sound of her pulse beating in her ears. The quilt slid down her bare breasts and fell to her lap.

Within the lighter shadows of the room, her gaze took in the king-sized bed, a hotel desk, and wall lamps. In the armoire across from her, a Sunday morning news program was on television, the sound turned down so low she could hardly hear it. The pillow beside hers was empty, but the heavy silver wristwatch on the bedside table and the sound of running water behind the closed bathroom door told her she was not alone.

She pushed the quilt aside and practically jumped out of bed. To her dismay, she wore nothing from the day before but a spritz of Escada and a pink thong. She scooped up the pink bustier at her feet and glanced quickly about for her dress. It was thrown across a small couch along with a pair of faded Levi's.

No doubt about it, she'd done it again, and like those few times years before, she couldn't remember the important details after a certain point in the evening.

She remembered Lucy's wedding at St. John's Cathedral and the reception afterward at the Double Tree Hotel. She remembered running out of champagne before the first round of toasts, forcing her to refill her glass several times. She recalled trading in her champagne glass for an old-fashioned filled with gin and tonic.

After that things got a little sketchy. Through a boozy haze, she recalled dancing at the reception, and she had a vague mortifying memory of singing "Fat Bottomed Girls." Somewhere. She had flashes of her friends, Maddie and Adele, renting a room in the hotel for her so she could sleep it off before she had to go home and confront Lonny. The hotel mini bar. Sitting at the bar downstairs? Maybe. Then nothing.

Clare wrapped the bustier around her middle and endeavored to fasten the hooks between her breasts as she moved across the room toward the couch. Halfway, she tripped over one pink satin sandal. The only crystal clear memory in her head was that of Lonny and the repairman.

Her heart pinched but she didn't have time to dwell on the pain and utter astonishment of what she'd seen. She would deal with Lonny, but first she had to get out of that hotel room.

With the corset hooked partway between her breasts, she reached for her pink fluff of a brides-maid's dress. She threw it over her head and battled yards of tulle, twisting and turning, fighting and pushing, until she had it down around her waist. Out of breath, she shoved her arms through the spaghetti straps and reached behind her for the zip-per and little buttons on the back of the dress.

The water shut off and Clare's attention flew to the closed bathroom door. She grabbed her clutch purse off the couch and in a rustle of tulle and satin raced across the room. She held up the front of her dress with one hand and scooped up shoes with the other. There were worse things than waking up in a strange hotel room, she told herself. Once she got home, she'd think of something worse too.

"Leaving so soon, Claresta?" said a rough male voice only a few feet behind her.

Clare came to an abrupt halt against the closed door. No one called her Claresta but her mother. Her head whipped around and her purse and one shoe fell to the floor with a muffled thud. The strap of her dress slipped down her arm as her gaze landed on a white towel wrapped around the bottom row of hard six-pack abs. A drop of water slid down the dark blond line of hair on his tanned stomach, and Clare lifted her gaze to the defined chest muscles covered in tight brown skin and short wet curls. A second towel circled his neck, and she continued to look up past his throat and stubble-covered chin to a pair of lips pulled into a wicked smile. She swallowed, then glanced into deep green eyes surrounded by thick lashes. She knew those eyes.

He shoved one shoulder against the bathroom door frame and folded his arms across his broad chest. "Good morning."

His voice was different from the last time she'd heard it. Lower, changed from a boy to a man. She hadn't seen that smile in over twenty years, but she recognized that too. It was the same smile he'd worn as he'd talked her into playing War or Doctor or Dare. Each game had usually ended with her losing something. Her money. Her dignity. Her clothes. Sometimes all three.

Not that he'd had to do all that much talking. She'd always been a sucker for that smile, and for him. But she was no longer a lonely little girl, susceptible to smooth-talking boys with wicked smiles who blew into her life each summer and made her little heart melt. "Sebastian Vaughan."

His smile creased the corners of his eyes.

"You've grown since the last time I saw you naked."

With her hand clutching the front of her dress, she turned and pressed her back into the door. The cool wood touched her skin between the open zipper. She pushed a dark brown tangle of hair behind her ear and tried to smile. She had to dig down deep inside, into the part of her that had been pounded with good manners. Into the part that brought gifts to dinner parties and sent thank-you notes the second she got home. The part that had a kind word—if not thought—for everyone. "How are you?"

"Good."

"Fabulous." She licked her dry lips. "I suppose you're visiting your father?" Finally.

He pushed away from the door frame and reached for one end of the towel around his neck. "We covered that last night," he said, and dried the side of his head. As a boy, his hair had been blond like the sun. It was darker now.

Obviously they'd covered quite a few things she couldn't remember. Things she didn't even want to think about. "I heard about your mother. I'm sorry for your loss."

"We covered that too." He dropped his hand to his hip.

Oh. "What brings you to town?" The last

she'd heard of Sebastian, he'd been embedded with the marines in Iraq or Afghanistan or God knew where. The last time she'd seen him, he'd been eleven or twelve.

"Ditto." His brows lowered and he looked at her more closely. "You don't remember last night. Do you?"

She shrugged one bare shoulder.

"I knew you were shit-faced, but I didn't think you were so gone you wouldn't remember anything."

It was just like him to point that out. He obviously hadn't developed manners along with those abs. "I've never really quite understood that term, but I'm sure I wasn't 'shit-faced.' "

"You always were too literal. It means you were drunk off your ass. And yeah, you were."

Her smile slid into a frown that she didn't even try to stop. "I had reasons."

"You told me."

She hoped she hadn't mentioned everything.

"Turn around."

"What?"

He made a turning motion with one finger. "Turn around so I can zip your dress."

"Why?"

"Two reasons. If my father found out I'd let you run out of here with your dress half off, he'd kill me. And if we're going to have a conversation, I'd rather not stand here wondering if you're going to fall the rest of the way out of that thing."

She stared at him for several moments. Did she want him to help her out? It would probably be best if she didn't dash from the room with her dress open in the back. Then again, she really didn't want to stick around and converse with Sebastian Vaughan.

"In case you hadn't noticed, I'm only wearing a towel here. In about two seconds it's going to be real obvious I'm hoping I get to see you naked." He smiled, showing a perfect row of straight white teeth. "Again."

Her cheeks caught fire as she got his meaning, and in a rustle of satin and tulle, she turned and faced the door. It was on the tip of her tongue to ask him exactly what they'd done together the previous night, but she didn't want the details. She also wondered what she'd told him about Lonny, but she supposed she didn't want to know that either. "I guess I drank more than I intended."

"You were entitled to tie one on. Finding your fiancé on all fours like a bronc would drive anyone to drink." The tips of his fingers brushed her spine as he reached for the zipper. He chuckled and said, "I guess the Maytag man isn't the loneliest guy in town after all."

"It's not funny."

"Maybe not." He brushed her hair aside and slowly slid the zipper up her back. "But you really shouldn't take it so hard."

She pressed her forehead into the wooden door. This could not be happening.

"It's not like it's your fault, Clare," he added as if it were a comfort. "You just don't have the right equipment."

Yes, there were worse things than waking up in a hotel room with a stranger. One of those things was seeing the love of your life with a man. The other was zipping up her dress. She sniffed and bit her bottom lip to keep from crying.

He let go of her hair and fastened the two hooks at the top of the zipper. "You're not going to cry, are you?"

She shook her head. She did not show excessive emotion in public, or at least she tried not to. Later, after she'd confronted Lonny and was alone, she would fall apart. But, she figured, if she'd ever had an excuse to cry, this was it. She'd lost her fiancé and slept with Sebastian Vaughan. Barring a flesh-eating disease, she didn't think her life could get any worse than it was at that moment.

"I can't believe I slept with you," she moaned. If her head hadn't already been pounding, she would have beat her forehead against the door.

He dropped his hands to his sides. "There wasn't a whole lot of sleeping going on."

"I was drunk. I never would have had sex with you if I hadn't been drunk." She looked at him over her shoulder. "You took advantage of me."

His gaze narrowed. "Is that what you think?"

"It's obvious."

"You didn't complain." He shrugged and moved toward the couch.

"I don't remember!"

"Now, that's a real shame. You told me I was the best sex you'd ever had in your life." He smiled and dropped the towel. "You couldn't get enough."

He obviously hadn't outgrown the habit of dropping trow, and she kept her gaze pinned to the bird painting on the wall behind his head.

He turned his back on her and reached for his jeans. "At one point you were so loud I thought sure hotel security was going to beat down the door."

She'd never been loud during sex. Never. But she knew she wasn't in a position to argue. She could have been yelling like a porn star and wouldn't remember.

"I've been with some aggressive women . . ." He shook his head. "Who would have thought that little Claresta would grow up to be so wild in bed?"

She'd never been wild in bed. Sure, she wrote about hot, steamy sex, but she never actually lost control enough to have it. She'd tried a few times, but she was too inhibited to scream and moan and . . .

She lost the battle and her gaze slid down the smooth planes of his back and slight indent of his spine as he pulled his Levi's over his bare butt. "I've got to get out of here," she muttered, and bent to retrieve her purse from the floor.

"Do you need a ride home?" he asked with his head bent over his task.

Home. Her heart squeezed and her head pounded as she straightened. What she faced at home was an even bigger nightmare than the one standing across the room from her. The one with those rock-solid abs and a really nice butt. "No. Thanks. You've helped enough."

He turned and his hands paused over his buttoned fly. "Are you sure? We don't have to check out till noon." One corner of his mouth slid up and his wicked smile was back. "Wanna create some memories you *won't* forget?"

Clare opened the door behind her. "Not a chance," she said, and walked out of the room. She'd made it about ten feet before he called after her.

"Hey, Cinderella."

She glanced over her shoulder as he picked up her pink sandal and tossed it to her. "Don't forget your slipper."

She caught the shoe in one hand and hurried down the hall without looking back. She raced down the stairs and rushed through the lobby, afraid she might run into out-of-town wedding guests staying at the hotel. How could she possibly explain her appearance to Lucy's great-aunt and uncle from Wichita?

The hotel doors whooshed open, and with the cruel morning sun stabbing her eyes, Clare walked barefoot across the parking lot and thanked God her Lexus LS was exactly where she recalled leaving it the day before. She gathered up her dress, shoved herself into the car, and fired it up. Popping it into reverse, she caught a glimpse of her face in the rearview mirror and gasped at the sight of black mascara under bloodshot eyes, wild hair, and pale skin. She looked like death. Like road kill. And Sebastian had looked like he belonged on a billboard selling Levi's.

As Clare backed out of the parking space, she reached into the console for her sunglasses. If she laid eyes on Sebastian again in this lifetime, she thought, it would be too soon. She supposed his offer to take her home had been nice enough, but then in typical Sebastian style, he'd ruined it by offering to create unforgettable memories. Putting the car into drive, she covered her eyes with her gold Versace's.

She supposed he was staying with his father, just as he had as a boy when his mother used to send him to Idaho from Seattle for the summer. Since she didn't plan to visit her own mother any-time soon, she knew there wasn't a risk she'd see Sebastian again.

She drove out of the parking lot and headed up Chinden Boulevard toward Americana.

Sebastian's father, Leonard Vaughan, had worked for her family for almost thirty years. For as long as Clare could remember, Leo had lived in the converted carriage house on her mother's estate on Warm Springs Avenue. The main house had been built in 1890 and was registered with the Idaho Historical Society. The carriage house sat at the back of the property, half hidden by old willow trees and flowering dogwood.

Clare couldn't recall if Sebastian's mother had ever lived in the carriage house with Leo, but she didn't think so. It seemed that Leo had always lived there alone, overseeing the house and grounds and playing chauffeur from time to time.

The traffic light strung across Americana connecting Ann Morrison and Katherine Albertson parks turned green as Clare blew through. She hadn't been to her mother's house in more than two months. Not since the morning Joyce Wingate had told a room full of her Junior League friends that Clare wrote romance novels, just to spite her. Clare had always known how her mother felt about her writing, but Joyce had always ignored her career, pretending instead that she wrote "women's fiction"—right up until the day Clare had been featured in the *Idaho Statesman* and the Wingates' dirty secret was out of the closet and splashed across the Life section. Clare Wingate, writing under the pen name Alicia Grey, graduate of Boise State University and Bennington, wrote historical romance novels. Not only did she write them, she was successful and didn't have any plans to stop.

Since the time Clare had been old enough to put words together, she'd made up stories. Stories about an imaginary dog named Chip or the witch she'd always believed lived in her neighbor's attic. It hadn't been long before Clare's naturally romantic nature and her love of writing melded and Chip found a poodle girlfriend, Suzie, and the witch in the neighbor's attic got married to a warlock that looked a lot like Billy Idol in his *White Wedding* video.

Four years ago her first historical romance novels had been published, and her mother had yet to recover from the shock and embarrassment. Until the *Statesman* article, Joyce had been able to pretend that Clare's career choice was a passing phase, and that once she got over her fascination with "trash," she'd write "real books."

Literature worthy of the Wingate library.

In the cup holder between the seats of her car, Clare's cell phone rang. She picked it up, saw it was her friend Maddie, and set it back down. She knew her friend was probably worried, but she didn't feel like talking. All three of her best friends were the very best women to have around, and she'd talk to them later, just not right now.

She didn't know how much Maddie knew about the prior evening, but Maddie wrote true crime and would probably put some kind of psychotic killer spin on it whatever it was. Adele was just as well-meaning. She wrote fantasy and had a tendency to cheer people up by relating bizarre stories from her personal life, and Clare didn't feel like being cheered up at the moment. Then there was Lucy, who had just gotten married. The rights to Lucy's latest mystery novel had recently been optioned by a major studio. And Clare knew that the last thing Lucy needed was to have her own problems steal an ounce of her happiness.

She turned onto Crescent Rim Drive and continued past houses that overlooked the parks and the city below. The closer she drove toward her home, which she'd shared with Lonny, the more her stomach twisted. As she pulled her car into the driveway of the light blue and white Victorian she'd lived in for five years, her eyes stung with the painful emotion she could no longer hold back.

Even though she knew it was over with Lonny, she loved him. For the second time that morning déjà vu tightened the back of her skull and settled in the top of her chest.

Once again she'd fallen in love with the wrong man.

Once again she'd given her heart to a man who could not love her as much as she loved him. And like those other times in the past, she'd turned to a stranger when it all fell apart. Although she supposed that technically Sebastian wasn't a stranger, it didn't matter. In fact, it made what she'd done worse.

Once again she'd turned self-destructive and ended up disgusted with herself.

TWO

Sebastian Vaughan pulled his white T-shirt over his head and tucked the bottom into his jeans. So much for doing a good deed, he thought as he picked up his BlackBerry from the couch. He glanced at the face and saw that he had seven e-mails and two missed calls. He slid it into the back pocket of his Levi's, figuring he'd get to those later.

He should have known better than to help Clare Wingate. The last time he'd helped her, he ended up royally screwed.

Sebastian moved to the nightstand, grabbed his Seiko, and looked down at the black face with its compass and mile marker dials and features. He had yet to set the stainless steel watch to reflect the time zone change, and he pulled out the crown. As he moved the hands forward one hour, he thought back to the last time he'd seen Clare. She must have been ten or so, and had followed him to a pond not far from the carriage house where his father lived. He'd had a net to catch frogs and tadpoles, and she stood on the bank beneath a huge cotton tree while he waded in and got busy.

"I know how babies are made," she'd announced, looking down at him through thick glasses magnifying her light blue eyes. As always, her dark hair had been pulled into tight braids at the back of her head. "The dad kisses the mom and a baby gets into her stomach."

He had already lived through two stepfathers, as well as his mother's boyfriends, and he knew exactly how babies got made. "Who told you that?"

"My mother."

"That's the stupidest thing I ever heard," he'd informed her, then proceeded to fill Clare in on what he knew. He told her in technical terms how the sperm and the egg got together in the woman's body.

Behind her glasses, Clare's big eyes had filled with horror. "That's not true!"

"Yeah. It is." Then he'd added his own observations. "Sex is loud and men and women do it a lot."

"No way!"

"Yes way. They do it all the time. Even when they don't want babies."

"Why?"

He'd shrugged and netted a few tadpoles. "I guess it must feel good."

"Gross!"

The year before, he'd thought it sounded pretty gross too. But since turning twelve the month before, he'd started to think differently about sex. More curious than disgusted.

He recalled that when Mrs. Wingate had found out about his sex talk with Clare, shit had hit the fan. He'd been packed up and sent back to Washington early. His mother was so angered by his treatment, she refused to send him to Idaho anymore. From then on, his father had been forced to visit him in whichever city they happened to be living. But things between his mother and father deteriorated into full-blown rancor, and there were years in his life when his father had been absent. Large holes where he hadn't seen Leo at all.

These days, if he had to characterize his relationship with the old man, he would have said it was mostly nonexistent. There had been a time in his life when he'd blamed Clare for that situation.

Sebastian snapped the watch on his wrist and looked around for his wallet. He saw it on the floor and bent to retrieve it. He should have left Clare on a bar stool last night, he told himself. She'd been sitting three stools down, and if he hadn't overheard her tell the bartender her name, he wouldn't have recognized her. As a kid, he'd always thought she looked like a cartoon, with big eyes and mouth. Last night she hadn't been wearing big thick glasses, but once he looked into those light blue eyes, seen those full lips and all that dark hair, he realized it was her. The light and dark coloring that had been contrary and a little freaky in a child, had turned her into a stunning woman. The lips that had been too full on a child now made him wonder what she'd learned to do with that mouth as an adult. She'd grown into a beautiful woman, but the second he'd recognized her, he should have left her all weepy and sad and some other sucker's problem. Screw it. He didn't need the headache.

"Just once, you try and do the right thing . . ." he muttered as he shoved his wallet into his back pocket. He'd walked her up to her hotel room to make sure she made it, and she invited him in. He'd stayed while she bawled some more, and when she passed out, he tucked her in bed. Like a freakin' saint, he thought. And then he'd made a tactical error.

It was around one-thirty in the morning, and as he'd pulled the sheet over Clare, he realized he'd knocked back a few too many Dos Equis and tequila chasers from her minibar. Instead of risking a night in a Boise jail, he decided he'd stick around and watch some tube while he sobered up. In the past, he had shared a cave with guerrilla leaders and an Abrams tank stuffed with Marines. He'd chased endless stories and been chased across the Arizona desert by pissed-off polygamists. He could handle one passed-out, fully clothed, smelling-like-gin, drunk girl. No problem. None at all.

He'd kicked off his shoes, propped up some pillows, and reached for the remote. These days, he hardly slept, and he'd been wide-awake when she got up and began to wrestle with her dress. Watching her was a hell of a lot more entertaining than the *Golden Girls* marathon on television, and he'd enjoyed the show as she stripped down to nothing but a pink thong and beige birth control patch. Who would have thought the girl with the thick glasses and terminally tight braids would have grown up to look so good in a stripper thong?

He moved across the room and sat on the couch. His shoes rested on the floor, and he shoved his feet inside without untying the laces. The last time he recalled looking at the clock, it had been five-fifteen. He must have fallen asleep somewhere during the *Golden Girls* fourth season and woken a few hours later with Clare's little bare ass against his button fly, her back pressed to his chest, and his hand on her bare breast like they were lovers.

He'd woken up painfully hard and ready to go. But had he violated her? Taken advantage of her? Hell, no! She had a great body and a mouth just made for sin, but he hadn't laid a hand on her. Well, except for her breast, but that wasn't his fault. He'd been asleep and having erotic dreams. But once he woke up, he hadn't touched her. Instead he'd jumped in the shower and let the cold water cool him down. And what did it get him? He was accused of having sex with her anyway. Oh, he could have screwed her every which way till Sunday. But he hadn't. He wasn't that kind of guy. He never had been; not even if the woman was begging for it. He preferred his women coherent, and it pissed him off that she accused him of taking advantage of her. He'd purposely let her think it too. He could have set her straight, but flat-out lied just to make her feel worse. And he didn't feel bad about it. Not even a little.

Sebastian stood and looked around the room one last time. He glanced at the big bed and the rumpled covers. Within the spill of sunlight, sparks of tiny blue and red color caught his eye. He moved to the bed and picked up a diamond stud earring from the center of Clare's pillow. At least two carats glistened from his palm, and for a moment he wondered if the diamond was real. Then he laughed without humor and slipped it into the small hip pocket of his Levi's. Of course it was real. Women like Clare Wingate did not wear cubic zirconias. Lord knew, he had dated enough rich women in his life to know they'd rather cut their throats than wear fakes.

He turned off the television, left the room, and walked out of the hotel. He didn't know how long he'd be in Boise. Hell, he hadn't even planned on visiting his father until the moment he started packing. One minute he was lining up his notes for a piece on homegrown terrorists he was working on for *Newsweek*, and the next he was on his feet and reaching for his suitcase.

His black Land Cruiser was parked next to the entrance, where he'd left it the previous night, and he climbed inside. He didn't know what was wrong with him. He'd never had a problem writing a story before. Not at this stage. Not when all his notes were in order and all he had to do was pound the damn thing out. But each time he tried, he ended up writing complete shit and hitting the delete key. For the first time ever, he was afraid he would miss his deadline.

A pair of black Ray-Bans sat on the dash, and he reached for them. He was tired, that's all. He was thirty-five and so damn tired. He covered his eyes with the sunglasses and started the SUV. He'd been in Boise for two days, having driven straight through from Seattle. If he could just get enough sleep—a good solid eight hours ought to do it—but even as he told himself that was what he needed, he knew it was a crock. He'd functioned on a lot less sleep, and had always done his job. Be it in sand or rainstorms—once, in southern Iraq, both at the same time—and had managed to complete his work and make his deadline.

It wasn't even noon, and the temperature in Boise was already eighty-five as he drove from the parking lot. He turned on the air-conditioning and angled it to blow on his face. He'd had a complete physical last month. He was tested for everything from the flu to HIV. He was in perfect health. There was nothing wrong with him physically.

Nothing wrong with his head either. He loved his job. He'd worked his ass off to get where he was. Fought for every inch and was one of the most successful journalists in the country. There weren't many guys like him around. Men who'd made it to the top, not by pedigree or résumé or a degree from Columbia or Princeton, but by what was in them. Yeah, talent and a love of the business had played a part, but mostly he'd made it by grit and spit and the hundred-proof determination flowing through his veins. He'd been accused of being an arrogant prick, which he figured was pretty much the truth. What bothered his critics most, however, was that the truth didn't keep him up at night.

No, something else was keeping him up. Something that had hit him from left field. He'd been all over the world, continually amazed by what he'd seen. He had reported on such diversities as prehistoric art in the caves of eastern Borneo to raging wild fires in Colorado. He'd traveled the Silk Road and stood on the Great Wall. He'd been privileged to have met the ordinary and the extraordinary, and had loved every minute of it. When he took a moment to look at his life, he was amazed all over again.

Yeah, he'd experienced some bad shit too. He'd been embedded with the First Battalion Fifth Marine Regiment as they'd pushed three hundred miles into Iraq and all the way into Baghdad. He'd been at the point of the spear and knew the sounds of men fighting and dying right in front of him. He knew the taste of fear and cordite in his mouth.

He knew the smell of famine and abuse, seen the flames of fanaticism burning from eyes of suicide bombers and the hopes of brave men and women determined to stand up for themselves and their families. Desperate people looking at him as if he could save them, but the only thing he could do for them was to tell their story. To report it and bring it to the attention of the world. But it wasn't enough. It was never enough. When it got right down to it, the world didn't give a damn unless it happened in their backyards.

Two years before 9/11 he'd done a piece on the Taliban and the strict interpretation of Sharia under the direction of Mullah Muhammad Omar. He'd reported on the public executions and floggings of innocent civilians, while powerful nations—the champions of democracy—stood on the sidelines and did little. He'd written a book, *Fragmented: Twenty Years of War in Afghanistan*, about his experience and the inherent consequences of a world that looked the other way. The book had earned critical praise, but the sales had been modest.

All of that changed on a clear blue day in September when terrorists hijacked four commercial airliners, and suddenly people turned their attention to Afghanistan and light was shed on the atrocities committed by the Taliban in the name of Islam.

A year after his book's release, it hit number one on the best-seller lists, and he suddenly found himself the most popular boy in school. Every media outlet, from the *Boston Globe* to *Good Morning America* wanted an interview. He'd granted some, rejected most. He didn't care for the spotlight, or for politics or politicians either. He was a registered independent and tended to vote all across party lines. He cared most about shining a light on the truth and exposing it for the world to see. It was his job. He'd fought his way to the top—sometimes kicking and shoving—and he loved it.

Only it wasn't coming as easy these days. His insomnia was both physically and mentally draining. He could feel everything he'd worked so hard to accomplish slipping away. The fire inside dimming. The harder he fought, the dimmer the fire, and that scared him to his core.

The drive from the Double Tree that would have taken a native Boisean fifteen minutes took him an hour. He made a wrong turn and ended up driving around the foothills until he admitted defeat and plugged the coordinates into the SUV's navigation system. He disliked consulting the GPS and preferred to pretend he didn't need it. It felt pansy ass. Like stopping to ask for directions. He didn't even like to ask for directions in a foreign country. It was a cliché, but one he knew was true about him. Just like he hated to shop and hated to see women cry. He would do just about anything to avoid a woman's tears. Some things were clichéd, he thought, because they happened to be true more times than not.

It was around eleven A.M. when he turned up

the drive of the Wingate mansion and drove past the three-story home made mainly of limestone that had been quarried by convicts from the old penitentiary several miles up the road. He recalled the first time he'd seen the imposing structure. He'd been about five and thought sure a huge family must live within its dark stone walls. He'd been shocked to hear that just two people lived there: Mrs. Wingate and her daughter Claresta.

Sebastian continued around to the back and parked in front of the stone garage. Joyce Wingate and his father stood within the garden, pointing at rows of rosebushes. As always, his father wore a starched beige shirt, brown trousers, and a tan Panama hat covered his dark, graying hair. A clear memory of helping his father in that garden entered his head. Of getting dirty and killing spiders with a handheld spade. He'd absolutely loved it. Back then, he'd looked up to the old man as if he were a superhero. He'd been fungible, and absorbed every word, everything from mulch to fishing to how to fly a kite. But of course, that all stopped, and for years bitterness and disappointment had replaced hero worship.

After his high school graduation, his father had sent him a plane ticket to Boise. He hadn't used it. The first year he'd attended the University of Washington, his father wanted to visit him, but he'd said no. He didn't have the time for a father who hadn't had the time for him. By the time he graduated, the relationship between his father and mother had become so acrimonious, he'd asked Leo not to attend the ceremony.

After graduating, he'd been busy building his career. Much too busy to stop and take time out of his life for his father. He'd interned at the *Seattle Times*, worked for several years for the Associated Press, and written hundreds of freelance pieces.

Sebastian had always lived his adult life untethered. Free-wheeling. Roaming the world without attachments to hold him back or tie him down. He always felt superior to the poor suckers who had to take time out to call home on a satellite phone. His attention was never split in different directions. He'd been dogged and determined and extremely focused.

His mother had always encouraged him in everything he'd done. She'd been his biggest supporter and most vocal cheerleader. He hadn't seen her as much as he would have liked, but she'd always understood. Or at least had always said she did.

She had always been his family. His life was full. He and his father didn't even know each other, and he'd never felt any desire to see him, always thought that if at some point in the future he felt the urge to reconnect with his father—perhaps in

his late forties when it was time to slow down—
there would be time.

All that changed the day he put his mother in
the ground.

He'd been in Alabama, deep into research, when
he received the call that she was dead. Earlier that
afternoon, while trimming her clematis, she'd taken
a fall off a step stool. No fracture or cuts or scrapes.
Just a bruise on her leg. That night, she died alone
in her bed when an embolus traveled from her leg
to her heart. She'd been fifty-four.

He hadn't been there. Hadn't even known she'd
fallen. For the first time in his life he felt truly
alone. For years he'd roamed the world, thinking
himself free of strings. His mother's death had truly
cut him free, and for the first time he knew what it
was like to be untethered. He also knew he'd been
fooling himself. He hadn't traveled the world without strings. They'd been there. The whole time.
Keeping his life stable. Until now.

He had one living relative. Just one. A father he
hardly knew. Hell, they didn't know each other. It
was no one's fault, just the way things were. But
maybe it was time they changed that. Time to
spend a few days reconnecting with the old man.
He didn't think it would take long. He wasn't looking for a Hallmark moment. Just something easy
and free of the strain that existed between them.

He got out of the Land Cruiser and made his way across the thick green lawn to the flower garden rich with explosive color. Sebastian thought about the diamond stud in his pocket. He thought about giving it to Mrs. Wingate to return to Clare. He'd have to explain where he found it, and the thought brought a smile to his lips.

"Hello, Mrs. Wingate," he greeted the older woman as he approached. Growing up, he'd hated Joyce Wingate. He'd blamed her for his sporadic and unfulfilled relationship with his father. He had gotten over it about the same time he'd quit blaming Clare. Not that he harbored any love toward Joyce. He didn't have feelings one way or the other. Until that morning, he hadn't had any thoughts one way or the other about Clare either. Now he did, and they weren't nice thoughts.

"Hello, Sebastian," she said, and placed a red rose in a basket hanging from her bent arm. Several ruby and emerald rings slid on her bony fingers. She wore a pair of cream-colored pants, a lavender blouse, and a huge straw hat. Joyce had always been extremely thin. The kind of thin that came from being in control of everything in her life. Her sharp features dominated her large face, and her wide mouth was usually pinched with disapproval. At least it had been whenever he was around, and he had to wonder if it was her acerbic personality or her domineering ways that had always kept Mr. Wingate firmly planted on the East Coast.

Probably both.

Joyce had never been an attractive woman, not even when she was younger. But if someone shoved a gun in Sebastian's ear and forced him to say something kind, he could say her eyes were an interesting shade of light blue. Like the irises growing at the edge in her garden. Like her daughter's. The harsh features of the mother were smaller and much more feminine in the face of her daughter. Clare's full lips softened the lines of her mouth, and she'd inherited a smaller nose, but the eyes were the same.

"Your father tells me you plan to leave him soon," she said. "It's a shame you can't be persuaded to stay longer."

Sebastian looked from the rose in Joyce's basket up into her face. Into eyes that had shot blue flames at him as a kid. A huge bumblebee bumped along on a slight breeze, and Joyce waved it away. The only thing he saw in her eyes today was polite inquiry.

"I'm trying to talk him into staying at least through the coming week," his father said as he pulled a handkerchief from the back pocket of his pants and wiped beads of sweat from his brow. Leo Vaughan was a few inches shorter than Sebastian and his once brown hair was turning two-tone gray. The corners of his eyes had deep lines. His brows had gotten bushy in recent years and his "twenty minute naps" now seemed to last an hour. Leo would turn sixty-five at the end of the week, and Sebastian noticed that his father didn't get around the Wingate garden as easily as he remembered. Not that he remembered a lot about his father. A few months here and a weekend there didn't exactly make for copious childhood memories, but the one thing he did remember quite clearly was his father's hands. They'd been big and strong enough to snap small branches and boards, gentle enough to pat a boy's shoulder and rub his back. Dry and rough, the hands of a hardworking man. Now they were spotted with age and by his profession, the skin loose over his enlarged knuckles.

"I don't really know how long I'll stay," he said, unable to commit to anything. Instead, he changed the subject. "I ran into Clare last night."

Joyce bent to cut another rose. "Oh?"

"Where?" his father asked as he shoved the handkerchief back into his pocket.

"I met an old U.W. buddy at a bar in the Double Tree. He was there covering a Steelhead's fundraiser, and Clare said she'd been attending a wedding reception."

"Yes, her friend Lucy was married yesterday." Joyce nodded and her big hat dipped. "It won't be long before Claresta marries her young man, Lonny. They're very happy together. They have talked about having the wedding here in the garden next June. The flowers will be in bloom, and it will be just lovely that time of year."

"Yeah, I think she mentioned Lonny." Obviously, Joyce hadn't heard the latest news. An awkward silence passed between them, or perhaps it was only awkward on his end because he knew there would be no June wedding. "I didn't get the chance to ask Clare what she does for a living," he said to fill the silence.

Joyce turned to her roses. "She writes novels, but not like your book."

He didn't know which shocked him more: that Mrs. Wingate knew enough about him to know he'd written a book, though his wasn't a novel, or that Clare was a writer. "Really?" He would have thought she was a professional volunteer, like her mother. But he did have a vague memory of her telling him boring stories about an imaginary dog. "What's she write? Women's fiction?" he asked.

"Something like that," Joyce answered, and the old blue flames he recognized flared in her eyes. . . .

* * *

It wasn't until later when Sebastian and his father were alone at dinner that he asked, "So, what does Clare really do for a living?"

"She's writes novels."

"I got that. What kind of novels?"

Leo pushed a bowl of green beans in Sebastian's direction. "Romance novels."

His hand stilled as he reached for the bowl. Little Claresta? The girl who thought kissing made babies? The weird-looking little girl with the thick glasses who'd grown into a beautiful woman? The beautiful woman who wore a little pink thong and made it look good? A romance writer? "No shit?"

"Joyce isn't happy about it."

He picked up the bowl and started to laugh. No shit.

Three

"He told me it didn't mean anything," Clare said, and took a sip of coffee. "As if it was okay because he didn't love the Sears repairman. It was the same excuse my third boyfriend used when I found him with a stripper."

"Bastard!" Adele swore, and stirred almond-flavored creamer into her cup.

"Gay or straight," Maddie added to the conversation, "men are dogs."

"Worse of all, he took Cindy," Clare informed them, referring to the Yorkshire terrier she and Lonny had chosen together last year. While he'd packed his things, she'd taken a shower and changed out of her bridesmaid's dress. Some of the items in the house were solely his or things they'd purchased together. He could have all that; she didn't care for any reminders, but it hadn't occurred to her that he'd wait until she was in the shower to abscond with Cindy.

"At the risk of repeating Maddie," Lucy said as she leaned forward and poured herself more coffee, "bastard." Lucy had been married for less than twenty-four hours, but left her groom when she'd heard about Clare's heartache.

"Are you sure Quinn doesn't mind your being here?" Clare asked, referring to Lucy's husband. "I hate interrupting your honeymoon."

"I'm positive." She sat back and blew a cooling breath into her china cup. "I made him so extremely happy last night, he can't quit smiling." The corners of her lips curved up, and she added, "Besides, we don't leave for Grand Bahama until tomorrow morning."

Even though Clare had seen Lonny with her own eyes, she still couldn't believe it had happened. Raw emotion burned in her veins and she vacillated between anger and pain. She shook her head and choked back tears. "I'm still in shock."

Maddie leaned forward and set her cup and saucer on the marble and mahogany coffee table. "Honey, is it really a complete shock?"

"Of course it's a shock." Clare brushed moisture from her left cheek. "What do you mean?"

"I mean, we all thought he was gay."

Her fingers stopped and she looked at her friends sitting in her living room on her great-grandmother's sofa and armchair. "What? All of you?"

Their gazes slid away.

"For how long?"

"Since we first met him," Adele confessed into her coffee.

"And none of you told me?"

Lucy reached for the delicate silver tongs and added a sugar cube to her cup. "None of us wanted to be the one to tell you. We love you and didn't want to cause you pain."

Adele added, "And we kind of figured you must already know on some level."

"I didn't!"

"You never suspected?" Maddie asked. "He made tables out of glass shards."

Clare placed her free hand on the front of her white sleeveless blouse. "I thought he was creative."

"You told us yourself the two of you didn't have sex all that often."

"Some men have low sex drives."

"Not that low," all three friends said at the same time.

"He hangs out at the Balcony Club." Maddie frowned. "You knew that right?"

"Yes, but not all men who have a drink at the Balcony Club are gay."

"Who told you that?"

"Lonny."

The three friends didn't say a word. They didn't have to. Their raised brows spoke for them.

"He wore pink," Lucy pointed out.

"Men wear pink these days."

Adele scowled and shook her head. "Well, someone needs to tell them that they shouldn't."

"I wouldn't date a guy in pink." Maddie took a drink, then added, "I don't want a man that in touch with his feminine side."

"Quinn would never wear pink," Lucy pointed out, and before Clare could argue further, she dropped the irrefutable proof. "Lonny cares way too much about his cuticles."

That was true. He was obsessive about neat cuticles and perfectly trimmed nails. Clare's hand fell to the lap of her green peasant skirt. "I just thought he was a metrosexual."

Maddie shook her head. "Is there really such a thing as a metrosexual?"

"Or," Adele inquired, "is that just another term for men on the down-low?"

"Men on the what-low?"

"I saw it on *Oprah* last year. Men on the down-low are homosexual men who pass themselves off as straight."

"Why would anyone do that?"

"I imagine it's easier to fit into society. Or perhaps they want children. Who knows?" Adele shrugged. "I don't care about Lonny. I care about you, and you should have told us yesterday instead of holding it all inside."

"I didn't want to ruin Lucy's day."

"You wouldn't have ruined it," Lucy assured her with a shake of her head, her blond ponytail brushing the collar of her blue shirt. "I did wonder if something might be up when you all went missing for a while. Then when Adele and Maddie appeared again, you weren't with them."

"I drank a bit too much," Clare confessed, and was relieved when no one brought up her episode at the karaoke machine belting out "Fat Bottomed Girls" or any other embarrassing moments of the previous evening.

For a second she debated whether to tell her friends about Sebastian, but in the end she didn't. There were just some humiliating moments a girl should keep to herself. Getting drunk and slutty at her age was one of them. *You told me I was the best sex you'd ever had in your life,* he'd said, and laughed as he dropped his towel. *You couldn't get enough.* Yeah, some things were most definitely best taken to the grave.

"Men are so evil," she said, thinking of Sebastian's laughter. If there was one thing Clare hated, it was being laughed at; especially by a man. More specifically, by Sebastian Vaughan. "It's like they can see when we're at our lowest, our most vulnerable, then they circle and wait until just the right moment to take advantage of us."

"That's true. Serial killers can size up the most vulnerable in a matter of seconds," Maddie added, causing her friends to groan inwardly. Because Maddie wrote true crime novels, she interviewed sociopaths for a living and had written about some of the most violent crimes throughout history. As a result, she tended to have a warped view of mankind and hadn't dated in about four years. "It becomes second nature."

"Did I tell you about my date last week?" Adele asked in an effort to change the subject before Maddie got started. Adele wrote and published science fiction and tended to date very strange men. "He's a bartender at a little place in Hyde Park." She laughed. "Get this, he told me that he is William Wallace reincarnated."

"Uh-huh." Maddie took a drink of her coffee. "Why is it that everyone who has ever claimed to be reincarnated is the reincarnation of someone famous? It's always Joan of Arc or Christopher Columbus or Billy the Kid. It's never some peasant girl with rotted teeth or the sailor who cleaned Chris's chamberpot."

"Maybe only famous people get to be reincarnated," Lucy provided.

Maddie made a rude snorting sound. "More likely it's all crap."

Clare suspected the latter, and asked what she thought was the first of two pertinent questions. "Does this bartender look like Mel Gibson?"

Adele shook her head. "Afraid not."

Now the second question, which was more important than the first. "You don't believe him, do you?" Because sometimes she had to wonder if Adele believed what she wrote.

"Nah." Adele shook her head, and her mass of long blond curls brushed her back. "I questioned him and he knew nothing of John Blair."

"Who?"

"Wallace's friend and chaplain. I had to research William Wallace for the Scottish time travel I did last year. The bartender was just trying to trick me into bed."

"Dog."

"Jerk."

"Did it work?"

"No. I'm not that easily tricked these days."

Clare thought of Lonny. She wished she could say the same. "Why do men try and trick us?" Then she answered her own questions. "Because they're all liars and cheats." She looked at the faces of her friends and quickly added, "Oh, sorry, Lucy. All men except for Quinn."

"Hey," Lucy said, and held up one hand, "Quinn isn't quite perfect. And believe me, he wasn't anywhere near perfect when I first met him." She paused and a smile crept across her lips. "Well, except in the bedroom."

"All this time," Clare said with a shake of her head, "I thought Lonny had a really low libido, and he let me think it. I thought I wasn't attractive enough for him, and he let me think that too. How could I have fallen in love with him? There has to be something wrong with me."

"No, Clare," Adele assured her. "You're perfect just the way you are."

"Yes."

"It was him. Not you. And someday," added Lucy the newlywed, "you're going to find a great guy. Like one of those heroes you write about."

But even after hours of reassurance, Clare still couldn't quite believe that there wasn't something wrong with her. Something that made her choose men like Lonny who could never love her fully.

After her friends left, she walked through her

house and couldn't recall a time when she'd felt so alone. Lonny certainly hadn't been the only man in her life, but he had been the only man she'd moved into her home.

She walked into her bedroom and stopped in front of the dresser she'd shared with Lonny. She bit her bottom lip and crossed her arms over her heart. His things were gone, leaving half of the mahogany top bare. His cologne and personal grooming brushes. His photo of her and Cindy, and the shallow bowl he'd kept for Chap Stick and stray buttons. All gone.

Her vision blurred but she refused to cry, fearing that once she started, she would not stop. The house was so utterly quiet, the only sound that of the air-conditioning blowing from the vents. No sound of her little dog as she barked at the neighborhood cats or of her fiancé as he worked on his latest craft.

She opened a drawer that had kept his neatly folded trouser socks. The drawer was empty, and she took a few steps back and sat on the edge of the bed. Overhead, a lacy canopy cut shadowy patterns across her arms and the lap of her green skirt. In the past twenty-four hours she'd experienced every emotion. Hurt. Anger. Sorrow. Confusion and loss. Then panic and horror. At the moment she was numb and so tired she could probably sleep for the coming week. She'd like that. Sleep until the pain went away.

When she'd returned home that morning from the Double Tree, Lonny had been waiting for her. He'd begged her to forgive him.

"It was just that once," he said. "It won't happen again. We can't throw away what we have because I messed up. It didn't mean anything. It was just sex."

When it came to relationships, Clare had never understood the whole concept of meaningless sex. If a person wasn't involved with someone, that was different, but she didn't understand how a man could be in love with a woman and yet have sex with someone else. Oh, she understood desire and attraction. But she just couldn't comprehend how a person, gay or straight, could hurt the one they professed to love for sex that meant nothing.

"We can work through this. I swear it just happened that once," Lonny said, as if he repeated it enough, she'd believe him. "I love our life."

Yes, he loved their life. He just hadn't loved her. There had been a time in her life when she actually might have listened. It wouldn't have changed the outcome, but she would have thought she had to listen. When she might have tried to believe him, or think she needed to understand him, but not today. She was through being the queen of denial. Through investing so much of her life with men who couldn't thoroughly invest theirs.

"You lied to me, and you used me in order to live that lie," she'd told him. "I won't live your lie anymore."

When he realized he wasn't going to change her mind, he'd behaved like a typical man and got nasty. "If you'd been more adventurous, I wouldn't have had to look outside the relationship."

The more Clare thought about it, the more she was certain it had been the same excuse her third boyfriend had used when she'd caught him with the stripper. Instead of acting ashamed, he had invited her to join them.

Clare didn't think it was outrageous or selfish for her to want to be enough for the man she loved. No third parties. No whips and chains, and no scary devices.

No, Lonny wasn't the first man in her life to break her heart. He was just the latest. There had been her first love, Allen. Then Josh, a drummer in a bad band. There'd been Sam, a base jumper and extreme mountain biker, followed by Rod, the lawyer, and Zack the felon. Each subsequent boyfriend had been different from the last, but in the end, whether she broke it off or they had, none of the relationships ever lasted.

She wrote of love. Big, sweeping, larger-than-life

love stories. But she was such an utter failure when it came to love in her real life. How could she write about it? Know it and feel it, yet get it so wrong? Time and again?

What was wrong with her?

Were her friends right? Had she known on some subconscious level that Lonny was gay? Had she known even as she'd made excuses for him? Even as she'd accepted his excuse for his lack of sexual interest? Even as she'd blamed herself?

Clare looked into the mirror above the dresser, at the dark circles beneath her eyes. Hollow. Empty. Like Lonny's sock drawer. Like her life. Everything was gone. She'd lost so much in the past two days. Her fiancé and her dog. Her belief in soul mates and her mother's two carat diamond earring.

She'd noticed the missing earring shortly after arriving home that morning. It would take some doing, but she could find a matching diamond to replace the one she'd lost. Finding something to replace the emptiness wasn't going to be as easy.

Despite her exhaustion, an urge to run out and fill the void forced her to her feet. A mental list of all the things she needed flew through her head. She needed a winter coat. It was August, but if she didn't hurry, the wool coat she'd seen on bebe.com would be sold out. And she needed the new Coach bag she'd had her eye on at Macy's. In black to match the bebe coat. Or red . . . or both. Since she'd be at Macy's, she'd pick up some Estée Lauder mascara and Benefits Browzing for her brows. She was running low on both.

On the way to the mall she'd stop at Wendy's and order a biggie fry with extra powdered salt. She'd get a gooey cinnamon roll from Mrs. Powell's, then swing into See's for a pound of toffee and . . .

Clare sat back down on the bed and resisted her urge to fill the emptiness with things. Food. Clothes. Men. If she was truly through being the queen of denial, she had to look at her life and admit that stuffing her face, filling her closet, and reaching for a man had never helped fill the terrifying hole in her chest. Not in the long run, and in the end she was left with a few pounds that forced her into the gym, clothes that went out of style, and an empty sock drawer.

Perhaps she needed a psychiatrist. Someone objective to look inside her head and tell her what was wrong with her and how to fix her life.

Maybe all she needed was a long vacation. She most definitely needed a time out from junk food, credit cards, and men. She thought of Sebastian and the white towel wrapped around his hips. She needed a long break from anything with testosterone.

She was physically tired and emotionally bruised,

and if she were honest with herself, still a little hung over. She raised a hand to her aching head and took a vow to stay away from alcohol and men, at least until she figured out her life. Until she had a moment of clarity. The ta-da moment when everything made sense again.

Clare stood and wrapped her arms around the bedpost and the swag of Belgian lace. Her heart and pride were in shreds, but those were all things from which she would recover.

There was something else. Something she had to take care of first thing in the morning. Something potentially serious.

Something that scared her more than an uncertain future with no shopping sprees and salty fries. And that was no future at all.

Vashion Elliot, Duke of Rathstone, stood with his hands behind his back as he lowered his gaze from the blue feather in Miss Winters' bonnet to her serious green eyes.

Clare's fingers hovered over the keys as she glanced at the time displayed at the bottom right of her computer monitor.

Miss Winters was pretty enough, despite the stubborn tilt of her chin. Pretty he could do without. The last pretty female in his life had displayed an excess of passion, in and out of bed, that he would not soon forget. Of course, that female had been his former mistress. Not a buttoned-up, prim and proper governess.

"I was lately in the employment of Lord and Lady Pomfrey. Governess to their three sons."

Her pelisse swallowed her slight frame and she looked as if a strong wind might carry her off. He wondered if she were stronger than she appeared. As stubborn as her chin implied. If he decided to hire her, she'd have to be. The fact that she stood in his study showed a certain strength and determination of character that he usually found lacking in the opposite sex.

"Yes. Yes." He waved an impatient hand over her letters of recommendation before him on his desk. "Since you are here, I assume you read my advertisement."

"Yes."

He came around his desk and pulled at the cuffs of his brown frock coat. He knew that he was considered tall and unfashionably built from many long hours of physical labor spent both on his estates in Devon and on his ship, the Louisa. "Then you are aware that if an occasion arises that requires travel, I expect to take

my daughter with me." He wasn't certain, but
he thought he detected a spark in those serious
eyes looking back, as if the thought of travel
excited her.

"Yes, your grace."

Clare wrote several more pages before she paused in her writing of *The Dangerous Duke*, the third book in her governess series. At nine A.M. she reached for the telephone. She'd lain awake most of the night, dreading this call. The thing she dreaded most, more than packing up the few reminders of Lonny, was calling Dr. Linden's office.

She punched the seven numbers, and when the receptionist picked up, she said, "I need to make an appointment, please."

"Are you a patient of Dr. Linden?"

"Yes. My name is Clare Wingate."

"Do you need to see the doctor, or do you need an appointment with Dana, the nurse practitioner?"

She wasn't sure. She'd never done this before. She opened her mouth to just spit it out. To just say it. Her throat got dry and she swallowed. "I don't know."

"I see that you had your yearly exam in April. Do you suspect that you're pregnant?"

"No . . . no. I . . . I recently found something out. I caught my . . . well, I discovered my boyfriend . . . I mean my former boyfriend has been unfaithful." She took a deep breath and placed her free hand on her throat. Beneath her fingers her pulse pounded. This was crazy. Why was she having such a hard time? "So . . . I need to be tested for . . . you know. HIV." Nervous laugher escaped her dry throat. "I mean, I don't think it's likely, but I have to know for sure. He said he cheated just the one time and used protection, but can you really trust a cheater?" Good lord. She'd gone from stammering to rambling. "As soon as possible, please."

"Let me look." From the other end of the line several taps on a keyboard, and then, "We'll get you in as soon as possible. I have a cancellation with Dana on Thursday. Is four-thirty okay?"

Thursday. Three days. It was an eternity. "That's fine." Silence filled the line, and Clare forced herself to ask, "How long will it take?"

"The test? Not long. You'll have the results before you leave the office."

When she hung up the phone, she leaned back in her chair and stared straight ahead at her computer screen. She'd told the receptionist the truth. She really didn't believe Lonny had exposed her to anything, but she was an adult and had to know for sure one way or the other. Her fiancé had been unfaithful, and if she'd caught him in the closet with a woman, she would have made the call too. Cheating was cheating. And despite what Sebastian had said, the fact that she didn't have male "equipment" didn't make it easier.

Her forehead felt tight and she raised her hands and massaged her temples. It wasn't even ten A.M. and she had a massive headache. Her life was a mess and it was all Lonny's fault. She had to get tested for something that could take her life, and she wasn't the one who'd messed around. She was monogamous. Always. She didn't hop into bed with . . .

Sebastian.

Her hands fell to her lap. She had to tell Sebastian. The thought made her throbbing temples just about burst. She didn't know if they'd used a condom, and she had to tell him.

Or not. More than likely the test would be negative. She should wait to say anything until she found out the results herself. She probably wouldn't have to tell him at all. What were the chances he'd have sex with someone else between now and Thursday? A vison of him dropping his towel entered her head.

Very likely, she concluded, and reached for a bottle of aspirin she kept in her desk drawer.

Four

My recorder beside my yellow legal pad, I look across the table at the man I know only as Smith. Around me locals chat and laugh, but it all feels forced as they keep a watchful eye on me and Smith. If I didn't know better, if the language around me was peppered with Arabic and scented with cumin, I would think I was in Baghdad sitting across from a fanatic named Mohammed. The inner beast shines just as bright in deep brown eyes as blue. Both men . . .

Sebastian reread what he'd written and scrubbed his face with his hands. What he'd written wasn't so much *bad* as it wasn't *right*. He returned his hands to the keyboard of his laptop and with a few strokes deleted what he'd written.

He stood and sent the kitchen chair sliding across the hardwood floor. He didn't understand it. He had his notes, an outline in his head, and a good workable nut graf. All he had to do was sit down and write a decent lead. "Fuck!" Something that felt a lot like fear bit the back of his throat and chewed its way down to his stomach. "Fuck! Fuck! Fuck!"

"Is there a problem?"

He took a deep breath and let it out as he turned and looked at his father standing just inside the back doorway. "No. No problem." Not any that he'd admit out loud, anyway. He'd get the lead paragraph. He would. He'd just never faced this kind of problem before, but he'd work it out. He moved to the refrigerator, reached inside and pulled out a carton of orange juice. He would have preferred a beer, but it wasn't even noon. The day he started drinking in the morning was the day he knew he had to truly worry about himself.

He lifted the carton to his mouth and took several long swallows. The cool juice hit the back of his throat and washed away the taste of panic in his mouth. He raised his gaze from the end of the carton to a wooden duck resting on top of the refrigerator. The brass plate identified the duck as an American wigeon. A Carolina wood duck and northern pintail rested above the fireplace in the living room. There were various wooden birds about the house, and Sebastian wondered when the old man had become so fascinated with ducks. He lowered the juice and glanced at his father, who was watching him from beneath the brim of his hat. "Do you need help with anything?" Sebastian asked.

"If you have a moment, you could give me a hand moving something for Mrs. Wingate. But I hate to interrupt you when you're hard at work."

He would give his left nut to be hard at work instead of writing and deleting the lead paragraph over and over. He wiped the back of his hand across his mouth and returned the carton to the refrigerator. "What does she want moved?" he asked, and shut the door.

"A sideboard."

He didn't know what the hell a sideboard was, but it sounded heavy. Like something to take his mind off his looming deadline and his inability to string together three cohesive sentences.

He moved across the small kitchen and followed his father out the door. Old elm and oak trees shaded the grounds and white iron furniture in deep shadowy patches. Sebastian walked beside his father across the yard shoulder-to-shoulder.

A perfect picture of father and son, but the picture was far from perfect.

"It's going to be nice today," Sebastian said as they passed a silver Lexus parked next to Sebastian's Land Cruiser.

"The weatherman said in the low nineties," Leo replied.

Then they fell into an uncomfortable silence that seemed to blanket most attempts at conversation. Sebastian didn't know why he was having such a difficult time talking to the old man. He'd interviewed heads of state, mass killers as well as religious and military leaders, yet he couldn't think of one damn thing to say to his own father beyond making a perfunctory comment on the weather or having a superficial conversation about dinner. Obviously, his father found it just as difficult to talk to him.

Together they walked toward the back of the main house. For some reason Sebastian couldn't explain, he tucked the ends of his gray Molson T-shirt into his Levi's and finger-combed his hair. Looking up at all that limestone, he felt like he was heading into church, and suppressed the urge to cross himself. As if he felt it too, Leo reached for his hat and pulled it from his head.

The hinges on the back door squeaked as Leo held open the door, and the sound of their boot heels filled the silence as the two of them continued up a set of stone steps and into the kitchen. It was too late for them. His father was just as uncomfortable being around him as he was being around his father. He should just leave, he thought. Put them both out of their misery. He didn't know why he'd come, and it wasn't as if he didn't have anything else to do besides sit around and not communicate with his father. There was a lot waiting for him in Washington State. He had to get his mother's house ready to put on the market, and he had to get on with his life. He'd been here three days now. Enough time to open a dialogue. Only it wasn't happening. He'd help his father move the sideboard and then go pack his things.

A huge butcher's block dominated the middle of the kitchen, and Leo tossed his hat on the scarred top as he passed. White cabinets lined the walls from the floor to the twelve-foot ceiling, and late-morning sunlight spilled through the windows and shined off of stainless steel appliances. The heels of Sebastian's Gortex hiking boots thudded across the old black and white tiles as he and his father walked through the kitchen and headed into a formal dining room. A huge vase of fresh-cut flowers sat in the center of a twenty-foot table covered in red damask cloth. The furniture, the windows and drapes, all reminded him of something he'd see in a museum. Polished and well-tended. It smelled like a museum too. Cold and a little musty.

A thick area rug muffled their footsteps as he and his father made their way toward an ornately carved piece of furniture on one wall. It had long spindly legs and a few fancy drawers. "I take it this is a sideboard."

"Yes. It's French and very old. It's been in Mrs. Wingate's family for more than a hundred years," Leo said as he removed a big silver tea service from the sideboard and set it on the table.

Sebastian had figured it was an antique and was not at all surprised that it was French. He preferred clean modern lines and comfort over old and fussy. "Where are we moving it?"

Leo pointed to a wall next to the doorway, and each of them grabbed an end of the sideboard. The piece wasn't heavy, and the two of them moved it easily. As they set it down in its new place, Joyce Wingate's raised voice carried from the next room. "What did you do?"

"I didn't know what to do," a second voice Sebastian recognized answered. "I was in shock," Clare added. "And I just left the house and went to Lucy's wedding."

"This doesn't make any sense. How does a man just go gay? Out of the blue?"

Sebastian looked at his father, who moved to the tea service and got busy arranging the silver sugar bowl and creamer.

"A man doesn't 'go gay,' Mother. In hindsight, the signs were all there."

"What signs? I didn't see any signs."

"Looking back, he had an unnatural fondness for antique ramekins."

Ramekins? What the hell was a ramekin? Sebastian's gaze returned to the empty doorway. Unlike the old man, he wasn't going to pretend he wasn't eavesdropping. This was juicy stuff.

"Lots of men love a beautiful ramekin."

And these two women didn't know the guy was gay?

"Name one man who loves ramekins," Clare demanded.

"That chef on television. I don't recall his name." There was a pause, and Joyce asked, "You're sure it's over, then?"

"Yes."

"That's a shame. Lonny had such beautiful manners. I'll miss his tomato aspic."

"Mother, I found him with another man. Having sex. In my closet. For God's sake, screw the aspic!"

Leo carried the tea service to the sideboard and for a fraction his gaze met Sebastian's. For the first time since he'd arrived, he saw a spark of laughter in the older man's green eyes.

"Claresta, watch your language. There's no need to yell profanities. We can discuss this without yelling."

"Can we? You're acting as if I should have stayed with Lonny because he uses the right fork and chews with his mouth closed."

There was another pause, and then Joyce said, "Well, I *suppose* it was necessary to call off the wedding."

"You suppose? I knew you wouldn't understand, and I debated about whether to even tell you. I only decided to tell you since I figured you'd notice him missing when he didn't show up for Thanksgiving dinner." Clare's voice became more clear as she walked into the large open entryway. "I realize he was the perfect man for you mother, but he turned out not to be the perfect man for me."

Her hair was pulled back into one of those inside out ponytails, all sleek and polished like the mahogany sideboard. She wore a white suit with big lapels, a deep blue blouse, and a long string of pearls. The skirt hit her just above the knee, and she had on a pair of white shoes that covered the front of her feet. The heels of the shoes looked like silver balls. She was spit polished and buttoned up tighter than a nun. Quite a change from the last time he had seen her, with her back pressed against a motel room door, falling out of that silly pink dress, black smudges beneath her eyes, and hangover hair.

Just outside the dining room door she turned back to the room she'd exited. "I need a man who not only knows where his pickle fork is located, but wants to put it to use more than once on holidays."

There was a shocked gasp followed by, "That's vulgar. You sound like a floozy."

Clare placed a hand on her chest. "Me? A floozy? I've been living with a gay man. I haven't had sex in so long, I'm practically a virgin."

Sebastian laughed. He couldn't help it. The memory of her stripping off her clothes didn't quite square with the woman claiming to be "practically a virgin." Clare turned at the sound and her gaze met Sebastian's. For a few unguarded seconds confusion wrinkled the smooth skin between her brows, as if she'd discovered something where it wasn't supposed to be. Like the sideboard on the wrong wall or the gardener's son in the dining room. A faint pink blush spread across her cheeks and the wrinkle between her brow deepened. Then, as had happened the other morning when she'd turned around and seen him standing behind her wearing nothing but a hotel towel and a few drops of water, she recovered quickly and remembered her manners. She pulled at the cuffs of her jacket and entered the dining room.

"Hello, Sebastian. Isn't this a wonderful surprise?" Her voice was pleasant enough, but he didn't believe she meant a word of what she said. She pushed up the corners of her lush mouth, and he didn't believe she meant that either. Maybe because that perfect smile didn't quite reach her blue eyes. "Your father must be thrilled." She held out her hand and he took it. Her fingers were a little cold, but he could almost feel her palm sweat. "How long do you plan to be in town?" she asked, all polished politeness.

"I'm not sure," he answered, and looked into her eyes. He couldn't say how "thrilled" his father felt about his visit, but he could practically read Clare's mind. She was wondering if he was going to spill the beans about the other night. He smiled and let her worry.

She tugged her hand, and he wondered what she'd do if he tightened his grasp, if she'd lose her composure. Instead he released her and she held out her arms for his father. "Hello, Leo. It's been a while."

The older man stepped forward and hugged her; his old hands patted her back as if she were a child. As they had Sebastian when he'd been a child. "You shouldn't stay away so long," Leo said.

"Sometimes I need a break." Clare leaned back. "A long break."

"Your mother isn't that bad."

"Not to you." She took a few steps backward and her hands fell to her sides. "I suppose you couldn't help but overhear my conversation about Lonny." Her attention remained fixed on Leo, as if she had dismissed Sebastian. As if he wasn't in the same room, standing so close he could see tiny stray wisps at her hairline.

"Yes. I'm not sorry he's gone," Leo said, lowering his voice a fraction and giving her a knowing look. "I always suspected there was something a little light in the loafers about him."

If the old man had known that Clare's fiancé was gay, Sebastian wondered how it was that Clare hadn't figured it out.

"I'm not saying there's anything wrong with being . . . you know . . . funny that way, but if a man has a preference for . . . ahh . . . other men, he shouldn't pretend he likes the ladies." Leo placed a comforting hand on Clare's shoulder. "That's not right."

"You knew too, Leo?" She shook her head and continued to ignore Sebastian. "Why was it so obvious to everyone but me?"

"Because you wanted to believe him, and some men are tricky. You have a kind heart and gentle nature, and he took advantage of that. You have a lot to offer the right man. You're beautiful and successful, and someday you'll find someone worthy of you."

Sebastian hadn't heard the old man string that many consecutive sentences together since he'd been in town. At least not when he'd been within hearing distance.

"Ahh." Clare tilted her head to one side. "You are the sweetest man alive."

Leo beamed, and Sebastian had a sudden overwhelming desire to knock Clare off her pins, to pull her perfect ponytail or throw mud on her and mess her up like he did when she used to irritate him when they were kids. "I told your mother and my father that I ran into you the other night at the Double Tree," he said. "It was a real shame you had to leave and we didn't get to, ahh . . . chat a little more."

Clare finally turned her attention to Sebastian and, through the fake little smile curving her full pink lips, said, "Yes. Truly one of the biggest regrets of my life." She looked back at Leo and asked, "How's the latest carving?"

"It's almost done. You should come and see it."

Sebastian shoved his fingers into the front pockets of his jeans. She'd changed the subject and dismissed him again. He'd let her change the subject, for now. But he'd be damned if he let her pretend he wasn't in the room. He leaned his behind against the sideboard and asked, "What carving?"

"Leo carves the most fabulous wildlife."

Sebastian hadn't known that. Of course, he'd seen them around the carriage house, but he hadn't known his father carved them.

"Last year he entered one of his ducks in the Western Idaho Fair and won. What kind of duck was it, Leo?"

"A shoveler drake."

"It was beautiful." Clare's face lit up as if she'd carved it herself.

"What did you win?" Sebastian asked his father.

"Nothing." Color rose up Leo's neck above the collar of his beige shirt. "Just a blue ribbon, is all."

"A *huge* blue ribbon. You're too modest. The competition was stiff. *Veni vidi vici.*"

Sebastian watched the flush creep into his father's cheeks. "I came, I saw, I kicked some bird-carving ass?"

"Well," Leo said as he looked down at the carpet, "it wasn't anything like the important awards you win, but it was nice."

Sebastian had been unaware that his father knew about his journalistic awards. He didn't recall mentioning them the few times they'd spoken throughout the years, but he must have said something.

Joyce entered the dinning room wearing all black, like the angel of doom, and put an end to the discussion of ducks and awards. "Hmm," she said, and pointed to the sideboard. "Now that I see it, I'm not sure I like it there." She pushed a side of her short gray bob behind her ear with one hand and twisted the pearl necklace around her throat with the other. "Well, I'll have to think about it." She turned to the three people in front of her and placed her palms on her bony hips. "I'm glad we're all in the same room because I've an idea." She looked at her daughter. "In case you've forgotten, Leo turns sixty-five on Saturday, and next month marks his thirtieth year of employment with us. As you know, he is invaluable and practically a member of the family. In certain respects, much more than Mr. Wingate ever was."

"Mother," Clare warned.

Joyce held up one slim hand. "I had thought to put together something next month to mark both occasions, but I really think that since Sebastian is in town, we should put together a small gathering of Leo's friends this weekend."

"We?"

"This weekend?" Sebastian hadn't planned to stay through the weekend.

Joyce turned to Clare. "I know you'll want to help with the arrangements."

"Of course I'll help as much as I can. I work most days until four, but after that I'm free."

"Surely you can take a few days off."

Clare looked as if she might argue, but at the last moment she pasted one of her fake smiles on her face. "Not a problem. I'll be happy to do whatever I can."

"I don't know." Leo shook his head. "It sounds like a lot of trouble, and Sebastian doesn't know when he might be leavin'."

"I'm sure he can stay a few more days." Then the woman who'd once banished him from her land like a queen asked, "Can't you please stay?"

He opened his mouth to tell her no, but something else came out instead. "Why not?" he heard himself say.

Why not? There were several good reasons why not. First, he wasn't sure more time wouldn't make his relationship with his father less awkward. Second, his *Newsweek* article obviously wasn't going to get written at his father's kitchen table. Third, he had to deal with his mother's estate, although calling it an estate was a stretch. The fourth and fifth good reasons stood in front of him: one was clearly relieved by his decision, the other annoyed and still pretending he was invisible.

"Wonderful." Joyce brought her hands together and placed her fingers beneath her chin. "Since you're here, Clare, we can get started right now."

"Actually, Mother, I need to leave." She turned to Sebastian and asked, "Would you walk me out?"

Suddenly he wasn't invisible after all. He was sure Clare had something to say about the other night, some blank spots that she wanted him to fill in for her, and he debated whether to leave her hanging. In the end he was curious about what she might ask. "Sure." He pushed away from the sideboard and pulled his hands from his pockets. He followed her from the dining room, the silver heels of her shoes making tiny *tap tap* sounds across the kitchen tile.

Sebastian walked down the stairs first and opened the back door for her. His gaze moved from the blue of her eyes to her slicked-back hair. As a kid her hair had always looked painful. As a woman it looked like dark silk that needed to be messed up. "You look different," he said.

The sleeve of her suit brushed the front of his T-shirt as she passed. "I wasn't exactly at my best Saturday night."

He chuckled and shut the door behind them. "I meant, you look different from when you were a kid. You used to wear thick glasses."

"Oh. I had Lasik surgery about eight years ago."

She looked down at her feet as they walked beneath an old oak tree toward the garage. A breeze played with the leaves above their head, and shadows fluttered in her hair and across the side of her face. "How much of the conversation with my mother did you overhear?" she asked as they stepped from the lawn and onto the stone driveway.

"Enough to know that your mother didn't take the news about Lonny very well."

"Actually, Lonny is the perfect man for my mother." They stopped by the back bumper of her Lexus. "Someone to arrange the flowers, who won't bother her in the bedroom."

"Sounds like an employee." Like my father, he thought.

She placed a hand on the car and looked at the back of the house. "I'm sure you've guessed why I asked you to walk out here with me. We need to talk about what happened the other night." She shook her head and opened her mouth to say more but nothing came out. She lifted her hand from the back of the Lexus, then set it back down again. "I'm not sure where to begin."

He could help her out. Clear things up real fast and tell her they hadn't slept together, but it wasn't his job to make her life easier. One thing he'd learned from his years as a journalist was to just sit tight and listen. He leaned his hip into the car, crossed his arms over his chest, and waited. Several thin strips of sunlight picked out deep auburn strands in her brown hair, and the only reason he could think why he even noticed was because he was trained to notice small details. It was his job.

"I'm guessing we met in the bar at the Double Tree," she began again.

"That's right. You were throwing back Jägermeister with some guy wearing a backward ball cap and a wife beater." Which was the truth. Then he broke his just-sit-back-and-listen rule and added a little lie for fun. "He had a nose ring and was missing a few teeth."

"Oh God." She pulled her fingers into a fist. "I'm not sure I want to know every detail. I mean, I probably should—up to a point anyway. It's just that . . ." She paused and swallowed hard. Sebastian's gaze slid from her mouth, down her throat, to the top button of her blouse. She was wound tight, but there was another side of her. One he'd seen the other night. One that didn't pull her hair back and string pearls around her neck before noon. He wondered if she was wearing that pink bustier beneath her bland suit. It had been dark in the hotel room, and he hadn't gotten a real good look at it before she'd whipped it off.

"I'm usually not the sort of woman to drink myself into oblivion or invite men to my hotel room. You probably don't believe that, and I don't blame you. I . . . had a really bad day, which you already know about," she rambled.

As Sebastian listened, he let his mind drift, and he wondered if she had a thong on beneath that virginal suit. Like the one she'd worn the other night. That thong had rocked. He wouldn't mind seeing that thong again. Not that he liked Clare much. He didn't, but not every woman could wear a thong and look that good in it. He'd traveled the world and seen his share of thong-clad women. It took a woman with a firm butt and just the right junk in her trunk to pull off a thong.

". . . condom."

Whoa. "What?" He looked back into her face. Her cheeks were turning a bright shade of red. "Come again?"

"I need to know if you used a condom the other night. I don't know if you were as inebriated as I was, but I hope you remembered. I realize that it was my responsibility . . . as much as yours, of course. But since I wasn't planning to . . . to . . . I didn't have any with me. So, I'm hoping you did and that . . . well, you were responsible and used it. Because in this day and age there are serious consequences from having unprotected sex."

She'd accused him of taking advantage of her when she'd been drunk. Pretended he didn't exist, and now it sounded like she was getting ready to accuse him of giving her something really unpleasant.

"I have an appointment with my doctor at the end of the week, and if we didn't use a condom, I think you would be wise to do the same. I thought I was in a committed relationship, but . . . You know what they say, it's not only the person you're sleeping with, but everyone they've ever slept with too." She gave a nervous little laugh and blinked her eyes a few times as if she were fighting back tears. "So . . ."

Sebastian looked at her standing there, with the shadows playing in her dark hair and touching one corner of her mouth.

He remembered the little girl with huge glasses who'd followed him around as a kid, and just as he had all those years ago, he began to feel a little sorry for her.

Damn it.

Five

"**W**e didn't have sex."

"Excuse me?" Clare's eyes stung, as she battled the tears she refused to shed. She was mortified and embarrassed, but she would not cry in public, especially in front of Sebastian. She was made of sterner stuff. "What did you say?"

"We didn't have sex." He shrugged his big shoulders. "You were too drunk."

Clare looked at Sebastian for several long seconds, not quite trusting her ears. "We didn't? But you said we did."

"Not at first. You woke up naked and you assumed that we did. I just let you assume it."

"What?" They hadn't had sex and she'd just gone through the agony of the past few moments.

For nothing? "You did more than let me assume. You said we were really loud and you were afraid someone was going to call security."

"Yeah, maybe I embellished a little."

"A little?" The sting in the back of her eyes turned to shooting anger. "You said I couldn't get enough!"

"Well, you deserved it." He pointed to the Molson beer on his T-shirt and had the audacity to act offended. "I've never taken advantage of a drunk woman. Not even one who strips naked right in front of me, crawls into bed, then spoons me all night."

"Spoons? Spoons!" Had she done that? She didn't know. How could she know? He was probably lying about that too. He'd lied about the sex. She took a calming breath and tried to remember that she didn't yell in public. Scream or pummel lying bastards to death. *Be nice,* the little voice in her head warned. *Don't lower yourself to his level.* She'd been raised to be a nice girl and look where it got her. Nice girls didn't finish first. They just sat around choking on everything they were too nice to say. Stuffing it down, terrified that someday they would burst, and the world would see that they weren't nice after all. "I don't believe you."

"You were all over me like white on rice."

"You're clearly delusional." He was pushing her

like he had when they'd been kids, but she wasn't going to fall into old childish patterns with him. "But I don't have to believe your wild fantasies."

"You wanted freaky, down and dirty sex. But I didn't think it was right to take advantage of a shit-faced drunk."

She felt her head get tight. "I'm not a drunk."

He shrugged. "You were, but I didn't give you what you were begging me for."

Her tight head exploded. "You lying dickhead," she said, and didn't care if her outburst was immature, or the sign of an ignorant mind, or if she'd responded to his baiting. It felt good to take her anger out on him. He deserved it. Or rather, it did feel good until he gave her that wicked grin of his. The one she recognized. The one that reached his green eyes and robbed her of satisfaction.

He took a few steps forward until only an inch or so of thin air separated his chest from the lapels of her jacket. "You were pressed against me so tight, my button fly left an imprint on your bare butt."

"Grow up." She tipped her head back and looked up past his clean-shaven chin and mouth to his eyes. "Why would I believe you? You've admitted that you lied. We didn't have sex and—" She stopped and sucked in a breath. "Thank God." She felt as if a heavy load had suddenly been lifted from her heart. "Thank God I didn't actually sleep with you," she said through a huge gush of relief. She shook her head and began to laugh like a lunatic. She wasn't a big drunk slut after all. She hadn't reverted to her old self-destructive pattern. "You don't know what a relief that is. I didn't have loud, hot, sweaty sex with you." She raised a palm to her forehead. Finally, a little good news after the week from hell. "Whew!"

He folded his arms across his chest and stared down at her. A lock of his sandy blond hair fell over his tan forehead. "You walk around so uptight, I doubt you've ever had loud, hot, sweaty sex. You wouldn't know loud, hot, sweaty sex if it threw you down and climbed on top."

She could practically feel his testosterone-infused indignation. He was right, she hadn't ever had loud, hot, sweaty sex. But she would probably know if it climbed on her. "Sebastian, I write romance novels for a living." She reached into the pocket of her jacket.

"Yeah?"

She pulled out her keys. There was no way she would ever let him know he was right about her. "Where do you think I get my ideas for all the *loud*, hot, sweaty *sex* I put in my books?" It was one of the most frequently asked questions of romance authors, and one of the most absurd. It was called romantic *fiction* for a reason, but if she were given a dollar for each time she was asked where she got her ideas for the love scenes she wrote, she could supplement her income quite nicely. "It's all carefully researched. You're a journalist. You know about research. Right?"

Sebastian didn't answer, but his wicked smile flat-lined.

Clare opened her car door and Sebastian was forced to take a step back. "You don't think I just make all that stuff up, do you?" She smiled and climbed into her car. She didn't wait for an answer as she fired up the Lexus and closed the door. As she drove away, she looked in her rearview mirror at Sebastian standing exactly where she'd left him, looking stunned.

He'd never read a romance novel. Thought they were sappy. For chicks. Sebastian buried his fingers in the front pockets of his jeans and watched Clare's taillights disappear. How much sex did she put into those books she wrote? And how hot was it?

The back door to the house closed and drew his attention to his father walking toward him. Was that why Mrs. Wingate didn't like to talk about what Clare wrote for a living? Was it porn, and more importantly, did Clare really research something like that?

"I see Clare left," his father said as he approached. "Such a nice sweet girl."

Sebastian looked at his father and wondered if he was talking about the same Clare who'd just called him a lying dickhead. Or the Clare who'd been so relieved that she hadn't had sex with him, she'd looked like a death row inmate who'd suddenly found God. Like she just might fall to the ground and praise Jesus.

"I know that Joyce put you on the spot in there." Leo stopped in front of Sebastian and shoved his hat on his head. "I know you weren't planning to stay the weekend." He looked across the yard and added, "Don't feel like you have to stay now. I know you got important things to do."

None of which he felt *compelled* to do. "I can stay the weekend, Dad."

"Good." Leo nodded. "Good, then."

Squirrels chatted in the trees overhead, and Sebastian asked, "What are your plans for the day?"

"Well, after I change my clothes, I was thinking of driving to the Lincoln dealership."

"You need a new car?"

"Yeah, the Lincoln just turned fifty."

"You have a fifty-year-old Lincoln?"

"No." Leo shook his head. "No. The speed-ometer just turned fifty thousand miles. I get a new Town Car every fifty thousand miles."

Yeah? His Land Cruiser had more than seventy thousand, but he couldn't see himself turning it in. Fact was, he just wasn't all that materialistic. Except when it came to wristwatches. He loved a good watch with lots of gadgets on it. "Do you want company?" he heard himself ask. Spending time with the old man away from the carriage house could be just what the two of them needed. Maybe do some father-son bonding over some cars. He could help his father out. It could be good.

The squirrels continued to chatter into the silence. Then Leo answered, "Sure. If you've got the time. I heard your cell phone ringin' earlier and I thought you might be busy."

The call had concerned a piece for a major news magazine that he and the managing editor had discussed several months ago. Now he wasn't so sure he wanted to hop a plane and travel to Rajwara, India, and chase an epidemic of black fever. The conventional methods of treatment in that part of the world had bred drug-resistant parasites and no longer worked. The projected death toll was as high as 200,000 worldwide.

When he'd spoken to the editor about the piece, it had seemed important, exciting. It was still important, vitally so, but now he wasn't so hot to see the drawn, hopeless faces or hear the suffering from hut after hut as he walked dusty streets. He was losing the fire to tell the story, and he knew it.

"I don't have anything to do for a few hours," he said, and the two of them walked toward the carriage house. He could feel the burning desire for his job cool a bit, and it scared the hell out of him. If he wasn't a journalist, wasn't chasing stories and tracking leads, who the hell was he? "Where else do you want to look besides the Lincoln dealership?"

"Nowhere. I've always been a Lincoln man."

Sebastian thought back to his childhood and remembered the car his father had driven. "You had a Versailles. Two-toned brown with beige leather seats."

"Fawn," Leo corrected him as they passed a marble fountain with a cherub peeing into a clamshell. "The leather was fawn that year. The two-tone paint was fawn and butternut."

Sebastian laughed. Who would have guessed that his father was the Rain Man of Lincolns? The BlackBerry hooked to his belt rang, and he stayed outside to answer it while his father entered the carriage house to change. A producer from the History Channel wanted to know if he was willing to be interviewed for a documentary they were putting together on the history of Afghanistan. Sebastian didn't consider himself an expert on Afghan history. He was more of an observer, but he agreed to do the interview and it was set for next month.

A half hour after the call ended, he and his father were on their way to the Lithia Lincoln Mercury dealership to look at Town Cars. Leo had spiffed himself up in a navy blue suit and a tie with the Tasmanian devil on it. His gray hair was slicked back like he'd combed it with a pork chop.

"What's with the suit?" Sebastian asked as they drove up Fairview past Rocky's Drive Inn. As they passed, a car hop in a short skirt skated down a row of cars with a tray held above her head.

"Salesmen respect a guy in a suit and tie."

Sebastian turned his attention to his father. "Not a Looney Toons tie."

Leo glanced over at him, then returned his green gaze to the road. "What's wrong with my tie?"

"It has a cartoon character on it," he explained.

"So? This a great tie. Lots of guys wear ties like this."

"They shouldn't," Sebastian mumbled, and looked out the passenger side window. Just because he didn't like to shop didn't mean he didn't know how to dress.

They drove for a few more moments in silence as Sebastian took in the sites up and down the busy street. Nothing looked familiar. "Have I ever been out this way?" he asked.

"Sure," Leo answered as they sped past a woman walking a big black dog and a beagle. "That's where I went to school," he said, and pointed to an old elementary school with a bell on top. "And remember when I took you and Clare to the drive-in theater?"

"Oh, yeah." They'd had popcorn and orange Fanta. "We saw *Superman II*."

Leo moved into the middle lane. "They tore it all down and now it's where they sell Lincolns." He turned into Lithia Motors and drove slowly past rows of shiny cars designed to create avarice in the least materialistic. Near the middle of the lot, they parked and were soon approached by J. T. Wilson, who wore a polo shirt with the dealership's insignia above the left pocket.

"Which of the Town Cars are you interested in looking at?" J.T. asked as the three of them moved across the parking lot. "We have three models of Signature Town Car."

"I haven't made up my mind. I'd like to test-drive a few and compare," Leo answered.

Sebastian just couldn't see why a guy would get worked up over a Town Car, but as they walked past two rows of SUVs, he stopped as if his feet had suddenly got stuck to the asphalt. "Why not test-drive the Navigator?" He glanced inside at the plush interior and ran a hand along the shiny black paint. He could see himself in that car and had visions of driving down the road fiddling with the stereo.

"I like the Town Car."

"You could add a set of chrome rims," Sebastian persisted, experiencing unexpected car craving. Perhaps he was more like Leo than he thought. "Maybe some custom grill work."

"I'd feel ridiculous. Like that Puff Daddy."

"P. Diddy."

"Huh?"

"Never mind. You could haul in a Navigator."

Leo shook his head and kept walking. "I don't want to haul anything."

"Most of the Navigators have a tow package with a heavy-duty receiver hitch," J.T. informed them.

Sebastian didn't bother informing the men he'd meant haul *ass*. Reluctantly, they moved on, and together Sebastian and Leo took a gold Town Car for a test-drive. "Why do you turn in a perfectly good car every fifty thousand?" he asked as they drove out of the dealership.

"Depreciation and trade-in value," Leo answered. "And I just like a new car."

Sebastian didn't know anything about depreciation and wasn't picky about the miles on his car. "This thing sure is smooth," he said.

"Hauls ass too."

Sebastian looked at his father, and across the car they shared a smile. Finally, they agreed on something. The importance of hauling ass.

The two of them spent the next half hour tearing up the streets and enjoying moments of comfortable silence punctuated by easy conversation. They talked about the changes he'd noticed in Boise, although he'd been young the last time he visited. The population had exploded and brought a lot of growth, but one thing that remained just as he'd remembered was the state capitol building made of sandstone and patterned after the Capitol Building in Washington, D.C. As a kid, his dad had taken him to visit, and he could recall the marble interior and crawling around on the cannon somewhere on the grounds. Mostly he remembered how it looked at night. All lit up with the golden eagle shining on top of the dome, 208 feet above.

When they returned to the dealership, playtime was over and Leo got down to business.

"I don't know." He shook his head. "You're going to have to come down."

"I've given you my best deal."

"He has a trade-in," Sebastian provided, in an effort to help out the old man. "Right?"

Leo turned his head and looked at him. Ten

minutes later they pulled out of the lot in the old Town Car, on their way back to the carriage house.

"You never tell a salesman that you have a trade-in unless he asks. I just about had him dickered down to where I want him," Leo said as they left the dealership behind. "You might think you know a thing or two about what tie to wear, but you don't know anything about buying a car." He shook his head. "Now I'll have to cross that dealership off. I'll never get a good deal there."

So much for father-son bonding.

After dinner that night, Leo worked in the garden, then went to bed after the ten o'clock news. Sebastian apologized for ruining his potential deal, and Leo smiled and patted his shoulder on his way to bed.

"I'm sorry I got a little hot. I guess we're just not used to each other's ways. It'll take time yet."

Sebastian wondered if they'd ever get used to "each other's ways." He had his doubts. They were both spinning their wheels, fighting to find common ground. But it shouldn't have been so hard.

Alone in the kitchen, he moved to the refrigerator and pulled out a beer. His life was in his apartment on Mercer Place in Seattle. And it wasn't like he didn't have a shitload waiting for him there—he had his own problems to contend with, and he had to pack up his mother's house in Tacoma. She'd lived in that house for close to twenty years, and getting it ready to put on the market was going to be a real bitch.

His mother had been married and divorced three times by the time he turned ten. Each time, she'd been filled with the promise of happily ever after. Each time, she'd fully expected the marriage to last a lifetime. But every husband had lasted less than a year. The boyfriends in her life hadn't even stuck around that long. And every time another relationship failed to work out, she'd put Sebastian to bed and cry herself to sleep while he lay awake, hearing her sobbing through the thin walls. Her tears made him cry too. They hurt his chest and made him feel helpless and afraid.

By his sophomore year in high school, Sebastian and his mother had moved half a dozen times. His mother had been a "beauty consultant," meaning she cut and styled hair. Which made it easy for her to get a job wherever they happened to move, each time hoping for a "new start." Which also meant a new neighborhood, and Sebastian would have to make new friends all over again.

The summer he turned sixteen, they landed in the small house in North Tacoma. For some reason—perhaps his mother had grown up or grown weary of moving—she'd decided to stay put in that small house on Eleventh Street. She must have grown weary of men too. She'd stopped dating almost altogether, and instead of putting so much of her energy into relationships, spent time converting the front room of the house into Carol's Clip Joint—naming it after herself—and outfitting it with two styling stations, shampoo bowls, and drier chairs. Her best friend, Myrna, had always worked alongside his mother, cutting hair, giving perms, and sharing the latest.

At Carol's Clip Joint, tight curls and superhold had never gone out of fashion, and filled the house with the scent of alkaline, peroxide, and alcohol. Except on Sunday. The salon was closed on Sunday and his mother always made him a big breakfast. For a few hours, blueberry pancakes chased away the scent of perm solution, dyes, and hair spray.

That same year, Sebastian got a job washing dishes at a local restaurant, and after a short time he'd been promoted to night manager. He bought a '75 Datsun pickup. Faded orange with a crumpled rear fender. From that job, he'd learned the value of hard work and how to get what he wanted. He got his first real girlfriend that year too. Monica Diaz had been two years older than him. Two very wise years. And from her he'd learned the difference between good sex, great sex, and mind-altering sex.

Sebastian grabbed a beer and moved from the kitchen, his footfalls the only sound in the silent carriage house. His sophomore year in high school, he'd signed up for journalism because he'd registered late and all the other elective classes were full. He'd spent the next three years reporting on the local music scene for the school newspaper. His senior year, he'd been the editor of the paper, but quickly learned that assigning stories and editing wasn't much fun. He preferred the reporting side of journalism.

He raised the beer to his lips and picked up the television remote on a table resting by his father's recliner. With his thumb, he flipped from channel to channel. His chest suddenly felt tight and he tossed the remote on the table. How was he going to put his mother's life neatly into cardboard boxes?

Thinking about packing up her life made his chest cramp. If he were honest with himself, thinking about clearing out that house was one of the reasons he was here in Boise—one of the things that was keeping him up at night.

He moved to a built-in shelf next to the fireplace and reached for the first bound photo album in the row. He flipped it open. Newspaper articles and magazine clippings fell to the floor and covered his feet. A snapshot of Leo stared back at him from the first page of the album. Leo held a baby in a sagging cloth diaper in his arms. The photo was faded and creased through the middle, and Sebastian assumed it had been taken by his mother. He figured he'd been about six months old at the time, which meant the three of them would have been living in Homedale, a small town east of Boise, and his father would have been working in a dairy.

Like all children of divorce, Sebastian remembered asking his mother why they didn't live with his father.

"Because your daddy's lazy," she'd said. At the time, he hadn't understood what lazy had to do with them not living together like a family. Later in his life, he would learn that his father wasn't lazy, he just wasn't ambitious, and that an unexpected pregnancy had brought two totally different people together. Two people who never should have shook hands, let alone made a baby.

He flipped through the rest of the album filled with different snapshots and school photos. One of the pictures was of him holding a fish just about as big as he'd been at the time. His chest was puffed out and a huge grin showed a missing front tooth.

He bent down on one knee and reached for the clippings. His hand paused as he recognized them as some of his old articles. There was the piece he'd done on the death of Carlos Castaneda, and *Time* articles on the Jarvis heart valve and the murder of James Bird. Seeing all his articles was a shock. He hadn't known the old man had kept up on his career. He placed the articles back inside the album and stood.

As he slid it back into the first slot, a pair of brass bookends on the mantel caught his attention. Between the shiny gold ducks was a collection of eight paperbacks by author Alicia Grey. He reached for the first two books in the row and pulled them out. The first had a purple cover and featured a man and woman in period clothing. The woman's red gown was pushed from her shoulders and her breasts were about to pop out of her gown. The man was shirtless and wore tight black pants and boots. In raised gold the title read, *The Devil Pirate's Embrace*. The second book, *The Pirate's Captive*, featured a man standing on the bow of a ship with the wind billowing his white puffy shirt. He didn't have a cutlass, or a pegleg or a patch. Just a Jolly Roger and a woman with her back pressed into his chest. Sebastian replaced one of the books and opened the other. He chuckled as he fanned the pages to the back. Clare stared back at him from a black and white publicity photo.

"This night is just full of surprises," he uttered as he read her bio.

Alicia Gray is a graduate of Boise State University and Bennington, it began, then went on to list her achievements, including something called a RITA® award from Romance Writers of America. *Alicia loves to garden and is waiting for her very own hero to sweep her off her feet.*

"Good luck with that," Sebastian scoffed. A guy would have to be desperate to attempt anything with Clare. Despite his father's opinion of her, Clare Wingate was a ballbuster, and it was a wise man who kept any part of him away from her.

Where do you think I get my ideas for all the loud, hot, sweaty sex I put in my books? she'd asked when she decided not to ignore him. *It's all carefully researched.* A ballbuster with soft curves in all the right places, and a mouth that made a man think of oral sex. Which Sebastian figured was a shame and a total waste.

He flipped to the little teaser page in front and moved to his father's leather recliner. He pulled the switch on the lamp and read as he sat.

"Why are you here, sir?" he read.
   "You know why I've come, Julia. Kiss me," the

*pirate demanded. "Kiss me and let me taste the
sweetness of your lips."*

"Holy Christ," Sebastian swore, and turned to
Chapter One. This should put him right to sleep.

Six

Clare raised her hand and knocked on the red door of the carriage house. Through the dark lenses of her sunglasses, she glanced at her gold watch. It was a little after two in the afternoon, and the relentless sun heated her bare shoulders as she stood on the porch. The temperature hovered at ninety-five, but was bound to reach a hundred.

Earlier, she'd written five pages, walked for half an hour on the treadmill in her spare bedroom, and made a list of names for Leo's party. For the past few days she'd run herself ragged with planning, but it kept her too busy to think about her life. For which she was grateful, although she'd never admit it to her mother. After she ran the names by Leo, she had to pick up her dry cleaning and buy party decorations. Then she would cook dinner and wash dishes, which she calculated would keep her busy until six or seven. After that, maybe she'd write some more. Each time she thought of Lonny, she felt a little piece of her heart chip away. Perhaps if she kept herself very busy for the next few months, her broken heart would heal and spare her some of the pain.

She was still waiting for an epiphany. A light to be shed on her life and show her why she'd chosen Lonny. A ta-da moment to explain why she hadn't seen the truth of her relationship with him.

Clare adjusted the small purse on her shoulder. It hadn't happened yet.

The door swung open. Light spilled across the threshold and shined into the house. "Holy mother of God," Sebastian swore as he raised one arm to shield his gaze from the sun.

"Afraid not."

Beneath his bare arm, he squinted down at her through bloodshot eyes as if he didn't quite recognize her. He wore the same jeans and Molson T-shirt he'd worn the day before. He was wrinkled and his hair stood up in front. "Clare?" he finally said, his voice rough and sleepy, as if he'd just rolled out of bed.

"Bingo." Light brown stubble shadowed the lower half of his face, and the shadow from his arm rested across the seam of his lips. "Did I wake you?"

"I've been up for a few."

"Late night?"

"Yeah." He scrubbed his face with his hands. "What time is it?"

"About a quarter after two. Did you sleep in your clothes?"

"It wouldn't be the first time."

"Out carousing again?"

"Carousing?" He dropped his hands to his sides. "No. I was up all night reading."

It was on the tip of her tongue to tell him picture books weren't really considered reading, but she was going to be nice today if it killed her. Calling him a dickhead the other day had felt good. For a while. But by the time she'd pulled into her garage, the elation had worn thin and she'd felt undignified and gauche. The nice thing—the ladylike thing— would be to apologize. She'd kill herself first. "It must have been a good book."

"It was interesting." A ghost of a smile curved his mouth.

She didn't ask what kind of book he'd read. She didn't really care. "Is your father around?"

"I don't know." He stepped aside, and she walked past him into the house. He smelled like bed linen and warm skin, and he was such a big man, he seemed to dwarf the space around him. Or perhaps it just seemed that way because she was used to Lonny, who stood a few inches taller than her own medium height and was quite thin.

"I searched for him in my mother's house and he's not there." She pushed her sunglasses to the top of her head and looked at Sebastian as he closed the door. He leaned his back against it, folded his arms across his chest and stared at her feet. Slowly, he lifted his gaze from the toes of her red sandals and up her halter dress with the deep red cherries on it. His attention paused on her mouth before continuing to her eyes. He tilted his head to one side, studying her as if trying to figure something out.

"What?" she asked.

"Nothing." He pushed away from the door and moved by her into the kitchen. His feet were bare. "I just put on a pot of coffee. Want some?"

"No. By two, I've usually moved on to Diet Coke." She followed close behind, her gaze taking in his broad shoulders. The arms of his T-shirt fit snugly around the bulge of his biceps, and the ends of his sandy blond hair touched the ribbed collar at the base of his neck. There was no doubt about it. Sebastian was a man's man. A guy. While Lonny had been particular about his clothing, Sebastian slept in his.

"My dad doesn't drink Diet Coke."

"I know. He's an RC Cola man, and I hate RC."

Sebastian glanced back at her and moved around the old wooden table stacked with notebooks, legal pads, and index cards. A laptop lay open, and a small tape recorder and three cassettes sat next to a BlackBerry. "He's the only person I know who still drinks RC," he said as he opened a cupboard and reached for a mug on the top shelf. The bottom edge of his T-shirt pulled up past the waistband of his jeans, riding low on his hips. The elastic band of his underwear looked very white against the tan skin of his lower back.

The memory of his bare behind flashed across her brain, and she raised her gaze to the back of his sleep-tousled hair. That morning at the Double Tree, he hadn't been wearing underwear. "He's a very loyal consumer," she said. The memory of that morning made her want to sink into the floor and hide. She hadn't had sex with him. While that was a huge relief, she had to wonder what they'd actually done, and how she'd ended up virtually naked. If she thought he'd give her a straight answer, she would ask him to fill in the blank spots.

"More like stubborn," Sebastian corrected with his back to her. "Very definitely set in his ways."

But she didn't believe he'd give her the truth without embellishing it for his own amusement.

Sebastian could not be trusted, but that wasn't exactly news. "That's part of his charm." A few feet from him, she leaned her behind against the table.

Sebastian grabbed the carafe with one hand and poured coffee into the mug he held with the other. "Are you sure you don't want any?"

"Yes." With both hands, she grasped the tabletop at her hips and purposely let her gaze once again slide down the back of his rumpled T-shirt and the long legs of his jeans. She couldn't help but compare him to Lonny, but supposed it was only natural. Besides the fact that they were both men, they had nothing in common. Sebastian was taller, bigger, and surrounded by a thick testosterone haze. Lonny was shorter, thinner, and had been in touch with his feelings. Perhaps that had been Lonny's appeal. He'd been nonthreatening. Clare waited for the ta-da bells to ring in her head. They didn't.

Sebastian set the carafe down, and Clare turned her attention to the tape recorder by her right hand. "Are you writing an article?" she asked. He didn't answer, and she looked up.

Sunlight spilled through the kitchen window across his shoulder and the side of his face. It poured across the stubble on his cheek and got tangled in his eyelashes. He raised the mug to his lips and watched her as he blew into the coffee.

"Writing? Not really. More like typing and deleting the same opening paragraph."

"You're stuck?"

"Something like that." He took a drink.

"Whenever I get stuck, it's usually because I'm trying to start a book in the wrong place or I'm going about it from the wrong angle. The more I try to force it, the more I get stuck."

He lowered the mug, and she expected him to say something deprecating about writing romance. Her grasp on the table tightened as she steeled herself and waited for him to point out to her that what he wrote was important, and to dismiss her books as nothing more than fantasies for bored housewives. Heck, her own mother trivialized her work. She did not expect better from Sebastian Vaughan, of all people.

Instead of launching into a condescending diatribe, however, he looked at her as he had earlier. Like he was trying to figure something out. "Maybe, but I don't 'get stuck.' At least I never have before, and never for this long."

Clare waited for him to continue. She was ready for him to jump on the literary bandwagon and say something derogatory. She'd been defending herself, her genre, and her readers for so long, she could handle what he threw at her. But he simply drank his coffee, and she tilted her head to the side and looked at *him* as if she couldn't figure *him* out.

Now it was his turn to ask, "What?"

"I think I mentioned yesterday that I write romance novels," she felt compelled to point out.

He raised a brow as he lowered the mug. "Yeah. You mentioned it, along with the fact that you do all your own sexual research."

That's right. Dang it. He'd made her mad, and she'd said things she wished she could take back. Things that were coming back to haunt her. Things said in anger that she'd learned long ago to keep behind the happy facade. "And you don't have one condescending thing to say?"

He shook his head.

"No smarmy questions?"

He smiled. "Just one." He turned and set the mug on the counter by his hip.

She held up a hand like a traffic cop. "No. I'm not a nymphomaniac."

His smile turned into a chuckle, laugh lines creasing the corners of his green eyes. "That isn't the smarmy question, but thanks for clearing that up." He folded his arms across his rumpled T-shirt. "The real question is: where do you *do* all your research?"

Clare dropped her hand to her side. She figured she had a couple ways to answer that question.

She could get offended and tell him to grow up, or she could relax. He seemed to be playing nice today, but this was Sebastian. The man who'd lied to her about having sex with him.

"Are you afraid to tell me?" he goaded her.

She wasn't afraid of Sebastian. "I have a special room in my house," she lied.

"What's in the room?"

He looked totally serious. As if he actually believed her. "Sorry, I can't divulge that sort of information to a reporter."

"I swear I won't tell anyone."

"Sorry."

"Come on. It's been a long time since anyone's told me anything juicy."

"Told or done?"

"What's in your kinky sex room, Clare?" he persisted. "Whips, chains, swings, slings, latex body suits?"

Slings? Holy heck. "You seem to know a lot about kinky sex closets."

"I know I'm not allergic to latex. Other than that, I'm a fairly straightforward guy. I'm not into being beaten or trussed up like a Thanksgiving turkey." He pushed away from the counter and took a few silent steps toward her. "Restraints?"

"Handcuffs," she said as he came to stand a foot in front of her. "Fuzzy, because I'm a nice person."

He laughed like she'd said something really amusing. "Nice? Since when?"

So, maybe she hadn't always been nice to Sebastian, but he loved to provoke her. She straightened and looked up past the stubble on his chin and into his green eyes. "I try to be nice."

"Babe, you might want to put a little more effort into that."

She felt her temper rise a bit, but refused to take the bait. Not today. She smiled and patted him on his rough cheek. "I'm not going to fight with you, Sebastian. There's nothing you can do to provoke me today."

He turned his face and lightly bit the heel of her palm. His green eyes stared into hers and he asked, "Are you sure about that?"

Her fingers curled against his scratchy cheek as a disturbing awareness curled in her stomach. She lowered her hand but could feel the warmth of his mouth and the sharp edge of his teeth in her palm. Suddenly she wasn't so sure of anything. "Yes."

"What if I nibbled . . ." He raised his hand and touched the corner of her mouth. ". . . here?" The tips of his fingers slid down her jaw and brushed the side of her neck. "And here." He slid his fingers down the edge of her halter dress and across her clavicle. "And here."

Her breathing stopped in her chest as she stared

up into his face. "Sounds painful," she managed as shock tightened her throat. It had to be shock, and not the heat of his touch brushing her throat.

"It won't hurt a bit." He raised his gaze from her neck to her eyes. "You'll like it, trust me."

Trust Sebastian? The boy who'd only been nice to her so he could tease and torture her? Who'd only pretended to like her so he could throw mud on her clean dress and make her cry? "I learned a long time ago not to trust you."

He dropped his hand to his side. "When was that?"

"The day you wanted me to show you the river and threw mud on my new dress," she said, and figured he'd no doubt forgotten that day long ago.

"That dress was too white."

"What?" How could something be *too* white? If it wasn't white, it was dingy.

He took a few steps back and grabbed his coffee. "You were always too perfect. Your hair. Your clothes. Your manners. It just wasn't natural. The only time you were any fun at all was when you were messed up and doing something you thought you shouldn't."

She pointed at her chest. "I was plenty fun." He lifted a dubious brow, and she insisted, "I'm still fun. All my friends think so."

"Clare, your hair was too tight then and you're

wound too tight now." He shook his head. "Either your friends are lying to you to spare your feelings or they're as much fun as a prayer circle."

She wasn't going to argue about how much fun she and her friends were, and she dropped her hand to her side. "You've been in a prayer circle?"

"You find that hard to believe?" His brows lowered and he scowled at her for about two seconds before the corner of his mouth tilted up and gave him away. "When I was in college, one of the first stories I was sent out to cover involved a group of evangelicals recruiting on campus. They were so boring, I fell asleep on a folding chair." He shrugged. "It probably didn't help that I was hung over as hell."

"Sinner."

"You know that old saying about finding something you're good at and sticking with it." The other side of his mouth slid up into a wicked smile, leaving little doubt that he'd turned sinning into an art form.

Her heart gave a little flutter, whether she wanted it to flutter or not. And she didn't. Clare reached for the glasses on top of her head, and her hair slid over her ear and across her cheek. "If you see your father, will you tell him I need to talk to him about the guest list for his party?" she asked, purposely turning the conversation away from thoughts of sinning.

"Sure." He raised the coffee to his lips. "You could leave the list and I'll make sure he sees it."

She pushed her hair back. "You'd do that?"

"Why not?"

Probably because being nice and helpful to her wasn't in his nature. "Thanks."

He took a drink and watched her over the top of the mug. "Don't mention it, E-Clare."

She frowned and pulled a piece of paper from the bag on her shoulder. Growing up, he'd called her any and every variation of her name. Her least favorite had been Hairy Clary. She set the list on the table and adjusted her purse. She remembered the time she'd thought she was so smart, and had tried to outwit Sebastian by calling him a numb nut. She'd heard the expression somewhere and thought she was calling him a stupid nut . . . until he pointed out that she was actually calling him a numb testicle. There'd never been any winning with Sebastian. "Tell him these are the people whom I've already contacted and who will attend. If he sees an omission, someone I've forgotten to include, I need to know ASAP." She looked up at him. "Thanks again," she said, and turned toward the door.

Without a word, Sebastian watched her leave. Warm coffee slid down his throat as his gaze moved down the shiny brown hair brushing her bare shoulders and back.

She was so thorough. So tidy. Somebody should do her a favor and mess her up a little. Wrinkle her clothes and smear her lipstick. At the front of the house, the door opened and closed, and Sebastian moved toward the table. That someone wasn't going to be him. No matter how tempting. She was too uptight for his tastes. But even if she did loosen up, he couldn't imagine that doing the deed with Clare would ever go over very well with the old man. Not to mention Joyce.

He kicked the chair away from the table and sat as he booted up his computer. The only reason he could come up with to explain his inexplicable attraction to Clare was that (a) he'd seen her naked, and (b) he hadn't had sex in a while, and (c) her damn book. He hadn't planned on reading it straight through, but she'd hooked him and he'd read every page. Every well-written, hot page.

On those rare occasions when Sebastian found the time to read something that wasn't related to his job, he picked up a Stephen King. As a kid, he'd loved horror and science fiction. As an adult it never once occurred to him to reach for a romance. From Chapter One, he'd been impressed with the smooth depth of her writing. Yeah, it had been emotionally overdone in some scenes, so much so that he'd groaned a few times, but it had also been exceedingly erotic. Not the *Penthouse Forum* sort of eroticism he'd found with some male writers. More of a soft lead by the hand rather than a slap across the face.

The night before, when he'd fallen asleep, he'd dreamed about Clare. Again. Only this time instead of a thong, she'd worn drawers and a white corset. And thanks to the clarity of her writing, he'd been able to picture every damn ribbon and bow.

Then today, he'd opened the door and found her on his doorstep as if he'd conjured her up. To make matters worse, her dress had cherries on it. *Cherries,* for God's sake. Like she was dessert. Which had instantly reminded him of the pirate throwing Lady Julia on his big table and licking Devonshire cream from her breasts.

He pulled his T-shirt over his head and brushed it across his chest. He needed to get laid. That was his problem. Only he didn't know anyone in Boise who could take care of that particular problem for him. He didn't pick up women for one-nighters anymore. He couldn't say for certain when sex with a total stranger had lost its appeal, but he figured it was about the same time he picked up a woman in a Tulsa bar and she'd about gone postal on him when he wouldn't give her his cell number.

His word processing system appeared on the screen, and he tossed his shirt on the floor by his feet. He glanced at his note cards and shuffled a few to the top. He moved them around in rapid succession, setting some aside, then picking them back up and placing them in a different order. For the first time in weeks he felt the beginning flick in his head. He glanced at his notes scribbled on a legal pad, picked up a pencil, and scribbled a little more. The flicker caught fire and he placed his fingers on the keyboard. He moved his neck from side to side and wrote:

I'm told his name is Smith, but it could be Johnson or Williams or any other typically American surname. He is blond and wears a suit and tie as if he plans to run for president someday. Only his heroes aren't Roosevelt, Kennedy, or Reagan. When he speaks of great men, he speaks of Tim McVeigh, Ted Kaczynski, and Eric Rudolph. Homegrown terrorists who've settled in the sediment of the American subconscious, overshadowed and forgotten for now by their foreign counterparts, until the next act of American extremism blows itself onto the nightly news and

*spills black ink across the nation's newspapers
as blood runs in the streets.*

Everything clicked and whirred and fell into
place, and for the next three hours the steady tapping of his keyboard filled the kitchen. He paused
to refill his coffee mug, and when he was finished,
he felt as if an elephant had stepped off his chest.
He leaned back in his chair and blew out a relieved breath. As much as he hated to admit it,
Clare had been right. He'd been trying to force it,
to start the piece in the wrong place, and he hadn't
been able to see. He'd been too tense. Holding on
too tight to look at what was so glaringly obvious.
If Clare had been in front of him, he would have
planted one on her beautiful mouth. Of course,
kissing Clare *anywhere* was completely out of the
question.

Sebastian rose from his chair and stretched. Earlier, when he asked her about her research, he'd
meant to tease her a little. Knock her off her pins.
Get her going, like he had as a kid. Only the joke
was on him. He was thirty-five. He'd traveled the
world and been with a lot of different women. He
did not get all hot and bothered by a romance novelist in a cherry dress as if he were a kid. Especially
that particular romance novelist.

Even if Clare was up for a few rounds of non-commital, no strings, hot and sweaty sex—and that was a big *if*—it would never happen. He was in Boise to try and build a relationship with his father. Something from the ashes, not set ablaze what little progress they'd made by sleeping with Clare. It didn't matter that Joyce wasn't Sebastian's employer. She was his father's boss, and that made her the boss's daughter. If shit had hit the fan years ago over a conversation about sex, he hated to think what might hit the fan if they actually *had* sex. But even if Clare weren't the boss's daughter, he instinctively knew she was a one man woman. The problem with a one man woman was that he was not a one woman man.

His life had slowed in the past few years, but he'd spent most of his twenties bouncing from town to town. Six months here, nine there, learning his job, honing his craft, making a name for himself. Finding women had never been a problem. It still wasn't, although he was a lot more particular at thirty-five than he'd been at twenty-five.

Perhaps someday he would marry. When he was ready. When the thought of it didn't make him put his hands up in the air and back away from the idea of a wife and kids. Probably because he hadn't exactly been raised in an ideal situation. He'd had two stepfathers. One he'd liked, the other he hadn't.

He'd liked some of his mother's boyfriends, but always knew that it was just a matter of time before they left and his mother would once again shut herself in her room.

Growing up, he'd always known that his parents loved him. They'd just loathed each other. His mother had been vocal about her hatred of his father, but to be fair to his dad, the old man hadn't ever *said* anything against his mother. Yet, sometimes it was what a person didn't say that spoke volumes. He didn't ever want to be stuck in that sort of vicious circle with a woman, and he certainly didn't want to raise a child in that environment.

Sebastian bent at the waist and picked up his T-shirt from the floor. No, he would never rule out marriage and family. Someday he might decide he was ready, but that day wasn't even in the pipeline.

The kitchen door opened and his father walked in. He moved to the sink and turned on the faucet. "Are you workin'?"

"I just finished."

Leo grabbed a bar of soap and washed his hands. "I have tomorrow off, and if you're not busy, I thought maybe you and me could drive up past Arrowrock dam and drop a hook."

"You want to go fishing?"

"Yeah. You used to like to fish, and I hear they're bitin' up there."

Fishing with the old man. It could work out to be just what the two of them needed, or it could turn into a disaster. Like shopping for a car. "I'd love to fish with you, Dad."

Seven

The day after Lucy's wedding, Clare had taken a vow of sobriety. The following Thursday evening at 5:32, she broke it. But really, a girl had to celebrate.

She held a bottle of Dom Perignon in her hands and worked the cork with her thumbs. After a few moments it popped and flew across her kitchen, hitting a deep mahogany cupboard and rebounding behind the gas stove. A gossamer mist rose from the mouth of the bottle as she poured into three tall champagne glasses. "This is going to be good," she said through an unrepentant smile. "I stole it from my mother."

Adele took a glass. "Stolen champagne is always the best kind."

"What year?" Maddie asked as she took a glass.

"Nineteen ninety. Mother was saving it for my wedding day. Just because I've given up on men, doesn't mean a vintage bottle of champagne should suffer." She clinked glasses with Maddie and Adele and said, "Here's to me." An hour earlier she'd been given an oral HIV test, and within minutes found out she was negative. One more weight lifted from her shoulders. Her friends had been with her when she'd received the good news. "Thanks for going with me today," she said, and took a sip. The only sad part of the celebration was that Lucy was not with them, but Clare knew that her friend was having a wonderful celebration of her own, soaking up the sun in the Bahamas with her new husband. "I know you both are busy, and it meant a lot that you were there with me."

"Don't thank us." Adele wrapped an arm around her waist. "We're friends."

"I'm never too busy for you." Maddie took a drink and sighed. "It's been so long since I've had a drink of anything that wasn't low carb. This is fabulous."

"Are you still doing the Atkins?" Clare asked. For as long as she could remember, Maddie had been on one diet or another. It was a constant battle for her to remain in her size six jeans. Of course, as writers, spending so much time sitting put on a few pounds and was something they all battled. But for Maddie it was a never-ending struggle.

"I'm doing South Beach now," she said.

"You should try going back to the gym," Adele advised, and leaned her behind into the black granite countertop. Adele jogged five miles every morning out of fear that she would someday inherit her mother's wide butt.

"No. I've belonged to four and quit each one after a few months." Maddie shook her head. "The problem is I hate to sweat. It's just so gross."

Adele raised her glass to her lips. "It's good for you to sweat out all the evil toxins in your body."

"No. It's good for *you*. I like my evil toxins to stay right where they are."

Clare laughed and grabbed the bottle by the neck. "Maddie's right. She should keep all her evil toxins buried deep and hidden from the unsuspecting world." The three of them moved to the living room, which was stuffed with the antique furniture that had been in Clare's family for generations. The arms of the medallion-back sofas and chairs were covered with doilies a great-grandmother or aunt had constructed with her own hands. She set the bottle on the marble-topped coffee table and took a seat in one of the high-backed chairs.

Maddie sat across from her on the sofa. "Have you ever thought of getting those guys from the *Antiques Roadshow* in here?"

"Why?" Clare asked, and picked a white thread from the left breast of her sleeveless black turtleneck.

"To tell you what some of this stuff is." Maddie pointed in the direction of the burgundy gout footstool and the cherub pedestal.

"I know what it is and where it all came from." She dropped the thread into a cloisonné dish.

Adele studied the Staffordshire figurines on the mantel. "How do you keep all this stuff clean?"

"It's a lot of work."

"Get rid of some of it."

"I can't do that." She shook her head. "I have the Wingate illness. I think it's in our genes. We can't seem to part with family heirlooms, not even the horrible stuff, and believe me, my great-grandmother Foster had truly hideous taste. The problem is, we used to have a large family tree but we've been winnowed down to just a few branches. My mother and myself, a few cousins in South Carolina, and a mountain of family antiques." She took a sip of champagne. "If you think my house is bad, you should see my mother's attic. Sheesh. It's like a museum up there."

Adele turned from the mantel and moved across

the Tulip & Lily rug to the sofa. "Did Lonny steal anything when he left? Besides your dog?"

"No." Lonny's fondness for her antiques had been something they had in common. "He knew he didn't want to make me that angry."

"Have you heard from him?"

"Not since Monday. I had the locks changed yesterday, and I get my new mattress delivered tomorrow." She looked down into her glass and swirled the light blond champagne. Less than a week ago she'd been naively happy. Now she was moving on without Lonny. New locks. New bed. New life. Too bad her heart wasn't moving as fast as the rest of her. Not only had she lost her fiancé, she'd lost a very close friend. Lonny had lied to her about a lot of things, but she didn't believe that their friendship had been a pretense.

"I don't think I'll ever understand men," Adele said. "They're seriously whacked in the head."

"What did Dwayne do this time?" Clare asked. For two years Adele had dated Dwayne Larkin and thought he just might be Mr. Right. She'd overlooked his undesirable habits, like smelling the armpits of his shirts before he put them on, because he was buff and very handsome. She'd put up with his beer-swilling, air-guitar-playing ways, right up to the moment when he told her she was getting a "fat ass." No one used the F word to describe her behind; she'd kicked him out of her life. But he wouldn't go completely. Every few weeks Adele would find one or two of the things she'd left at his house sitting on her front porch. No note. No Dwayne. Just random stuff.

"He left a half-empty bottle of lotion and one no-skid footie on the porch." She turned to Clare. "Remember the no-skid ladybug footies you gave me when I had my appendix out?"

"Yeah."

"He only gave me the one back."

"Bastard."

"Creepy."

Adele shrugged. "I'm more annoyed than afraid. I just wish he'd get tired and stop." She'd called the police about it, but an old boyfriend returning his former girlfriend's stuff wasn't against the law. She could try and get a restraining order, but wasn't sure it was worth the hassle. "I know he probably has more of my stuff."

"You need a big boyfriend to go scare the crap out of him," Clare provided. "If I still had a boyfriend, I'd lend him to you."

Maddie lowered her brows as she gazed across at Clare. "No offense honey, but Lonny wouldn't have scared the crap out of Dwayne."

Adele leaned back against the sofa. "That's true. Dwayne would have tied him into a knot."

Yeah, that was probably the truth, Clare thought, and took a sip of her champagne. "You should talk to Quinn when he and Lucy get back from their honeymoon." Quinn McIntyre was a detective with the Boise Police Department and might know what to do.

"He investigates violent crimes," Adele pointed out, which was how Lucy had met the handsome detective. She'd been researching online dating, he'd been searching for a female serial killer. Lucy had been his number one suspect, but he'd saved her life in the end. In Clare's heart and mind, it had all been very romantic. Well, except for the creepy part.

"Do you think there is a right man out there for every woman?" Clare asked. She used to believe in soul mates and love at first sight. She still wanted to believe, but wanting to believe and actually believing were two different things.

Adele nodded. "I like to think so."

"No. I believe in Mr. Right Now."

"How's that working for you?" Clare asked Maddie.

"Fine, Dr. Phil." Maddie leaned forward and set her empty glass on the coffee table. "I don't want hearts and flowers. I don't want romance, and I don't want to share my remote. I just want sex. You'd think that wouldn't be too hard to find, but damn if it isn't."

"That's because we have standards." Adele tipped her glass and drained it. "Like a paying job. No artists who sponge, and no false teeth that pop out when he talks, unless he plays hockey and is extremely hot."

"He can't be married or homicidal." Maddie thought a moment and, typical of her, she added, "And heft would be nice."

"Heft is always nice."

Clare stood and refilled the glasses. "Not gay is a must." She was still waiting for the bing-bing moment. When she would know and could see why she picked cheaters and liars time and again. "The only good thing to come out of the breakup with Lonny is that my writing is going surprisingly well." She found comfort in her writing. Comfort in being transported for several hours a day into a world she created when the reality of her real life sucked.

The doorbell chimed and the Muzak version of "Paperback Writer" filled the house. She set down a glass and looked at the porcelain clock on the mantel. She wasn't expecting anyone. "I don't know who that could be," she said as she got up. "I forgot to enter the Publisher's Clearinghouse Sweepstakes this year."

"It's probably the missionaries," Adele called after her. "They've been casing my neighborhood on their bikes."

"If they're cute," Maddie added, "invite them in for a drink and a little corruption."

Adele laughed. "You're going to hell."

Clare glanced over her shoulder and paused long enough to say, "And you're trying to pull the rest of us down with you. Don't even think about sinning in this house. I don't need that kind of bad karma." She moved into the entry, opened the door, and came face-to-face with the poster boy for sin and corruption standing in the shade of her porch and gazing back at her through a pair of dark sunglasses. The last time she'd seen Sebastian he'd looked sleepy and unkept. Tonight his hair was combed and he'd shaved. He wore a dark green Stucky's Bar T-Shirt tucked into beige cargo pants. She didn't think she would have been more shocked to discover that Prize Patrol really was standing on her porch with a big check and balloons.

"Hey, Clare."

She leaned to the left and looked behind him. A black Land Cruiser was parked at the curb.

"You got a minute?" He pulled the sunglasses from his face, slid one earpiece down the loose collar of his shirt and hooked them slightly left of his chin. He stared back at Clare through green eyes surrounded by thick lashes that she'd found so hard to resist as a little girl.

"Sure." These days she didn't have that problem,

and stepped aside. "My friends are here and we're just about to form a prayer circle. Come on in and we'll pray for you."

He laughed and walked in. "Sounds like my idea of good time."

She shut the door behind him, and he followed her into the living room. Maddie and Adele looked up, their glasses suspended in midair, their conversation hung in mid-sentence. Clare could practically read the cartoon bubbles above their heads. The same "Whoa, baby" bubble she would have had over her head if she didn't know Sebastian. But just because Maddie and Adele had paused to appreciate a good-looking man didn't mean they were suckers for a pretty face and would start checking their breath or flipping their hair anytime soon. They weren't that easy to impress. Especially Maddie, who viewed all men as potential offenders until proven otherwise.

"Sebastian, these are my friends," Clare said as she crossed the room. The two women stood, and Clare looked at them as a stranger might. At Adele, with her long blond hair curling halfway down her back and magical turquoise-colored eyes that sometimes appeared more green than blue, depending on her mood. And Maddie, with her lush curves and Cindy Crawford mole at the corner of her full lips. Her friends were beautiful women, and around them she sometimes felt like the little girl with the tight braids and thick glasses. "Maddie Jones writes true crime under the pen name Madeline Dupree, and Adele Harris writes science fiction fantasy under her own name."

While Sebastian shook the hand of each woman, he looked into their eyes and smiled, a smooth tilt of his mouth that might have charmed more susceptible women. "It's a pleasure to meet you both," he said, and sounded as if he meant it. The sudden appearance of his well-hidden manners was another shock to Clare. Almost as big as opening her door and seeing him on her porch.

"Sebastian is Leo Vaughan's son," she continued. Both women had been to her mother's house on several occasions and had met Leo. "Sebastian is a journalist." Since she'd invited him in, she supposed she would have to be hospitable. "Would you care for champagne?"

He removed his gaze from her friends and looked at her over his shoulder. "No, but I'll take a beer if you have one."

"Of course."

"Who do you write for?" Maddie asked as she raised her glass to her lips.

"I'm primarily a freelancer, although these days I work for *Newsweek*. For the glossies, I've written pieces for *Time*, *Rolling Stone*, *National*

Geographic," he answered, listing his impressive bona fides as Clare left the room.

She grabbed a bottle of Lonny's Hefeweizen from the refrigerator and popped the top. She could no longer hear what he said, just the low rumble and deep texture of his voice. For a year she'd lived with a man in the house, but having Sebastian in the next room felt very odd. He'd brought a different energy into her home. One she couldn't put her finger on at the moment.

When she returned to the living room, he'd sat in her chair, relaxed and comfy, as if he wasn't going anyplace soon. He obviously intended to stay longer than a "minute," and Clare wondered what had brought him to her door.

Maddie and Adele were seated on the couch, listening to Sebastian's journalistic tales. "A few months ago, I did a real interesting piece for *Vanity Fair* on a Manhattan art dealer who faked the histories of Egyptian antiquities in order to get around Egyptian export laws," he said as she handed him the beer. He glanced up at her. "Thank you."

"Would you like a glass?"

He looked the bottle over and read the label. "No, this is good," he said, and Clare took a seat in one of the matching high-backed chairs. He crossed one foot over his knee and rested the bottle on the heel of his boot. "For a lot of years I bounced around from state to state and wrote articles for a lot of different news organizations, but I don't write for the black-and-whites anymore." He shrugged his big shoulders. "Not for a few years, since I was an embed with the First Battalion Fifth Marine Regiment during the invasion of Iraq." He took a drink of his beer while Clare waited for him to get to the reason behind his visit. "How many books have you ladies published?" he asked, and Clare realized he wasn't going to talk about why he'd appeared on her porch, leaving her to wonder but have absolutely no clue. Other than to drive her insane with speculations.

"Five," Maddie answered. Adele had eight publishing credits to her name, and like a good reporter, Sebastian followed up each answer with another question. Within fifteen minutes the two women who were hard to impress had become willing victims of Sebastian's born-again charm.

"Sebastian published a book about Afghanistan," Clare felt compelled by good manners to point out. "I'm sorry, I don't recall the name of your book." It had been years since she'd borrowed it from Leo and read it.

"*Fractured: Twenty Years of War in Afghanistan.*"

"I remember that book," Adele admitted.

"So do I," Maddie added.

Clare was not surprised that her friends recalled it. It had taken up the top slots on the *USA Today* and *New York Times* best-seller lists for weeks. Authors didn't tend to forget or easily forgive a list hog. Except Adele, apparently. Clare watched as her friend wound a spiral lock of hair around her finger.

"What was it like being embedded with the Marines?" Adele asked.

"Cramped. Dirty. Scary as hell. And those were the good days. For months after I returned to the States, I'd just stand outside and breathe in air that wasn't permeated with powdered sand." He paused, and a slight smile touched the corner of his mouth. "If you talk to the military guys who are home now, that's one of the things they appreciate most. Dust-free air."

Maddie studied Sebastian as he took a drink, and the suspicious scrutiny that she subjected upon all men melted from her brown eyes. "They all look so young."

Sebastian licked the beer from his bottom lip, then said, "The sergeant who commanded the vehicle I rode in was twenty-eight. The youngest soldier was nineteen. I was the old guy, but they saved my ass on more than one occasion." He pointed at the champagne bottle with his beer and changed the subject. "Are you ladies celebrating?"

Adele and Maddie looked at Clare but didn't answer. "No," Clare lied, and took a sip. She didn't feel like sharing that afternoon's doctor visit with Sebastian. He might look normal and talk like a regular guy, but she didn't trust him. He'd come to her house because he wanted something. Something he didn't want to discuss in front of her friends. "We always drink when we get together to pray."

He glanced at her out of the corners of his eyes. He didn't believe her, but didn't press her either. Maddie raised her glass and asked, "How long have you known Clare?"

For several heartbeats Sebastian looked into Clare's eyes before he turned his attention to the women across from him. "Let's see. I was five or six the first time I spent the summer with my father. The first time I remember seeing her, she was wearing a little dress that was kind of gathered at the top." He pointed to his chest with the mouth of his bottle. "And little girl socks that fold over around the ankles. She dressed like that for years."

Growing up, she and her mother had fought a lot about clothing. "My mother was into smocked dresses and Mary Janes in a big way," she said. "When I was ten it was pleated skirts."

"You still wear a lot of dresses and skirts," Adele pointed out.

"It's what I'm used to, but as a child, I didn't have a choice. My mother bought my clothes and I had to look perfect all the time. I was terrified of getting dirty." She thought back and said, "The only time I got dirty was when Sebastian was around."

He shrugged, clearly unrepentant. "You looked better messed up."

Which showed his contrary nature. No one looked good messed up. Except maybe him. "When I visited my father," Clare said, "he'd let me wear whatever I wanted. Of course, my clothes had to stay in Connecticut, so the next time I visited him they didn't fit. My favorite was a Smurf T-shirt." She remembered Smurfette and sighed. "But what I really wanted, and not even my father would get for me, was a 'boy toy' belt buckle like Madonna. I wanted one of those in the worst way."

Maddie frowned. "I can't imagine you ever wanting to be a boy toy."

"I didn't even know what it meant, but I thought Madonna was so cool rolling around in that wedding veil with all that gaudy costume jewelry hanging off her. I wasn't allowed costume jewelry because Mother thinks it's vulgar." She looked at Sebastian and confessed, "I used to sneak into your father's house when he was working and watch MTV."

Tiny laugh lines creased the corners of his eyes. "Rebel."

"Yeah, right. Rebel, that's me. Remember when you taught me to play poker and you won all my money?"

"I remember. You cried, and my dad made me give it all back."

"That's because you told me we weren't really playing for keeps. You lied."

"Lied?" He took his foot from his knee, leaned forward and placed his forearms on his thighs. "No, I had an ulterior motive and big plans for that money."

He'd always had an ulterior motive. "What plans?"

The bottle dangled from one hand between his knees as he thought a moment. "Well, I was ten, so I wasn't into porn and alcohol yet." He tapped the bottle against the leg of his cargo pants. "So, probably a stack of *Mad* magazines and a six-pack of Hires. I would have shared with you, if you hadn't been such a crybaby."

"So, your ulterior motive was to take all my money so you could share magazines and root beer with me?"

He grinned. "Something like that."

Adele laughed and set her empty glass on the table. "I bet you were cute running around in your little dresses and polished shoes."

"No. I wasn't. I looked like a bug."

Sebastian was conspicuously silent. *Jerk.*

"Honey, it's better to be a homely child and a beautiful adult than a beautiful child and a homely adult," Maddie pointed out in an effort to comfort Clare. "I have a cousin who was a gorgeous little girl, but she is one of the ugliest women you don't ever want to lay your eyes on. Once her nose started to grow, it just didn't stop. You may have started out a little short on looks, but you're certainly a beautiful woman."

"Thank you." Clare bit her bottom lip. "I think."

"You're welcome." Maddie set her glass on the table and stood. "I've got to get going."

"You do?"

"Me too," Adele announced. "I have a date."

Clare stood. "You didn't mention that."

"Well, today is about you, and I didn't want to talk about my date when your life isn't so great."

After both women said their good-byes to Sebastian, Clare walked them to the front door.

"Okay. What is between you and Sebastian?"

Maddie asked just above a whisper as she stepped out onto the porch.

"Nothing."

"He looks at you like there's something more."

Adele added, "When you left the room to get his beer, his gaze followed you."

Clare shook her head. "Which doesn't mean a thing. He was probably hoping I'd trip and fall or something equally mortifying."

"No." Adele shook her head as she reached into her purse for her keys. "He looked at you like he was trying to picture you naked."

Clare didn't point out that he didn't have to try. Pretty much, he already knew.

"And while I would normally find that disturbing in a man, it was really hot when he did it." Maddie also dug around in her purse for her keys. "So, I think you should go for it."

Who are these women? "Hello. Last week I was engaged to Lonny. Remember?"

"You need a rebound man." Adele took a step off the porch. "He'd be perfect in that capacity."

Maddie nodded and followed Adele down the sidewalk toward their cars, parked in the driveway. "You can tell by looking at the man that he has heft."

"Good-bye, you two," she said, and closed the

door behind her. As far as Clare was concerned, Maddie was preoccupied with heft, probably because she hadn't been anywhere near heft in several years. And Adele . . . Well, she had always suspected that Adele sometimes lived in the fantasyland in which she wrote.

Eight

When Clare walked into the living room, Sebastian stood with his back to her, gazing up at a portrait of her and her mother taken when Clare had been six. "You were cuter than I remember," he said.

"That was retouched several times."

He chuckled as he turned his attention to a photo of Cindy, all groomed and polished in her pink hair bow. "This must be your wussy-looking mutt."

Cindy was AKC certified and belonged to the Yorkshire Terrier Club of America. Hardly a mutt. "Yes. Mine and Lonny's, but he took her when he left." Looking at the photo made her miss her dog a lot.

He opened his mouth to say more, but shook his head and glanced about the room instead. "This is a lot like your mother's house."

Her house didn't look anything like her mother's. Her tastes were much more Victorian while her mother's tastes leaned toward the French classics. "How' s that?"

"Lots of stuff." His gaze landed on her. "But your house is more girly-girl. Like you."

He set his beer on the mantel. "I have something for you, and I didn't want to take it out in front of your friends. Just in case you hadn't mentioned that night at the Double Tree." He reached into the front pocket of his cargo pants. "I believe this is yours."

He held up her diamond earring between his fingers. Clare didn't know which was more stunning, that he'd found the earring and brought it to her or that he hadn't mentioned it in front of her friends. Both gestures were uncharacteristically thoughtful. Nice, even.

He took her hand in his and placed the diamond earring in her palm. "I found it on your pillow that morning."

The heat from his hand seeped into her skin and spread to the tips of her fingers. The sensation was disturbing, and as unwanted as the memory of what he'd been wearing, or rather, not been wearing, which seeped into her head and got stuck in her brain. "I thought I'd lost this for good." She looked up into his eyes. There was something purely physical about Sebastian. A combination of cool strength and hot sexual energy that was impossible to ignore. "I would have had a difficult time matching it."

"I kept forgetting to give it to you when you were at your mother's."

His thumb brushed hers and heat spread to her palm. She closed her hand into a fist to hold the hot tingles inside, pressing her fingers tightly together to keep the feeling from traveling to her wrist and spreading across her chest. Too late, she pulled her hand away. She was old enough to recognize the warmth brushing across her flesh. She didn't want to feel anything for Sebastian. Or any man, for that matter. Nothing. She'd just finished a two-year relationship. It was too soon, but this feeling had nothing to do with deep emotion and everything to do with lust. "Tell me what happened in the Double Tree Saturday night."

"I did."

She took a step back. "No. Not everything. From the time you found me sitting on a bar stool talking to a toothless man in a wife beater until I woke up naked, something more had to have happened."

He smiled as if he found something she'd said amusing. The smile chilled the warm little tug of lust. "I'll tell you, if you tell me what you and your friends were celebrating."

"What makes you think we were celebrating anything?"

He pointed to the champagne. "I'm guessing that bottle cost someone a hundred and thirty dollars. Nobody drinks Dom Perignon for the hell of it. Plus, I just met your friends, so don't give me that crap about a prayer circle."

"How do you know how much the champagne cost?"

"I'm a reporter. I have an incredible capacity for minutiae. Your friend with the curly hair said today was about you. So, don't make me work too hard for the answer, Clare."

She folded her arms beneath her breasts. Why did she care if he knew about the HIV test? He already knew she'd planned to take one. "I went to the doctor today and . . . remember Monday when I talked to you about getting tested?"

"For HIV?"

"Yes." She couldn't quite look him in the eyes and lowered her gaze to the sunglasses hooked to the neck of his T-shirt. "Well, I found out that I was negative today."

"Ah. That's good news."

"Yes."

He placed his fingers beneath her chin and brought her gaze up to his. "Nothing."

"What?"

"We didn't do anything. Not anything fun, anyway. You cried until you passed out, and I raided your minibar."

"That's it? How did I end up naked?"

"I thought I told you."

He'd told her a lot of things. "Tell me again."

He shrugged. "You stood up, stripped out of your clothes, then crawled back in bed. It was quite a show."

"Is there more?"

He smiled a little. "Yeah. I lied about the guy in the bar at the Double Tree. The one with the baseball cap and wife beater."

"About drinking Jägermeister?" she asked hopefully.

"Oh no. You were definitely knocking back the Jägermeister, but he wasn't missing any teeth and he didn't have a nose ring."

Which wasn't much of a relief. "Is that it?"

"Yeah."

She didn't know if she believed him. Even though he'd brought her the earring and spared her the embarrassing explanation in front of her friends, she didn't think he'd lie to spare her feelings. God knew, he never had in the past. Her hand tightened around the diamond in her palm. "Well, thank you for bringing the earring to me."

He grinned. "I have an ulterior motive."

Of course he did.

"You look worried." He raised his hands in the air as if surrendering. "I promise it won't hurt a bit."

She turned away and placed the earring in the cloisonné dish on the coffee table. "The last time you said that, you talked me into playing doctor." She straightened and pointed to her chest. "I ended up buck naked."

"Yeah," he said as he laughed. "I remember, but it wasn't like you didn't want to play."

Saying no had always been her problem. Not any longer. "No."

"You don't even know what I was going to ask."

"I don't have to know."

"How about if I promise that you won't end up naked this time?" His gaze slid to her mouth, down her throat, and to her finger, resting on her dress, between her breasts. "Unless you insist."

She picked up the three empty glasses and

champagne bottle. "Forget it," she said through a sigh as she walked from the room.

"All I need are a few ideas about what I should get my father for the party Saturday."

She looked back at him. "Is that all?" There had to be more.

"Yeah. Since I had to drop off the earring, I thought you could point me in the right direction. Give me some ideas. Although Dad and I are trying to get to know each other again, you know him better than I do."

Okay, so now she felt bad. She was being judgmental, and that wasn't fair. He'd been a smooth-talking flimflammer as a child, but that was a long time ago. She certainly didn't want to be judged by things she'd said and done as a girl. "I got him an antique wooden duck," she answered, and entered the kitchen, the heels of her sandals tapping across the hardwood floors. "Maybe you could get him a book on wood carving."

"A book would be good." Sebastian followed. "What do you think of a new fishing pole?"

"I wasn't aware that he fished these days." Clare set the glasses and bottle on the granite island in the middle of the kitchen.

"He and I pulled a few trout out of the reservoir this afternoon." He leaned back against the counter and folded his arms across his chest. "His gear is fairly dated, so I thought I'd get him a newer setup."

"With him, you have to pay attention to brands."

"That's why I thought you could help me out. I wrote down what we'll need."

She stopped and slowly turned toward him. "We'll?"

He shrugged. "Sure. You'll go along. Right?"

Something wasn't quite right. He wasn't looking her in the eyes and . . . She sucked in a breath and the real reason for his unannounced visit became crystal clear. "There's no 'we'll,' is there? You came here to talk me into getting your father a fishing pole. By myself."

He looked at her then and gave her his most charming smile. "Honey, I don't know where the sporting goods stores are in this town. And really, there's no point in both of us going."

"Don't honey me." She was such a fool. She'd given him the benefit of the doubt, felt bad for misjudging him, and here he was, standing in her kitchen attempting a bait and switch. She folded her arms across her chest. "No."

"Why not?" He dropped his hands to his sides. "Women love to shop."

"For shoes. Not fishing poles. Duh!" She groaned

inwardly and closed her eyes. Had she just said *Duh*? Like she was ten again?

Clearly amused, Sebastian laughed. "Duh? What's next? Are you going to call me a numb nut?"

She took a deep breath and opened her eyes. "Good-bye, Sebastian," she said as she moved to the kitchen doorway. She stopped and pointed to the front of her house. "You are on your own."

He pushed away from the counter and moved toward her. Slow and easy, as if he wasn't in a big hurry to comply to her demand. "Your friends are right, you know."

Good God! Had he overheard the heft conversation?

As he walked past her, he paused and said next to her ear, "You might not have been the cutest little girl in patent leather shoes, but you've grown into a beautiful woman. Especially when you're all worked up."

He smelled good, and if she turned her face just a little she could bury her nose in his neck. The desire to do so alarmed her, and she kept as still as possible. "Forget it. I'm not doing your shopping for you."

"Please?"

"Not a chance."

"What if I get lost?"

"Get a map."

"Don't need one. The Land Cruiser has a navigation system." He chuckled and pulled back. "You were more fun as a kid."

"I was more gullible. I'm not a little girl now and you can't trick me, Sebastian."

"Clare, you wanted me to trick you." He smiled and moved to the front door. "You still do," he said, and was gone before she could argue or utter a good-bye or good riddance.

She walked back into the kitchen, reached for the champagne glasses, and set them next to the sink. Ridiculous. She hadn't wanted to be tricked. She'd just wanted him to like her. She turned on the faucet and added a few drops of lemon fresh Joy. *She'd just wanted him to like her.* She supposed that was the story of her life. Sad and a little pathetic, but true.

The water ran for a few moments before she turned off the faucet and placed the glasses in the warm soapy water. If she were honest and took a good hard look at her past, she could see the same destructive patterns in her life. If she were honest, the kind of honest that was painful to look at, she'd admit that she was letting her childhood influence her adult life.

Admitting that really did bite the big one, but it

was too obvious to ignore. She'd absolutely refused to consider it for so long because it was such a cliché, and she hated clichés. She hated to write them, but more than that, she hated being one.

In college she'd taken sociology classes and read the studies conducted on children raised in single parent homes. She had thought she'd escaped the statistics, which found that girls raised without fathers were more likely to engage in greater and earlier sexual activities and were at a greater risk of suicide and criminality. She'd never had one single thought of suicide, never been arrested, and was a freshman in college when she'd lost her virginity. Her friends from two-parent homes had lost theirs in high school. Therefore, she'd convinced herself that she did not have the classic "daddy issues."

No, she hadn't been sexually promiscuous. Just emotionally hollow and subconsciously seeking male approval to fill the empty places inside. And she didn't have to look very hard at her life to discover why she always searched for male attention to make herself feel whole.

Clare washed the glasses and set them on a towel to dry. For all intents and purposes, she'd been raised without a father. On those occasions when she visited her dad, he always had a beautiful woman living with him. A different beautiful woman. To a little girl with thick glasses and a wide mouth that didn't fit her face, all those beautiful women had made her feel even more unattractive and insecure. It hadn't been their fault. Most of the women were kind to her. Nor had it been her fault. She'd been a child—it was just life, her life—and she was still letting those old insecurities influence her relationships with men. After all these years.

Clare reached into a drawer and pulled out a towel. As she dried her hands, she came to a painful realization. She'd settled for men unworthy of her because, deep inside, she'd felt lucky to have them. It wasn't exactly the bing-bing moment she'd been waiting for to explain her relationship with Lonny. It didn't answer why she hadn't seen what had been so obvious to everyone else, but it did explain why she'd settled for a man who could never love her the way any woman deserved to be loved by the man in her life.

The telephone sitting next to the porcelain canisters rang, and she glanced at the caller ID. It was Lonny. He'd been calling every day since she'd kicked him out. She never picked up, and he never left a message. This time she decided to answer. "Yes."

"Oh, you're there."

"Yes."

"How are you?"

Hearing his voice made all the hollow places ache. "Fine."

"I thought maybe we could get together and talk."

"No. There's nothing to say." She closed her eyes and pushed past all the pain. The pain of loss, and of loving a man that did not exist. "It's best if we both just move on."

"I never meant to hurt you."

She opened her eyes. "I've never understood what that means." She laughed without humor. "You dated me, made love to me, and asked me to marry you, but you weren't physically attracted to me. Exactly what part of that wasn't meant to hurt me?"

He was silent for several long moments. "You're being sarcastic."

"No. I sincerely want to know how you could lie to me for two years, then claim you never meant to hurt me."

"It's true. I'm not gay," he said, lying to her and probably himself. "I've always wanted a wife and kids and the house with the picket fence. I still do. That makes me a normal man."

She almost felt sorry for him. He was even more confused than she was. "That makes you trying to pass for something you're not."

"What does it matter anyway? Gay or straight, men are unfaithful all the time."

"That doesn't make it right, Lonny. It makes them just as guilty of lying and cheating as you."

When she hung up, she knew she was saying good-bye to him for the last time. He would not phone again, and there was a piece of her that missed him. That still loved him. Not only had he been her fiancé, he'd been one of the best male friends she'd ever had, and she would miss that friendship for a very long time.

She dried the glasses and placed them in the china hutch in the dining room. Her thoughts turned to Sebastian and his irritating sneaky ways. And of the pheromones that rolled off him like heat waves tumbling across the Mojave Desert. Those pheromones had stunned Maddie and Adele and left them both dazed. And no matter how much she hated to admit it, there was no denying that she was very aware of him too. The way he looked and smelled, and the touch of his hand on hers.

What was wrong with her? She'd just ended a serious relationship, and was already thinking about the touch of another man. But now that she thought about it for a rational moment, she realized that her reaction to Sebastian probably had more to do with not having good-quality sex in ages rather than the man himself.

He wants you, Maddie had said, and Adele had added, *You need a rebound man*. But they were wrong. Both of them. The last thing she needed, rebound or permanent, no matter how long it had been since she'd had good sex, was a man. No, she needed to be okay by herself before she even *considered* allowing a man in her life.

By the time she crawled into bed that night, Clare was certain that her reaction to Sebastian had been purely physical. It was the reaction of any woman to a handsome man. That was all. Normal. Natural. And it would pass.

She turned off the bedside light and chuckled into the darkness. He'd thought he'd come over to her house and sucker her into doing his shopping for him. Charm her just like he had in the past.

"Who's the sucker now?" she whispered. For the first time in her life, she hadn't been tricked by Sebastian.

But the next morning, while her coffee brewed, she opened the front door to get her newspaper and a fishing pole fell into the house. A note written on the back of a Burger King napkin was stuck in one of the eyes of the pole. It read:

Clare,

Could you please wrap this and bring it to the party tomorrow night? I'm horrible at this sort of thing and don't want to embarrass the old man in front of his friends. I'm sure you'll do a great job.

Thanks, Sebastian

Nine

She'd wrapped the fishing pole and reel in pink ribbon and glittery bows. It was so girly and gaudy, Sebastian had hid it behind the sofa in the carriage house where no one would see it.

"Such a sweet girl."

Sebastian stood beneath a big awning constructed in the Wingate backyard. There were about twenty-five guests, none of whom Sebastian had ever met before. He'd been introduced to everyone and recalled most of their names. After years of reporting, he'd developed a knack for recalling people and events.

Roland Meyers, one of Leo's oldest friends, stood next to him, munching on foie gras. "Who?" Sebastian asked.

Roland pointed across the lawn at a large knot of people, the setting sun bathing them in burnt orange. "Clare."

Sebastian speared a little weenie with a toothpick and stuck it on his plate next to crab-stuffed Camembert. "So I've heard." His father, he noticed, had dressed himself up in charcoal trousers, white dress shirt, and a god-awful tie with a howling wolf on it.

"She and Joyce put this whole thing together for your father." Roland took a drink of something on the rocks, and added, "They've been like family to Leo. Always taken real good care of him."

Sebastian detected a note of censure. It wasn't the first time that evening that he felt as if he were being politely admonished for not visiting sooner, but he didn't know Roland well enough to be certain.

Roland's next words removed any doubt. "Never were too busy for him. Not like his own family."

Sebastian smiled. "The interstate runs two ways, Mr. Meyers."

The older man nodded. "That's true enough. I have six kids and can't imagine not laying eyes on one of them for ten years."

It had been more like fourteen years, but who was counting. "What do you do for a living?" Sebastian asked, purposely changing the subject.

"Veterinarian."

Sebastian moved down the table filled with hors d'oeuvres. Directly behind him, sixties music played from speakers hidden by planters of tall grasses and cattails. One of the strongest memories Sebastian had of his father was his love of the Beatles, Dusty Springfield, and especially Bob Dylan—of reading Fantastic Four comics and listening to "Lay Lady Lay."

Sebastian ate the Camembert on thin crackers and followed that up with a few stuffed mushrooms. He raised his gaze to the people milling about the lawn amidst lit torches and candles floating in various fountains. His gaze moved to the group of people standing near a nymph fountain, and once again landed on one brunette in particular. Clare had curled her straight hair, and the setting sun caught in the big waves and touched the side of her face. She wore a tight blue dress with tiny white flowers that hit her just above the knee. The thin straps of the dress looked like bra straps, and a white ribbon circled her ribs and was tied beneath her breasts.

Earlier, before the guests had arrived that evening, he'd watched the caterer set up while Clare and Joyce had placed Leo's carved wildlife along the tables and in the cattails. Roland had been right. The Wingate women did take good care of his father. A twinge of guilt plucked his conscience. What he'd said to Roland had been true too. The interstate did run two ways, and he'd never bothered heading in the direction of his father until a week ago. They'd let things fall to nothing, and whether it was the old man's fault or his didn't seem to matter anymore.

They'd had a great time fishing together, and Sebastian had felt the first real hint of optimism. Now, if neither of them did anything to mess it up, they might actually have some kind of framework on which to build. Funny that he'd had a fuck-it attitude toward his father only a few short months ago. But that was before he'd stood in a mortuary picking out a casket for his mother. That day, his world shifted, turned him 180 degrees around and changed him, whether he'd wanted it to or not. Now he wanted to know the old man before it was too late. Before he once again had to make a decision on cherrywood or bronze. Crepe or velvet. Cremated or buried.

He polished off the remaining hors d'oeuvre and threw the plate in the trash. Or, given his job, before his father might have to make arrangements for him. He preferred to be burned rather than buried and wanted his ashes dumped rather than kept in a columbarium or on someone's mantel. During the course of his life, he'd been shot at numerous times, he'd chased stories and been chased, and he didn't have any illusions about his own mortality.

With that happy reflection, he ordered a scotch on the rocks at the open bar, then made his way to his father. When he'd packed for his impromptu trip to Boise, he'd thrown jeans, a couple pairs of cargo pants, and a week's worth of T-shirts into the suitcase. It hadn't occurred to him to pack anything to wear to a party. Earlier that afternoon, his father had brought him a blue and white striped dress shirt and a plain red tie. He'd left the tie sitting on the dresser, but he'd been grateful for the loan of the shirt, whose tails he'd tucked into his newest Levi's. Every now and again he caught the scent of the old man's laundry soap and realized it was coming from him—a little disconcerting after all these years, but comfortable.

At Sebastian's approach, his father made a place for him. "Are you having a good time?" Leo asked.

Good time? No. Good time meant something entirely different in Sebastian's personal lexicon, and he hadn't had that kind of good time in months. "Sure. The food is good." He raised his drink to his mouth. "But pass on the cheese ball with the chunks in it," he advised from behind his glass.

Leo smiled and asked just above a whisper, "What are the chunks?"

"Nuts." Sebastian took a drink and his gaze slid to Clare, standing a few feet from his father, chatting it up with a man in green and blue plaid who looked to be in his late twenties. "And some sort of fruit."

"Ah, Joyce's ambrosia cheese ball. She makes it every Christmas. Horrible stuff." The corner of Leo's smile quivered. "Don't tell her. She thinks everyone loves it."

Sebastian chuckled and lowered his glass.

"Excuse me while I go grab some of the Camembert before it's all gone," his father said, and made a beeline for the buffet table.

Sebastian watched his father walk away, his gait a little slower than it had been earlier. It was getting close to his bedtime.

"I bet Leo is just thrilled to death to finally have you here," said Lorna Devers, the neighbor from across the hedgerow.

Sebastian pulled his gaze from his father and looked over his shoulder. "I don't know if he's thrilled or not."

"Of course he is." Mrs. Devers was in her fifties, although it was hard to tell which end of fifty, given that her face was frozen from Botox. Not that Sebastian had a real opinion one way or the other about plastic surgery. He just thought it shouldn't be so obvious to the casual observer exactly where a person had gotten herself nipped, tucked, sucked, or injected. Case in point, Lorna's Pamela-Anderson-sized breasts. Not that he had anything against big, or even fake. Just not that big and that fake on a woman that age.

"I've known your father for twen—a few years," she said, then proceeded to talk about herself and her poodles, Missy and Poppet. As far as Sebastian was concerned, that was strike three and four. He had nothing against poodles, although he couldn't see himself owning one, but Missy and Poppet? Lord, just the sound of those two names siphoned off a few ounces of testosterone. If he listened much longer, he was afraid he'd grow a vagina. To preserve his sanity and his manhood, Sebastian eavesdropped on the different conversations taking place around him while Lorna rambled on.

"I'll have to buy one of your books," the guy next to Clare said. "I might learn a thing or two." He laughed at his own joke, but didn't seem to notice that he was the only one laughing.

"Rich, you always say that," Clare managed as smooth as butter. Light from the torches flickered and seeped through the soft strands of her dark curls, touching the corners of her phony-as-hell smile.

"I'm going to do it this time. I hear they're real sexy. If you need research, give me a call."

Somehow, when Rich said it, it sounded sleazy. Not like when Sebastian said it. Or . . . perhaps it sounded just as sleazy and he didn't want to think he was as ignorant as Rich.

The corners of Clare's fake smile went higher, but she didn't answer.

Standing directly across from Sebastian, Joyce conversed with several women who looked to be about her age. He seriously doubted they were friends of his father's. They looked too rich and too old-guard Junior League.

"Betty McLeod told me Clare writes romance novels," one of them said. "I love trashy books. The trashier the better."

Instead of defending Clare, Joyce asserted in a voice that brooked no disagreement, "No. Claresta writes *women's fiction*." Within the wavering light, Sebastian watched Clare's phony smile fade. Her gaze narrowed as she excused herself from Rich and moved across the lawn to disappear behind pots of tall grasses and cattails.

"Excuse me, Lorna," he said, interrupting the woman's fascinating tales of Missy and Poppet's love of car rides.

"Don't stay away so long next time," she called after him.

He followed Clare and found her looking through a stack of CDs next to the sound system. The light from the torches barely leached through the grasses as she read the titles by the blue LCD light.

"What are you putting on next?" he asked.

"AC/DC." She glanced up, then returned her gaze to the CD in her hand. "Mother hates 'racket.' "

Sebastian chuckled and moved behind her. "Shoot To Thrill" would probably spike Joyce's blood pressure and give her heart failure. While that might be amusing, it would ruin Leo's party. He looked over Clare's shoulder at the stack of music. "I haven't hard Dusty Springfield in years. Why don't you play that?"

"Fine, party pooper," Clare said, and picked up Dusty's CD. "How'd Leo like the fishing pole?"

He'd rather be whipped than admit he hadn't given it to him yet. "He loved it. Thanks for the wrapping job."

"You're welcome," she said, and Sebastian could hear the laughter in her voice as she popped a CD into the stereo. "You two will have to break it in while you're here."

"That'll have to wait. I'm leaving in the morning. Got to get back to work."

She glanced over her shoulder at him. "When will you be back?"

"I don't know." After he finished the piece on the black fever outbreak in Rajwara, he was headed to the Arizona border with Mexico to do a follow-up piece on illegals entering the country. After that he was off to New Orleans to write an update on conditions and progress in the Big Easy. At some point he still had to deal with his mother's estate, but he figured that could wait. There was no rush.

"I noticed Leo's new Lincoln in the driveway. I guess the old one must have turned fifty."

"It did. He bought the new Town Car today at a dealership in Nampa," he said as the delicate scent of her perfume surrounded his head and he felt an urge to lower his face to the side of her neck. "You know a lot about my father."

"Of course." She shrugged and one thin strap slid down her arm. "I've known him most of my life." She pushed Play and Dusty Springfield's lush, soulful voice flowed like a sexy whisper from the speakers. She shook her head and her hair brushed her bare shoulders. Sebastian felt a second, stronger urge to raise his hand and reach for a curl resting against her skin. To feel the texture with his fingers. He took a few steps back, retreating deeper into the darkness. Away from the scent of her neck and the inexplicable compulsion to touch her hair.

"For as long as I can recall, he's lived in my mother's backyard," she continued while Dusty sang about getting a little lovin' in the morning. She turned and looked up at him through the variegated shadow. "In a lot of ways, I know him better than my own father. I've certainly spent more time with him."

He supposed his insides were getting all tied up in hot knots over Clare because he hadn't been laid in months. That had to be the reason. With his mother's funeral and everything else going on, he'd put off his sex life. As soon as he got home, he was going to have to do something about that. "But he's not your father."

"Yes. I know."

A man just shouldn't put off something like sex. Especially when he wasn't used to going without. He raised his glass to his lips and polished off his scotch. "As a kid, I used to wonder."

"If I knew Leo wasn't my father?" She laughed, a breathy little sound of amusement, and took a step toward him. "Yeah. I knew. The term 'serial cheater' was invented for my father. Every time I visited him, he had a new woman. Still does, and he's seventy." A shaft of light cut across the darkness and lit up Clare's cleavage but left her face in inky shadow.

The memory of her naked except for a tiny pink thong flashed in his head and got all mixed and confused with the woman standing in front of him. Desire crawled down his belly and tightened his groin. He pulled his gaze from her cleavage and looked behind him. The very last thing he needed to complicate his life was Clare Wingate.

"He still thinks he's quite the lady's man," she said through a breathy laugh.

He turned and moved a few feet toward a wrought-iron bench sitting beneath a pruned dogwood tree. If it hadn't been painted white, it would have been undetectable in the darkness. "I don't even know if my father has a girlfriend or a special woman in his life." He sat and leaned back against the cool metal.

"He's had a few. Not many." Dusty's soulful voice drifted on the warm night breeze.

"I always wondered if there was anything going on between your mother and my dad."

Again she gave a breathy little laugh. "Nothing romantic."

"Because he's the gardener?"

"Because she's frigid."

That he could believe. One more thing mother and daughter did not have in common.

"Aren't you going to rejoin the party?" she asked.

"Not yet. If I have to listen to Lorna Devers for one more second, I'm afraid I'll grab one of the torches and set myself on fire." Mrs. Devers was only one reason he didn't plan to rejoin that party for a while. The other reason wore a blue and white dress and was stalking him.

"Ouch." Clare laughed and moved in front of him.

"Believe me, it'll be less painful than listening to her silly stories about Missy and Poppet."

"I don't know who is worse, Lorna or Rich."

"Her son is an idiot."

"Rich isn't her son." She sat beside him on the bench, and Sebastian gave up, resigned himself to his tormented fate. "He's her fifth husband."

"No shit?"

"No shit." She sat back and the night almost swallowed her. "If I hear my mother tell one more person that I write women's fiction, I'm afraid I'll grab one of the torches and set *her* on fire."

"What's wrong with her saying you write women's fiction?" Moonlight filtered through the dogwood and cut across her nose and mouth. Her fantasy of a mouth that made him wonder if she tasted as good as she looked.

"It's the reason why she says it. I embarrass her." The corners of her lips rose in a smile. "Who else should we throw on the pyre? Besides Lorna and my mother?"

He leaned forward and placed his elbows on his knees. He set his glass on the ground and looked through the darkness before him. He could just see the outline of his father's house and the porch light above the red door. "Everyone who has taken the time to point out to me that my relationship with my father sucks."

"Your relationship with Leo *does* suck. You should try to work on it. He's not getting any younger."

He glanced at the hypocrite across the iron bench. "Hello, pot? This is the kettle calling."

"What is that supposed to mean?"

"That before you start giving me advice, you should take a good hard look at your relationship with your mother."

Clare folded her arms beneath her breasts and looked across at the man beside her, the white stripes of his shirt the most visible thing about him. "My mother is an impossible woman."

"Impossible? If there is one thing I've learned over the past few days, it's that there is always a way to compromise."

She opened her mouth to argue, then closed it again. She'd given up on compromise years ago. "There is no use trying. I can't please her. I've tried my whole life, and my whole life I've disappointed her. I quit the Junior League because I didn't have the time, and I don't belong to any other charitable organization anymore. I'm thirty-three, single, and haven't produced a grandchild. To her, I'm wasting my life away. In fact, the only thing I've ever done that she approved of was my engagement to Lonny."

"Ah, so that's the reason."

"What?"

"I've been trying to figure out why a woman would choose to live with a gay man."

She shrugged and the other strap of her dress slid down her arm. "He lied to me."

"Maybe you wanted to believe the lie to please your mother."

She thought a moment. It still wasn't the ah-ha epiphany she'd been waiting for, but there was some truth in it. "Yeah, maybe." She pushed both straps back up. "But that doesn't mean I didn't love him and that it hurts less because he wasn't unfaithful with a woman." She felt an appalling sting in the backs of her eyes. She hadn't had a good soul-cleansing cry all week, and she certainly couldn't allow it to happen now. "It doesn't mean that all the hopes I had for a future suddenly go away and I feel relieved, and I think, 'Wow, dodged that bullet.' Maybe I should, but—" Her voice broke and she rose to her feet as if someone had yanked her up.

Clare walked farther from the party and stopped beneath an old oak. She placed her hand on the rough, uneven bark and stared out through rapidly blurring eyes at the outline of wild growth beyond. Had it only been a week? It seemed longer, and yet . . . it also seemed like yesterday. She rubbed beneath her eyes and wiped away her tears. She was in public. She didn't cry in public.

Why was the crying jag hitting her now? Here, of all places? She took a deep breath and let it out slowly. Perhaps because she'd kept herself busy. Worrying about the HIV test and planning Leo's party had taken a lot of mental and physical energy. Now that she didn't have those worries blocking her emotions, she was having a breakdown.

And it was damn inconvenient.

She felt Sebastian move up behind her. Not touching, but so close she could feel the heat of his body.

"Are you crying?"

"No."

"Yes you are."

"If you don't mind, I just want to be alone."

Of course, he didn't leave. Instead he placed his hands on her shoulders. "Don't cry, Clare."

"Okay." She wiped the moisture from her cheeks. "I'm fine now. You can rejoin the party. Leo's probably worried about where you are."

"You're *not* fine, and Leo knows I'm a big

boy." He slid his hands down her bare arms to her elbows. "Don't cry over someone who isn't worth it."

She looked down at her feet, her pedicured toes barely visible in the dark. "I know you think because I don't have the right equipment that I shouldn't take it so hard, but you don't understand that I loved Lonny. I thought he was the person I'd spend the rest of my life with. We had a lot in common." A tear rolled down her cheek and fell on her chest.

"Not sex."

"Yeah, except for that, but sex isn't everything. He was very supportive of my career and we took care of each other in every way that really matters."

His warm, rough palms slid up her arms to her shoulders. "Sex matters, Clare."

"I know, but it's not the *most* important thing in a relationship." Sebastian made a scoffing sound, but she ignored it. "We were planning to go to Rome on our honeymoon so I could research a book, but that's all gone now. And I feel foolish and . . . empty." Her voice broke and she raised a hand and wiped at her eyes. "How do you love someone one day and not the next? I wish I kn-knew."

Sebastian turned her and placed his hands on

the sides of her face. "Don't cry," he said, and brushed her wet cheeks with his thumbs.

The distant sound of crickets chirping mixed and mingled with "Son of a Preacher Man" softly pouring from the stereo. Clare looked up at Sebastian's smeared dark outline. "I'll be okay in a minute," she lied.

He lowered his face, and the light touch of his lips stopped the air in her lungs. "Shh," he whispered at the corner of her mouth. His hands slid toward the back of her head and his fingers plowed through her hair. He placed soft kisses on her cheek, her temple, and her brow. "Don't cry anymore, Clare."

She doubted she could if she wanted to. While Dusty sang about the only boy who could ever teach her, shock clogged everything in the center of Clare's chest and she could hardly breathe.

He kissed her nose, then said just above her mouth, "You need something else to think about." He gently pulled her head backward and her lips parted slightly. "Like how it feels to be held by a man who can get it up for a woman."

Clare placed her hands his chest and felt the solid muscles beneath the thin dress shirt. This could not be happening. Not with Sebastian. "No," she assured him a little desperately. "I remember."

"I think you've forgotten." His lips pressed into

hers, then eased back a fraction. "You need a little reminding by a man who knows how to use his pickle fork."

"I wish you'd forget I said that," she managed past the constriction in her chest.

"Never. Although I can't imagine anything the size of a pickle fork being much use to anyone."

She gasped as his mouth opened over hers and his tongue swept inside. He tasted like scotch and something else. Something she hadn't tasted in a very long time. Sexual desire. Hot and intoxicating, focused directly at her. She should have been alarmed, and she was a little. But mostly she liked the taste in her mouth. Like something luscious and rich she hadn't had in a while, and it poured all through her, warming the pit of her stomach and the empty places inside.

Everything around her receded away like a low tide. The party. The crickets. Dusty. Thoughts of Lonny.

Sebastian was right. She'd forgotten what it was like to have a man make love to her mouth. She couldn't recall it being so good. Or perhaps it was that Sebastian was so good at it. Her palms slid to his shoulders and the side of his neck as his slick tongue teased and coaxed until she gave in and kissed him back, returning the passion and possession he fed her.

Her toes curled in her Kate Spade sandals and she ran her fingers through the short hair brushing the collar of his shirt. His mouth never left hers, yet she felt the kiss everywhere. His wet mouth on hers turned every cell in her body needy and greedy and wanting more.

She rose to the balls of her feet and pressed into him. He groaned into her mouth, a deep sound of lust and yearning that fanned her ego, flamed the feminine fire deep inside that she'd allowed to die to a small ember. She turned her head to the side and her mouth clung to his.

His hands slid to her waist and his thumbs fanned her stomach through the thin cotton of her dress. His fingers pressed into her and he held her against his lower belly, where he was hard and swollen. He wanted her; she'd forgotten how truly good that felt. She kissed him like she wanted to eat him up, and she did. Every last bite. At that moment, she didn't care who he was, only how he made *her* feel. Wanted and desired.

He pulled back and gasped for breath. "Jesus, stop!"

"Why?" she asked, and kissed the side of his throat.

"Because," he answered, his voice sounding both rough and tortured, "we're both old enough to know where this will lead."

She smiled against his neck. "Where?"

"To a quicky in the weeds."

Clare wasn't that far gone. She dropped to her heels and retreated a few steps, leaned her back against the tree and took several mind-clearing breaths. She watched Sebastian comb his fingers though his hair and tried to make sense of what had happened. She'd just kissed Sebastian Vaughan, and as crazy as that sounded inside her head, she wasn't sorry. "You've been practicing since you were nine," she said, still a little dazed by it all.

"That shouldn't have happened. Sorry, but I've been thinking about it since the night you stripped in front of me. I remember exactly what you look like naked, and things got out of control and—" He scrubbed his face with his hands. "It wouldn't have happened if you hadn't started crying."

Her brows lowered as she stared into the darkened shadows and raised her fingers to her lips, still moist from his kiss. She wished he hadn't apologized. She knew she should probably be mad or appalled or offended by the way they'd both behaved, but she wasn't. At the moment, she didn't feel offended, appalled, or even sorry. She just felt alive. "You're blaming me? I'm not the one who grabbed and assaulted your mouth."

"Assaulted? I didn't assault you." He pointed at her. "I can't stand to see a woman cry. I know it sounds clichéd, but it's true. I would have done just about anything to get you to stop."

She was sure she'd be sorry later, though. Like when she had to see him in the light of day. "You could have walked away."

"And you'd still be bawling your eyes out like you were the night at the Double Tree." He took a deep breath and let it out slowly. "Once again, I did you a favor."

"Are you kidding?"

"Not at all. You stopped crying, didn't you?"

"Is this your ulterior motive crap again? You kissed me to help me out?"

"It's not crap."

"Wow, how noble of you." She laughed. "I suppose you got turned on because . . . why?"

"Clare," he said through a sigh, "you're an attractive woman and I'm a man. Of course you turn me on. I don't have to stand here and try to imagine what you look like naked, I *know* you're beautiful all over. So of course I felt something. If I hadn't felt some measure of desire, I'd be damn worried about myself."

She didn't bother pointing out that his desire measured about eight hard inches. She wished she could conjure up some righteous indignation or anger, but she couldn't. To do that meant she'd have to be sorry. Right now, she wasn't. With one kiss he'd given her back something she hadn't even known she'd let slip away. Her power to make a man want her with nothing more than a kiss.

"You should thank me," he said.

Right. She probably should thank him, but not for the reason he thought. "And you should go right ahead and kiss my butt." Lord, she sounded like she was ten again, but she didn't feel like it. Thanks to the man in front of her.

He chuckled, low and deep in his chest.

"In case you're confused, Sebastian, that wasn't an invitation."

"It sure sounded like an invitation," he said. He took a few steps back and added, "The next time I'm in town, I just might take you up on it."

"I don't know. Will I have to thank you?"

"No. You won't have to, but you will." Then, without another word, he turned and walked away, not in the direction of the party but toward the carriage house.

She'd known Sebastian all of her life. Some things hadn't changed. Like his attempts to talk around her and make her think day was night, to feed her lines of bull, and on occasion make her feel wonderful. Like the time he'd told her that her eyes were the color of the irises growing in her mother's garden. She couldn't remember her age, but she did remember that she'd lived on the compliment for days.

Clare felt the sharp edges of the tree against her back as she watched Sebastian step onto the porch of the carriage house. The light above his head turned his hair gold and the white of his shirt almost neon. He opened the red door and disappeared inside.

She once again raised her fingers to lips made sensitive by his kiss. She'd known him most of her life, but one thing was for certain, Sebastian was no longer a boy. He was definitely a man. A man who made women like Lorna Devers eye him like a piece of smooth, mouth-watering decadence. Like something she wanted to sink her teeth into just once.

Clare knew the feeling.

Ten

The second week of September, Sebastian boarded an international flight bound for Calcutta, India. Seven-thousand-plus miles and twenty-four hours later, he boarded a smaller aircraft for the plains of Bihar, India, where life and death depended on the whim of the annual monsoon and the ability to find a few hundred dollars to battle *kala azar*—black fever.

He landed in Muzaffarpur and drove four hours to the village of Rajwara with a local doctor and a photographer. From a distance the village looked bucolic and untouched by modern civilization. Men in traditional white dhoti kurta cultivated the fields with wooden carts and water buffalo, but like all underdeveloped parts of the globe that he'd reported on in the past, Sebastian knew this peaceful scene was an illusion.

As he and the other two men walked the dirt lanes of Rajwara, swarms of excited children surrounded them, kicking up dust along the way. A Seattle Mariners baseball cap shaded his face from the sun, and he'd filled the pockets of his cargo pants with extra batteries for his tape recorder. The doctor was well known in the village, and women in bright saris emerged from thatched huts one after the other, speaking rapidly in Hindi. Sebastian didn't need the doctor to translate to know what was said. The sound of the poor begging for help spoke a universal language.

Over the years, Sebastian had learned to place a professional wall between himself and what took place around him. To report on it without sinking into a black fog of hopeless depression. But scenes like these were still hard to encounter.

He stayed on the Bihar plains for three days interviewing One World Health and Doctors Without Borders relief workers. He visited hospitals. He spoke with a pharmaceutical chemist in the U.S. who'd developed a stronger more effective antibiotic, but like all drug development, money was the key to its success. He visited one last clinic and walked between the crammed rows of beds before he headed back to Calcutta.

He had an early flight out in the morning and was more than ready to relax in the hotel lounge, away from the teeming city, the overwhelming smells, and the constant noisy barrage. India possessed some of the most astounding beauty on earth and some of the most appalling poverty. In some places the two lived side by side, and nowhere was that more in evidence than Calcutta.

There had been a time when he'd scorned the journalist he considered soft—those "old" guys who kicked back in nice comfy hotel bars and ordered hotel food. As a young journalist, he'd felt that the best stories were out there in the streets, in the trenches and on the battlefields, in the flea bag hotels and slums, waiting to be told. He'd been right, but they weren't the only worthy stories or always the most important. He used to believe he needed to feel bullets whizzing past his head, but he'd learned that high-octane reporting could make a journalist lose perspective. The rush to report could lead to a loss of objectivity. Some of the best reporting came from a thorough and unbiased gaze. Through the years, he'd perfected the sometimes difficult craft of journalistic balance.

At thirty-five, Sebastian had suffered through several cases of dysentery, been robbed, stepped in running streams of raw sewage, and seen enough death to last him a lifetime. He'd been there and done that, and earned every bit of his success. He didn't have to fight for a byline anymore. After years of running full tilt, balls to the walls, chasing stories and leads, he'd earned some kickback time in an air-conditioned hotel.

He ordered a Cobra beer and tandoori chicken while he checked his e-mail. Halfway through his meal, an old colleague spotted him.

"Sebastian Vaughan."

Sebastian looked up and a smile spread across his mouth as he recognized the man walking toward him. Ben Landis was shorter than Sebastian, with thick black hair and an open, friendly face. The last time Sebastian had seen him, Ben had been a correspondent with *USA Today,* and they'd both been in a Kuwaiti hotel, awaiting the invasion of Iraq. Sebastian stood and shook Ben's hand. "What are you up to?" he asked.

Ben sat down across from him and signaled for a beer. "I'm writing a piece on the Missionaries of Charity ten years after the death of Mother Teresa."

Sebastian had done a piece on the Missionaries of Charity in 1997, a few days after the death of the Catholic nun, the last time he'd been in Calcutta. Little had changed, but that was no surprise. Change was slow in India. He raised his beer and took a drink. "How's it going?" he asked.

"Ah, you know how things move around here. Unless you're in a taxi, everything seems to stand still."

Sebastian set his bottle on the table and the two of them caught up, swapping war stories and ordering a second beer. They reminisced about what a pain in the ass it had been to climb into hot, sweaty, chemical-protection suits everytime there'd been a chemical threat during the push into Iraq. They laughed about the Marine's FUBAR, with forest green suits sent to the troops instead of sandstorm beige, though at the time it hadn't been a laughing matter. They recalled stories of waking every morning in a shallow hole with fine dust covering their faces, and laughed some more about the knockdown, drag-out between a Canadian peace activist, who'd called Rumsfeld a warmonger, and an American wire service reporter, who'd taken exception. The fight had been fairly evenly matched until two women from Reuters joined the fray and broke it up.

"Remember that Italian reporter?" Ben asked through a smile. "The woman with big red lips and . . ." He held his hands in front of his chest as if he were holding melons. "What was her name?"

"Natala Rossi." Sebastian raised the bottle to his lips and took a drink.

"Yeah. That was her."

Natala had been a reporter with *Il Messaggero,* and her gravity-defying breasts had been a constant source of fascination and speculation for her male colleagues.

"Those had to be fake," Ben said as he took a long pull off his beer. "Had to be."

Sebastian could have cleared things up for him. He'd spent a long night with Natala inside a Jordanian hotel and had firsthand knowledge—so to speak—that her lovely breasts were real. He'd understood very little Italian; she'd spoken very poor English; but conversation hadn't been the point.

"The rumor was, she took you up to her hotel room."

"Interesting." He'd never been the kind of guy to kiss and tell. Not even when the retelling was really good stuff. "Did the rumor mention if I had a good time?" When he thought back on that night, he could hardly recall Natala's face or her passionate cries. For some reason he couldn't fathom, a different brunette rose up and got stuck center brain.

"So, the rumor isn't true?"

"No," he lied, rather than give a blow by blow—so to speak—description of his night with the Italian reporter. While the memory of Natala had faded, the memories of Clare in a pink thong and the kiss they'd shared seemed to grow more vivid

with each passing day. He could recall perfectly
the soft curves of her body pressed against him,
the soft texture of her lush lips beneath his, and the
warmth of her slick mouth. He'd kissed a lot of
women in his life, good, bad, and hot as hell. But
no woman had ever kissed him like Clare. Like she
wanted to use her mouth to suck out his soul. And
the confusing thing was, he'd wanted to let her.
When she told him to kiss her nice little butt, he
knew just the spot he wanted to kiss.

"I hear you got married," he said in an effort to
change the subject and get his thoughts off Clare,
her smooth behind, and soft mouth. "Congratula-
tions."

"I did. My wife's expecting our first child any
day now."

"And you're here, waiting around to talk to
nuns?"

"I've got to make a living." A waiter set Ben's
third beer on the table and disappeared. "You
know how it goes."

Yeah, he knew. It took a lot of hard work and a
good deal of luck to make a living in journalism.
Especially for a freelance reporter.

"You haven't said what you're doing in Calcutta," Ben said, and reached for the bottle.

Sebastian filled him in on what he'd been in-
vestigating in the Bihar plains and the newest

outbreak of black fever. The two men shot the breeze for another hour, then Sebastian called it a night.

On the flight home the following day, he listened to the interviews he'd taped and scribbled down notes. While he wrote an outline, he recalled the abject hopelessness he saw in the faces of the peasants. He knew there was nothing he could do but tell their story and shed some light on the epidemic that had plagued the region. Just as he knew that there would be a new plague and a new epidemic to report next month. Bird flu, malaria, HIV/AIDS, cholera, drought, hurricane, tidal waves, starvation. Take your pick. War and disasters were a never-ending cycle and a constant employer. On any given day there was a new breakout of disease, or if not, some little dictator, terrorist leader, or Boy Scout gone bad, was going to start shit somewhere on the planet.

During a two-hour layover in Chicago he got a bite to eat in a sports pub and pulled out his laptop. As he'd done hundreds of times in the past, he pecked out an opening while he ate a pastrami on rye. He struggled a bit, but nothing compared to what he'd gone through with the piece he'd written on homegrown terrorism.

On the flight from O'Hare, he caught up on some sleep, waking just in time for the Boeing 787 to set down at Sea-Tac. Rain pelted the runway and strings of water streamed from the wings of the big aircraft. It was ten A.M., Pacific time, when he deplaned, and he maneuvered easily though the airport toward his Land Cruiser parked in the long-term lot. He couldn't recall how many times he'd walked through Sea-Tac over the years. Too many to count, but this time was different. For some reason he couldn't explain, he knew this would be his last international flight. Flying halfway across the globe to report a story didn't appeal to him as it once had, and now he was thinking about Ben Landis and his pregnant wife.

As he drove up Interstate 5, an irritating little peck of loneliness nagged at him. Before the death of his mother, he'd never been lonely. He had male friends. Women too, a number of whom he could ring and who'd meet for a drink or anything else he wanted.

His mother was gone, but life was fine, just the way he liked it, just the way he'd always envisioned. But with every silent swipe of his windshield wipers, the feeling scratched a little deeper. He figured it was the jet lag and once he got home to his condo and relaxed, the feeling would go away.

He'd purchased the condo two years after his book had hit number one on the *New York Times* and *USA Today* best-seller lists. The book had sat on the lists for fourteen months, earning him more money than he'd ever made or would ever hope to make from journalism. He'd invested the money in real estate, luxury goods, and a few risky tech stocks that were paying off nicely. Then he'd moved on up, à la the Jeffersons, from a small apartment in Kent to the deluxe condo in the Queen Anne district of Seattle. He had a million-dollar view of the bay, the mountains, and Puget Sound. The 2,500-square-foot space had two bedroom suites with shower stalls and sunken jet tubs in each bathroom. Everything from the ceramic tile and hardwood floors to the plush carpet and leather furniture were done in rich earth tones. The polished chrome and glass shined like new money, a symbol of his success.

Sebastian pulled his SUV into his parking space, then moved to the elevator. A woman in a power suit and a boy wearing a lizard T-shirt waited by the doors and stepped into the elevator with him. "What floor?" he asked as the doors closed.

"Six, please."

He pressed the buttons for six and eight, then leaned back against the wall.

"I'm sick," the little boy informed him.

Sebastian looked down into the kid's pale face.

"Chicken pox," the woman said. "I hope you've had them already."

"When I was ten." His own mother had turned him pink with calamine lotion.

The elevator stopped and the woman gently placed her hand on the back of her son's head and they stepped into the hallway. "I'll make you some soup and a bed in front of the TV. You can curl up with the dog and watch cartoons all day," she said as the doors closed.

Sebastian rode the elevator two more floors, got out, and entered the condominium on his left. He dropped his carry-on suitcase in the entryway, the sound inordinately loud on the tile floor. There was nothing to break the silence that greeted him. Not even a dog. He had never had a dog, not even as a kid. He wondered if he should get one. Maybe a beefy boxer.

Sunlight poured through the huge windows as he walked from the great room and set his laptop on the marble countertop in the kitchen. He started a pot of coffee and tried to explain away his sudden interest in a dog. He was tired. That's what was wrong with him. The last thing he needed was a dog. He wasn't home enough to take care of a plant, let alone an animal. There was nothing missing in his life and he wasn't lonely.

He moved from the kitchen to the bedroom and thought perhaps it was the condo itself. Maybe it needed something more . . . homey. Not a dog, but something. Maybe he should move. Maybe he was more like his mother than he'd ever guessed and had to try on a dozen or so homes before he found one that felt just right.

Sebastian sat on the edge of his bed and took off his boots; the dust from the streets of Rajwara still clung to the laces. He kicked off his socks and took off his watch as he headed to the bathroom.

Several years before, he'd tried to talk his mother into retiring and moving into a nicer house. He'd offered to buy her something newer and fancier, but she'd flat-out refused. She'd liked her house. "It took me twenty years to find a place that feels like a home," she told him. "I'm not leaving."

Sebastian stripped naked, then stuck his hand into the shower stall. The brass fixture was cool to the touch as he turned on the faucet and stepped within the glass closure. If it had taken his mother twenty years to find a comfortable space, he figured he had a few more years to figure it out. Warm water rained down upon his head and over his face. He closed his eyes and felt the tension wash away. There were plenty of things to stress about. At the moment, where he lived wasn't one of them.

He had to sell his mother's house. Soon. Her best friend and business partner, Myrna, had moved all the beauty supplies out of the salon and taken all the plants. She'd donated the canned and dry goods to the local food bank. All that was left for him was to figure out what to do with the rest of his mother's things. Once he got that off his shoulders, his life would get back to normal.

He reached for the soap, lathered his hands and washed his face. He thought of his father and wondered what the old man was up to. Probably pruning roses, he supposed. And he thought of Clare. More specifically, of the night he'd kissed her. What he'd told Clare had been the truth. He would have done just about anything to get her to stop crying. A woman's tears were just about the only thing in the world that made him feel helpless. And, he reasoned, kissing Clare had seemed like a better idea than hitting her or throwing a bug in her hair, like he had as a kid.

He lifted his face and rinsed away the soap. He had lied to her. When he apologized for kissing her, he hadn't been all that sorry. In fact, he hadn't been sorry in the least. One of the most difficult things he'd ever done was turn away and leave her standing in the shadows. One of the most difficult—but the wisest. Out of all the single women he knew, Clare Wingate was not available for kissing and touching and rolling around naked. Not for him.

But that didn't stop him from thinking about her. About her round breasts and dark pink nipples. Lust churned low in his belly as he closed his eyes and thought about making her nipples hard as his fingers followed the pink string of her thong across her hip to the triangle of silk material covering her crotch.

His testicles ached and he turned rock hard. He thought of her using her beautiful mouth on him, and sexual need pounded through his veins, but there wasn't anyone to slip into the shower and take care of that need for him. He could call someone to come over, he supposed, but he didn't feel right having one woman finish something another woman had started. With the thought of Clare in his head, he took care if it himself.

After Sebastian's shower, he wrapped a towel around his waist and headed into the kitchen. He felt a little ridiculous having just fantasized about Clare. Not only was she the weird little girl from his youth, but she didn't even like him. Usually he tried to fantasize about women who didn't think he was a dickhead.

He poured a mug of coffee and reached for the phone sitting on the counter. He dialed and waited as it rang.

"Hello," Leo answered on the fifth ring.

"I'm back," he said, pushing thoughts of Clare

from his head. Even after the time they'd spent together recently, it still felt a bit strange to just dial
up the old man.

"How was your trip?"

Sebastian raised the mug. "Good."

They talked about the weather, then Leo asked,
"Are you going to be heading this way anytime
soon?"

"I don't know. I have to pack up Mom's house
and get it ready to sell." Even as he said it, a part of
him shrank from the thought of packing his mother's life in boxes. "I've been putting it off."

"It's going to be tough."

That was an understatement, and Sebastian
laughed without humor. "Yeah."

"Would you like me to help?"

He opened his mouth to give an automatic re-
fusal. He could pack up a few boxes. No problem.
"Are you offering?"

"If you need me."

It was just stuff. His mother's stuff. She most
definitely *wouldn't* have wanted Leo in her house,
but his mother was gone and his father was offering
a helping hand. "I'd appreciate that."

"I'll tell Joyce I've got to be gone a few days."

Packing up the kitchen was easier than Sebastian
had anticipated. He was able to detach himself as

he and Leo worked side by side. His mother had never been into china or crystal. She ate off Corelle, plain white, so if she broke a plate she could replace it. She bought her glasses at Wal-Mart, so if she dropped one, it was no big deal. Her pots and pans were old and in fairly good shape because she'd rarely cooked, especially once Sebastian had moved out of the house.

But just because his mother hadn't been materialistic didn't mean she hadn't been meticulous about her appearance till the day she'd died. She'd been picky about her hair, the color of her lipstick, and whether her shoes clashed with her purse. She'd loved to sing old Judy Garland songs, and when she was in the mood to splurge, she'd bought snow globes. She had so many, she'd converted his old bedroom into a showplace for her collection. She'd lined the walls with custom-made shelving, and Sebastian had always suspected she'd done it so he couldn't move back home again.

After Leo and Sebastian packed up the kitchen, they grabbed some newspapers and cardboard boxes and headed for Sebastian's old bedroom. The wood floors creaked beneath their feet, and through the white sheer curtains sunshine flowed into the room and through the rows of globes. He half expected to see her, pink feather duster in hand, dusting the shelves.

Sebastian set two boxes on a card table and a stack of newspapers on a folding chair he'd placed in there earlier. He deliberately pushed memories of his mother and her feather duster from his head. He reached for a globe he'd brought back from Russia and turned it in his hand. White snow fluttered about Saint Basil's Cathedral in Red Square.

"Well, I'll be . . . Who woulda thought Carol would have kept this all these years."

Sebastian looked over at Leo as the older man reached for an old globe from Cannon Beach, Oregon. A mermaid sat on a rock combing her blond hair while bits of glitter and shells floated about her.

"I bought this for your mother on our honeymoon."

Sebastian grabbed a piece of newspaper and wrapped the Russian globe. "That's one of her oldest. I didn't know you gave it to her."

"Yeah. At the time, I thought that mermaid looked like her." His father glanced up. The deep lines at the corners of his eyes got even deeper and a faint smile played across his mouth. "Except your mother was about seven months pregnant with you."

"Now that, I did know." He set the globe in the box.

"She was so beautiful and full of life. A real

corker." Leo bent and grabbed a piece of paper. "She liked everything full-tilt, like a roller coaster, and I . . ." He paused and shook his head. "I liked calm." He wrapped the globe. Over the sound of the paper he said, "Still do, I guess. You're more like your mother than you are me. You like to chase lots of excitement."

Not so much anymore. At least not as much as he had a few months ago. "Maybe I'm slowing down."

Leo looked up at him.

"After this last trip, I'm seriously thinking about hanging up my passport. I have a few more assignments, and then I think I'll go strictly freelance. Maybe take some time off."

"What will you do?"

"I'm not sure. I just know I don't want to take foreign assignments. At least for a while."

"Can you do that, then?"

"Sure." Talking about work kept his mind off what he was doing. He reached for a Reno, Nevada, globe and wrapped it up. "How's the new Lincoln?"

"Rides like butter."

"How's Joyce?" he asked, not that he cared, but thinking about Joyce was better than thinking about what he was doing.

"Planning a big Christmas to-do. That always makes her happy."

"It's not even October."

"Joyce likes to plan ahead."

Sebastian set the wrapped globe in the box. "And Clare? Is she over her breakup with the gay guy?" he asked, just to keep up the small talk with the old man.

"I don't know. I haven't seen much of her lately, but I doubt it. She's a very sensitive girl."

Which was yet one more reason to stay away from her. Sensitive girls liked long-term commitments. And he had never been the kind of guy to commit to anything long term. He reached for a Wizard of Oz globe with Dorothy and Toto following the yellow brick road. Even though it would never happen, he let his mind wonder to the possibility of spending a night or two with Clare. He wouldn't mind getting her naked, and he was certain she'd benefit from a few rounds of sex. Get her to relax and lighten her up. Put a smile on her face for weeks.

In his hand, the first notes of "Somewhere Over the Rainbow" began to play from the music box within the base of the globe. The Judy Garland classic was his mother's favorite, and everything inside Sebastian stopped. A thousand tingles raced

up his spine and tightened his scalp. The globe fell
from his hands and smashed to the floor. Sebastian
watched water splash his shoes, and Dorothy, Toto,
and a dozen little flying monkeys washed across the
floor. The detached front he'd kept inside his soul
shattered like the broken glass at his feet. The one
steady anchor in his life was gone. Gone, and she
wasn't coming back. She was never going to dust
her snow globes or fuss about clashing shoes. He'd
never hear her sing in her faulty soprano voice or
nag him to come over for a haircut.

"Fuck." He sank to the chair. "I can't do this."
He was numb and charged at the same time, like
he'd stuck a key in the light socket. "I thought I
could, but I can't pack her up like she's never coming back." The backs of his eyes stung and he swallowed hard. He placed his elbows on his knees and
covered his face with his hands. A sound like a
freight train clambered in his ears, and he knew it
was from the pressure of holding it all back. He
wasn't going to cry like a hysterical woman. Especially not in front of the old man. If he could just
hold it back for a few more seconds, it would pass
and he'd be okay again.

"There's no shame in loving your mother," he
heard his father say over the crashing in his head.
"In fact, it's a sign of a good son." He felt his father's hand on the back of his head, the weight

heavy, familiar, comforting. "Your mother and I didn't get along, but I know she loved you something fierce. She was like a pit bull when it came to you. And she never would admit that her boy did any wrong."

That was true.

"She did a fine job raising you mostly on her own, and I always was grateful to her for that. The Good Lord knows I wasn't around as much as I shoulda been."

Sebastian pressed his palms against his eyes, then dropped his hands between his knees. He glanced up at his father standing next to him. He took a deep breath and the pinch behind his eyes eased. "She didn't exactly make it easy."

"Don't make excuses for me. I could have fought more. I could have gone back to court." His hand moved to Sebastian's shoulder and he gave a little squeeze. "I could have done a lot of things. I should have done something, but I . . . I thought that the fighting wasn't good and that there would be lots of time once you were older. I was wrong, and I regret that."

"We all have regrets." Sebastian had a ton of his own, but the weight of his father's hand felt like an anchor in a suddenly vertiginous world. "Maybe we shouldn't dwell on them. Just move on."

Leo nodded and patted Sebastian's back like

when he'd been a boy. "Why don't you go get yourself a Slurpee. That'll make you feel better, and I'll finish here."

He smiled despite himself. "I'm thirty-five, Dad. I don't get Slurpees anymore."

"Oh. Well, go take a break and I'll finish this room."

Sebastian stood and wiped his hands down the front of his jeans. "No. I'll go find a broom and a dustpan," he said, grateful for his father's steady presence in the house.

Eleven

The first week of December, a light snow dusted the streets of downtown Boise and covered the foothills in pristine white. Holiday wreaths hung suspended from lampposts, and storefront windows were decked out for the season. Bundled-up shoppers crowded the sidewalks.

On the corner of Eighth and Main, "Holly Jolly Christmas" played softly inside The Piper Pub and Grille, the muted Muzak a fraction or two lower than the steady hum of voices. Gold, green, and red garlands added a festive air to the second-story restaurant.

"Happy holidays." Clare held up her peppermint mocha and lightly touched glasses with her friends. The four women had just finished lunch and were enjoying flavored coffee instead of dessert.

"Merry Christmas," Lucy toasted.

"Happy Hanukkah," Adele said, although she wasn't Jewish.

To cover all bases, Maddie added, "Happy Kwanzaa," although she wasn't African American, Pan African, or had ever set foot in Africa.

Lucy took a drink and said as she lowered her glass mug, "Oh, I almost forgot." She dug around in her purse hanging on the back of her chair, then pulled out several envelopes. "I finally remembered to bring copies of the picture of us all together at the Halloween party." She handed an envelope to Clare, who sat on her right, and two others across the table.

Lucy and her husband, Quinn, had thrown a costume party in their new house on Quill Ridge overlooking the city. Clare slipped the photo from the envelope and glanced at the picture of her in a bunny costume standing beside her three friends. Adele had dressed as a fairy with large gossamer wings, Maddie as a Sherlock Holmes, and Lucy had worn a naughty cop outfit. The party had been a lot of fun. Just what Clare needed after a difficult two and a half months. By the end of October her heartache had started to mend a little, and she'd even been asked out by Darth Vader.

Without his helmet, Darth had been attractive in a macho-cop sort of way. He'd had a job, all his teeth and hair, and appeared to be one-hundred-percent heterosexual. The old Clare would have accepted his invitation to dinner with the subconscious hope that one man would ease the loss of another. But though she'd been flattered, she said no. It had been too soon to date.

"When's your book signing?" Adele asked Clare.

She looked up and slipped the photo into her purse. "I have one at Borders on the tenth. Another at Walden's on the twenty-fourth. I'm hoping to cash in on all those last-minute shoppers." It had been almost five months now since she found Lonny with the Sears repairman, and she'd moved on. She no longer had to battle tears and her chest didn't feel so tight and empty these days, but she still wasn't ready to date. Not yet. Probably not for quite a while.

Adele took a sip of her coffee. "I'll come to your signing on the tenth."

"Yeah, I'll be there," Lucy said.

"Me too. But I'm not going near the mall on the twenty-fourth." Maddie looked up from the photo. "With the place so crowded, I'm more likely to run into an old boyfriend."

Clare raised a hand. "Me too."

"That reminds me, I have gossip." Adele set her

mug on the table. "I ran into Wren Jennings the other day, and she let it slip that she can't find anyone interested in her next book proposal."

Clare didn't particularly like Wren, thought she had a huge ego but little talent to back it up. She'd done one book signing with Wren, and one was enough. Not only had Wren monopolized the whole two hours, she kept telling anyone who approached the table that she wrote "real historical romance. Not costume dramas." Then she'd looked pointedly at Clare as if she were a felon. But not finding a publisher for your next book would be horrible. "Wow, that's scary."

Lucy nodded. "Yeah, no one tortures verbiage quite like Wren, but not having a publisher would be frightening."

"What a huge relief for the Earth Firsters. No more trees have to die for Wren's crappy books."

Clare looked at Maddie and chuckled. "Meow."

"Come on. You know that woman can't even construct an intelligent sentence and wouldn't know a decent plot if it bit her on the ass. And that's a lot of ass." Maddie frowned and glanced about at her friends. "I'm not the only catty one at this table. I just say what everyone is thinking."

That was true enough. "Well," Clare said, and raised her peppermint mocha to her lips, "every now and again I do have an overwhelming urge to lick my hands and wash my face."

"And I have a desire to nap in the sun all day," Lucy added.

Adele gasped. "Are you pregnant?"

"No." Lucy held up her drink, which was laced with kahlua.

"Oh." Adele's excitement was instantly deflated. "I was hoping one of us hurries up and has a baby. I'm getting broody."

"Don't look at me." Maddie shoved the Halloween photo in her bag. "I don't have any desire to have children."

"Never?"

"No. I think I'm one of the only women on the planet who was born without a burning desire to procreate." Maddie shrugged. "I wouldn't mind practicing with a good-looking man, though."

Adele raised her coffee. "Ditto. Celibacy sucks."

"Double ditto," Clare said.

Lucy smiled. "I've got a good-looking man to practice with."

Clare finished her coffee and reached for her purse. "Bragger."

"I don't want a man on a permanent basis," Maddie insisted. "Snoring and hogging the blankets. That's the good thing about having big Carlos.

When I'm finished, I throw him back in the night-stand."

One brow lifted up Lucy's forehead. "Big Carlos? You named your . . ."

Maddie nodded. "I've always wanted a Latin lover."

Clare looked around to see if anyone had overheard Maddie. "Sheesh, lower your voice." None of the other diners were looking their way, and Clare turned back to her friends. "Sometimes you're not safe in public."

Maddie leaned across the table and whispered, "You have one."

"I didn't name it!"

"Then whose name do you call out?"

"No one's." She'd always been very quiet during sex and didn't understand how or why a woman could or would lose her dignity and start hollering. She'd always thought she was good in bed. At least she tried to be, but a soft little murmur or moan was as loud as she got.

"If I were you, I'd practice with Sebastian Vaughan," Adele said.

"Who?" Lucy wanted to know.

"Clare's hot friend. He's a journalist, and you can tell by looking at him that he knows what to put where and how often."

"He lives in Seattle." Clare hadn't seen Sebastian

since the night of Leo's party. The night he'd kissed her and made her remember what is was like to be a woman. When he'd flamed the desire deep inside that she'd almost allowed her relationship with Lonny to extinguish. She didn't know firsthand if Sebastian knew the who, what, where, when, and why, but he certainly knew *how* to kiss a woman.

"I don't think I'll see him for another twenty years or so." Leo had spent Thanksgiving in Seattle, and the last Clare had heard, he planned to spend Christmas there also. Which was sad. Leo had always spent Christmas day with her and Joyce. Clare would miss him. "I've got to get going," she said, and stood. "I told my mother I'd help her with her Christmas party this year."

Lucy looked up. "I thought you refused to help her after last year."

"I know, but she behaved herself over Thanksgiving and didn't mention Lonny's aspic." She reached for her wool peacoat on the back of her chair and shoved her arms inside. "It about killed her, but she didn't mention Lonny at all. So as a reward, I said I'd help her." She looped her red scarf around her neck. "I also made her promise to stop lying about what I write."

"Do you think she'll be able to keep her promise?"

"Of course not, but she'll try." She grabbed her

red alligator skin purse. "See you all on the tenth," she said, bid her friends good-bye, and walked from the restaurant.

The temperature outside had risen, and the snow on the ground began to melt. Cold air brushed her cheeks as she walked along the terrace toward the parking garage. She pulled her red leather gloves from her coat pocket and put them on. The heels of her boots tapped across white and black tile as she hooked a right at an Italian restaurant. If she'd walked straight ahead, she would have ended up in the Balcony Bar—the place Lonny had always assured her *wasn't* a gay bar. She knew now that he'd lied about that, just as he'd lied about a lot of things. And she'd been perfectly willing to believe him.

She pushed open the doors to the garage and walked toward her car. At the thought of Lonny, her heart no longer pinched in her chest. What she mostly felt was anger, at Lonny for lying to her, and at herself for wanting so desperately to believe him.

The temperature inside the concrete garage was colder than it was outside, and her breath hung in front of her face as she unlocked her Lexus and got behind the wheel. If she thought about it, she truly wasn't all that angry anymore. The one good thing that had come out of her failed relationship with

Lonny was that she'd forced herself to stop and take a good hard look at her life. Finally. She was going to turn thirty-four in a few months and she was tired of relationships that were doomed to failure.

The obvious ta-da moment she'd been waiting to reveal itself and solve all her problems had never happened. About a month earlier, while she'd been folding laundry and watching *The Guiding Light*, she'd realized that the reason she hadn't been able to experience the big eureka moment was because there wasn't just one—there were several. Starting with her issue with her father and sliding right into her subconscious desire to either rile or please her mother. And Clare had dated men who'd fit both bills. She hated to admit that her mother had that much influence on her personal life, but she did. To top it all off, she was a love junkie. She loved love, and while that helped her career, it wasn't so good for her personal life.

She pulled out of her parking space and headed toward the toll booth. She was a little embarrassed that she'd reached thirty-three and was only now changing the destructive patterns in her life.

It was past time she took control. Time to break the passive-aggressive cycle with her mother. Time to stop falling in love with every man who paid attention to her. No more love at first sight—ever—and she meant it this time. No more settling—ever—and that included, but was not limited to, cheaters, liars, and fakes. If and when she got involved with a man—and that was a big *if* and a cautious *when*—he was going to feel *damn* lucky to have *her*.

The day before Joyce Wingate's annual Christmas party, Clare dressed in old jeans and a cable-knit sweater. Over that she wore her white ski parka, wool gloves, and light blue wool scarf wrapped around her neck and the lower half of her face. She spent the afternoon adding the finishing touches to the outside of the house on Warm Springs Avenue.

The last two weeks since she'd met her friends for lunch, she'd helped her mother and Leo decorate the big home inside and out. A twelve-foot Douglas fir stood in the middle of the foyer, adorned with antique ornaments, red bows, and golden lights. Every downstairs room had been decorated with pine greenery, brass candlesticks, nativity scenes, or Joyce's extensive nutcracker collection. The Christmas Spode and Waterford crystal had been cleaned, and the linens pressed and waiting in the truck of Clare's car to be brought inside.

The day prior, Leo had come down with a cold, and she and Joyce insisted that he abandon the remaining tasks outside for fear his cold would worsen. He was given the job of polishing the silver and wrapping pine garland and red velvet ribbon up the mahogany banisters.

Clare had taken over outside, and every time she ventured into the house for a coffee refill or just to thaw her toes, Leo fussed and argued that he was well enough to hang lights on the remaining shrubs. He might have been, but at his age, Clare didn't want to take a chance that the cold would get worse and turn into pneumonia.

The work outside was neither hard nor heavy, just freezing and tedious. The big house was festooned with lighted boughs that hung about the door, along the porch, and around each stone column. A pair of five-foot pepperberry reindeer stood in the front yard, and lighted candy canes lined the sidewalk and driveway.

Clare moved the ladder to the last shrub and untangled one remaining string of C-9 lightbulbs. After this string, she was finished, and she was looking forward to going home, filling her jet tub with hot water and sitting in it until her skin wrinkled.

The sun was out, warming the valley to a balmy thirty-one degrees, which was an improvement over the twenty-seven high of the day before. Clare climbed onto the ladder and wrapped the lights around the top of the eight-foot tree. Leo could have told her both the common and scientific name of the shrub. He was amazing that way.

The frozen foliage made a rasping sound as it slid across the sleeve of Clare's coat, and the toes inside her boots had turned numb about an hour ago. She could no longer feel her cheeks, but her fingers still worked inside her fur-lined gloves. She leaned into the shrub to wrap the lights around the back and felt her cell phone slip from her coat pocket. She reached for it a second too late, and the thin phone disappeared into the shrub.

"Dang it." Her hands dove into the greenery and pushed it apart. She caught a glimpse of the silver and black flip phone as it slid deeper into the middle of the shrub. She leaned forward, bending over the top of the ladder and reaching as far as she could into the middle. The tips of her gloves brushed the phone, and it disappeared into denser foliage. As she pulled her head out of the shrub, a vehicle turned into the driveway and continued to the back of the house. By the time she looked around, the car was out of view. She assumed the florist delivering her mother's poinsettias, crocuses, and amaryllis for the party was a little early.

She moved to the back of the shrub closest to the house and pushed the branches apart. The frozen stems brushed her face, and her thoughts turned to spiders. For the first time since she'd stepped outside, she was glad it was below freezing. If it had been summer, she would have bought a new phone rather than risk spiders in her hair.

"Hey there, frosty."

Clare straightened and turned so fast she almost tripped herself. Sebastian Vaughan walked toward her, the sunlight catching his hair, lighting him up like an archangel come down from heaven. He wore jeans, a black down parka, and a smile that hinted at less than heavenly thought. "When did you get here?" she asked, and came out from behind the heavy greenery.

"Just now. I recognized your butt when I pulled in the driveway."

She frowned. "Leo didn't mention you were coming." The last time she'd seen him, he'd kissed her, and the memory brought a flush to her frozen face.

"He didn't know until I landed about an hour ago." His breath left his lungs in white wisps, and he took one bare hand from the pocket of his coat and reached toward her.

She pulled back and wrapped her gloved hand around his wrist. "What are you doing?"

His smile creased the corners of his green eyes. "What do you think I was going to do?"

Her chest got tight when she recalled with startling clarity what he'd done to her at his father's birthday party. More than what he'd done, she remembered her response. And the disturbing thing was, she wanted to feel that way again. She wanted what every woman wanted, to feel desire and be desired. "With you, I never know."

He picked a twig from her hair and showed it to her. "Your cheeks are red."

"That's because it's below freezing out here," she said, and blamed it on the weather. She removed her hand from his wrist and took a step back. Needing a man to make her feel good about herself was the old Clare, she told herself. The newer and wiser Clare had learned that she didn't need a man to feel okay. "Why don't you do something useful and call my cell number."

"Why?"

She pointed behind her. "Because I dropped it in there."

He chuckled and reached for the BlackBerry hooked to his belt. "What's the number?"

She gave it to him, and within a few moments "Don't Phunk With My Heart" played from within the tall shrub.

"Your ring is the Black Eyed Peas?"

Clare shrugged and dove into the shrub once more. "It's my new motto." She pushed several branches apart and caught a glimpse of the phone.

"Does that mean you're over the gay boy-friend?"

"Yes." She didn't love Lonny anymore. She stretched her arm as far as possible and grabbed the phone. "Got it," she whispered, and backed out of the shrub. She turned and the front of her coat brushed Sebastian's. He grabbed the tops of her arms to keep her from falling. Her gaze moved up the zipper of his coat to his throat and chin, past his lips to his eyes, staring down into hers.

"What are you doing out here?" he asked. Instead of letting go, his grasp tightened and he pulled her onto the balls of her feet, bringing her face closer to his. "Besides losing your phone."

"Christmas lights." She could have stepped back, pulled away.

His gaze moved to her mouth. "It's colder than a well digger's ass out here."

Yeah, she could have stepped back, but she didn't. "Have you ever felt a well digger's ass?"

He shook his head.

"Then how do you know how cold it is? And why his ass as opposed to his elbow?"

"It's just an expression. It isn't . . ." His voice trailed off with the white puffs of his breath. He looked up into her eyes and drew his brows together. "You always did take everything too literally." He let go of her arms and pointed to the string of lights. "Need help?"

"From you?"

"Is there anyone else around?"

Her toes were frozen and her thumbs were turning numb. With help, she wouldn't have to waste time climbing up and down the ladder and moving it around. She could be in the house warming up in about ten minutes instead of half an hour. "What's the ulterior motive?"

He chuckled and climbed up the ladder. "I hadn't thought of one." He grabbed the string of lights and wrapped it around the top of the shrub. His reach was so long, he didn't have to climb down and move the ladder. "But I will."

And fifteen minutes later he did.

"This is my favorite," Sebastian said as he handed Clare a cup of cocoa. He'd had to sweet-talk her into coming with him into the carriage house, and he wondered why he'd bothered. It wasn't like he was hard up for female company. "I like the crunchy little marshmallows." She took a drink of the cocoa and looked up at him through her light blue eyes, and he knew why he'd bothered talking her out of her coat and wrestling it from her grasp. He didn't necessarily like it, but there was no denying that he'd thought a lot about her in the past few months. He took a drink from his cup. For reasons he could not even begin to explain to himself, he could not get Clare Wingate out of his head.

"This is pretty good," she said as she lowered her cup. He watched her as she licked chocolate from her top lip, and he felt it in his groin. "Are you here for Christmas?"

He wanted Clare, and not as a friend. Sure, he liked her well enough, but standing so close to her, he wanted to lick chocolate off her mouth. "I hadn't thought that far ahead. I was in Denver this morning and I called Dad. He started hacking and wheezing and I switched my flight from Seattle to Boise."

"He has a cold."

His attraction to her was purely physical. That was all. He wanted her body. Too bad she wasn't the sort of woman who might be up for some mutual using. "He sounded like he couldn't catch his breath," he said, and didn't even want to think about how much that had scared the shit out of him. He'd immediately called the airline and changed destinations. During the nearly two hours it took him to get to Boise, he'd imagined different scenarios. Each one worse than the last. By the time he landed, he had a lump in his stomach and several coffins picked out in his head. That just wasn't like him. "But I guess I overreacted, because when I called him from the Boise airport, he was polishing silver in your mother's kitchen and bitching about being cooped up in the house like a baby. He sounded irritated that I was checking up on him."

The corners of her full lips tilted up and she leaned one hip into the counter. "I think it's nice that you're concerned. Does he know you're here?"

"I haven't gone to the big house yet. I got distracted by the sight of your butt sticking out of the shrub," he said, rather than admit he felt foolish. Like a paranoid old woman. "I'm sure he's seen the rental car and will be here when he's through."

"What were you doing in Denver?"

"I spoke last night in Boulder, at the University of Colorado."

One brow moved up her smooth forehead as she blew a breath into her cup. "About?"

"The role of journalism in wartime."

One side of her hair fell across her cheek. "Sounds interesting," she said, and took a drink.

"Riveting." He pushed her hair behind her ear, and she didn't jump out of her skin nor grab his wrist this time. "I've decided on my ulterior motive." He dropped his hand.

She tilted her head to the side and set her cup on the counter next to his. A frown pulled at the corners of her porn-star mouth.

"Don't worry. All you have to do is come with me to find a Christmas gift for my father."

"You forget what happened when you wanted a birthday gift for Leo."

"I didn't forget. It took me a good fifteen minutes to cut all that pink crap off the fishing pole."

Her scowl turned into a pleased smile. "I guess you learned your lesson."

"What lesson is that?"

"Not to mess with me."

Now it was his turn to smile. "Clare, you like it when I mess with you."

"What have you been smoking?"

Instead of answering, he took a step forward and closed the distance between them. "The last time I messed with you, you kissed me like you didn't want me to stop."

She tilted her head back and looked up at him. "You kissed me. I didn't kiss you."

"You practically sucked the air out of my lungs."

"That isn't how I remember it."

He slid his palms up the arms of her thick, bumpy sweater. "Liar."

A furrow appeared between her brows, and she leaned back a little. "I was raised not to lie."

"Honey, I'm sure you do a lot of things your mama raised you not to do." His hands slid to the middle of her back and he brought her closer. "Everyone thinks you're nice. Sweet. Such a good girl."

She put her hands on his chest and swallowed. Through the blue wool of his shirt, the soft pressure of her touch heated his skin and warmed the pit of his stomach. "I try to be a nice person."

Sebastian chuckled and plowed his finger through her soft hair. He held the back of her head in one of his hands. "I like it when you don't try so hard." He looked into her eyes and saw the desire she tried so hard to hide from him. "When you let the real Clare out to play."

"I don't think . . ." He kissed the corner of her mouth. "Sebastian, I don't think this is a good idea."

"Open up," he said as he brushed his lips across hers. "And I'll change your mind." Just once. Just for a minute or two. Just to make sure he wasn't mistaken about the last time he'd kissed her. Just to make sure he hadn't exaggerated that kiss in his own mind to fulfill his X-rated fantasies.

He started slow. Teasing and coaxing. The tip of his tongue touched the seam of her full lips, and he placed soft kisses at the corners. She stood perfectly still. Stiff, except for her fingers curling into the front of his shirt. "Come on, Clare. You know you want to," he whispered just above her mouth.

Her lips parted and she sucked in a breath, his breath, deep into her lungs. He took full advantage and his tongue touched the inside of her hot, moist mouth. She tasted like chocolate and like the desire she was trying to deny herself. Then she turned her head to one side and melted into his chest. Her hands slid up to his shoulders and the sides of his neck. Sebastian turned the heat up a bit and applied a little more pressure. She responded with a sweet moan that spread heat across his flesh and gripped his lower belly in a white hot fist. But just as the kiss was starting to get real good, the front door of the house opened and closed and Clare practically jumped out of her skin. She took a few steps back and Sebastian's hands fell to his sides. Her eyes were wide and her breathing uneven.

Sebastian heard his father's footsteps a moment before Leo walked into the kitchen. "Oh," the old man said, and came to a stop on the other side of the table. "Hello, son."

Sebastian had never been more relieved to be wearing an untucked Pendleton wool shirt in his life. "How are you feeling?" Sebastian asked, and reached for his mug.

"Better." Leo looked over at Clare. "I didn't know you were here."

Clare, being Clare, smiled and wiped her face free of expression. "Sebastian helped me with the lights."

"Good. I see he gave you something nice and hot to warm up your insides."

Her eyes widened. "What?"

Sebastian tried not to laugh—for about half a second. Then his amused chuckle filled the kitchen.

"He always did like the cocoa with crunchy marshmallows," Leo added, then turned his attention to his son. "What are you laughing about?"

"Oh," Clare said through a huge sigh of relief, and saved Sebastian an explanation. "Cocoa. Yes, Sebastian was kind enough to make cocoa." She took a few steps and reached for her coat. "I need to get the linens out of my trunk and then I think I'm done for the day," she said as she shoved her arms into her coat. "Unless Mother has more for me to do." She wrapped her scarf around her neck. "What am I saying? Of course she'll have more for me to do. She always does." She looked across the kitchen. "Leo, take care of yourself so that your cold doesn't get worse, and I'm sure I'll see you tomorrow at Mother's party." She turned her gaze to Sebastian. "Thank you for your help."

"I'll walk you out."

She held up one hand and her blue eyes got wide. "No!" Her smile wavered but remained in place. "Stay and visit with your father." She picked up her gloves and walked out of the kitchen. A few moments later the door closed behind her.

Leo glanced across at Sebastian. "That was

odd. Did something happen that I should know about?"

"No. Nothing happened." Nothing that he was going to talk to his father about. Leo definitely shouldn't know about the kiss. "I think she's stressed about the party."

"You're probably right," Leo said, but he didn't sound convinced.

Twelve

Clare moved among various members of her mother's social clubs and charity organizations, smiling and making small talk. Several decibels below the hum of conversation, Bing Crosby crooned "The First Noel." For the annual Christmas party, Clare had stuck a sprig of holly berries in the small breast pocket of her fuzzy angora sweater. The sweater closed with pearl buttons down the front, and the bottom hit just below the waistband of her black wool pants. She'd strapped red high-heeled sandals on her feet and pulled her hair back in a simple covered ponytail. Her cosmetics were flawless and her red lipstick matched her sweater. She looked good. She knew she did. No use denying it. It was just too bad she was having a harder time denying that she'd dressed with a certain reporter in mind. She could tell herself that she always tried to look her best, which was pretty much the truth. Only she'd never been quite so picky with her coal eyeliner, or applied mascara and separated her lashes quite so perfectly, just to attend one of her mother's parties.

She didn't know why she'd gone to so much trouble. She didn't even *like* Sebastian. Well, not that much. Certainly not enough to get all anal about her appearance. Too bad she tended to forget that she didn't really care for him the second his lips touched hers. He had a way of making every rational thought melt. Of heating her up inside and making her want to be absorbed into his big chest.

She told herself that it had little to do with Sebastian himself and more to do with the fact that he was a healthy heterosexual man. Testosterone clung to his skin like an intoxicating drug, while he manufactured enough pheromones to overdose any women within a hundred yards. After Lonnie, she was especially vulnerable to that kind of sexual force.

The last time he'd kissed her, she'd had every intention of just standing there, aloof and uninvolved. The best way to discourage a man was to remain unmoved in his embrace, but of course that hadn't happened. If Leo hadn't entered the carriage house, she didn't know how far she would have let things go before stopping him.

But she would have stopped him because she did not need a man in her life. *Then why the red lipstick and fuzzy sweater?* an inner voice asked. A few months ago she would not have even paused to ask herself the question, let alone consider an answer. She made small talk with her mother's friends as she thought about it and decided it was plain old vanity, exacerbated by lingering insecurities from childhood. But it didn't matter anyway. His rental car was no longer parked in front of the garage. He'd probably returned to Seattle, and she'd gone to all the trouble of looking good for a house full of her mother's friends.

An hour into the Christmas party Clare had to admit things were progressing surprisingly well. The gossip ranged from the mundane and disapproving to the ultra juicy. From the latest fundraiser and overall appalling quality of the younger club members, to Lurleen Maddigan's heart surgeon husband running off with thirty-year-old Mary Fran Randall, the daughter of Dr. and Mrs. Randall. Understandably, both Lurleen and Mrs. Randall had declined the yearly invitation to the Wingate Christmas party.

"Lurleen hasn't been quite right since her hysterectomy," Clare heard someone whisper as she carried a silver tray of canapés to the dining room table.

Clare had known Mrs. Maddigan most of her life and figured Lurleen had *never* been quite right. Anyone who made Joyce Wingate look like a slacker had severe control issues. Still, cheating wasn't right, and getting dumped for a woman half her age must have been humiliating and hurtful. Perhaps even more humiliating and hurtful than finding your fiancé with the Sears man.

"How is your writing, dear?" asked Evelyn Bruce, one of Joyce's closest friends. Clare turned her attention to Mrs. Bruce and fought the urge to squint. Evelyn refused to believe she'd actually reached the age of seventy, and still dyed her hair bright red. The color made her look as white as a corpse and clashed horribly with her scarlet St. John suit.

"Good," Clare replied. "Thank you for asking. My eighth book is out this month."

"That's wonderful. I've always thought that someone should write a book about my life."

Didn't everyone? The problem was, most people thought their lives were more interesting than they actually were.

"Perhaps I could tell you and you could write it for me."

Clare smiled. "I write fiction, Mrs. Bruce. I'm

sure I couldn't tell your story as well as you. Excuse me." She escaped into the kitchen, where Leo was preparing a new batch of eggnog. A potpourri of cinnamon and clove simmered on the stove, filling the house with the smells of the season.

"What can I do?" she asked as she came to stand beside the older gentleman.

"Go enjoy yourself."

That wasn't likely to happen. The old guard Junior Leaguers weren't exactly fun gals. She glanced out the back window at her Lexus parked next to Leo' s Town Car—no sign of the rental.

"Did Sebastian go home?" she asked, and reached for a corkscrew.

"No. We returned the car. There's no use in having it when Sebastian can drive the Lincoln while he's here." Leo folded beaten egg whites into the eggnog mixture. "He's over at the carriage house by himself. I'm sure he wouldn't mind if you went over there to say hello."

The news that Sebastian was still in town sent a zap along her nerves, and she tightened her grasp on the bottle. "Oh . . . ah, I couldn't leave you to do everything."

"There isn't that much to do."

Which was absolutely true, but the last thing she needed was to be alone with Sebastian. Sebastian made her forget she was on a man hiatus.

She grabbed a bottle of chardonnay and stuck the corkscrew into the top. "The ladies can always use more wine," she said.

"Did something happen yesterday between you and Sebastian?" Leo asked as he placed one bowl of eggnog in the refrigerator and took out another bowl he'd prepared earlier. "When I walked in the house, you looked a little rattled."

"Ahh, no." She shook her head and felt her cheeks get warm as she recalled the kiss the day before. One moment she'd been enjoying cocoa, and the next, she'd been enjoying Sebastian.

"Are you sure? I remember how he'd get you all riled up when you were a girl." Leo set the bowl on the counter and sprinkled nutmeg on top. "I think he liked to pull your pigtails just to hear you scream."

Clare pulled the cork out and let a pleasant smile curve her lips. These days he had a whole new way of riling her. "Nothing happened. He didn't pull my hair or swindle me out of my money." No, he'd just kissed her and made her want more.

Leo looked closely at her, then nodded. "If you're sure."

Lord, she was a good liar. "I am." She grabbed the wine and moved to the pantry.

Leo chuckled and called after her, "He can be a rascal."

"Yes," Clare said, although there were other words that fit him better than rascal. She opened the pantry door inward and moved inside, turned on the light and walked past a stepladder and rows of canned goods. On a back shelf, she grabbed a box of Wheat Thins and Rye Crisps.

Returning to the dining room, Clare set the wine beside the other bottles. She replenished a red wicker tray with crackers and plucked a green grape from its vine. From the parlor, she heard her mother's laugh above the group of voices in the foyer next to the Christmas tree.

"They let anyone in the club these days," someone said. "Before she married into that family, she was working at Wal-Mart."

Clare frowned and popped the grape into her mouth. She didn't see anything wrong with working at Wal-Mart, only the people who thought there was something wrong with it.

"How's your love life?" Berni Lang asked from across the narcissus centerpiece.

"Nonexistent at the moment," Clare answered.

"Weren't you engaged? Or was that Prue Williams's daughter?"

Clare was tempted to lie, but she knew Berni wasn't confused. She was just using her false naiveté like a crowbar to do a little stealth prying. "I had a short engagement but it didn't work out."

"That's too bad. You're an attractive girl, I just don't understand why you're still single." Bernice Lang was in her mid- to late seventies, had a slight case of osteoporosis and a severe case of old lady-itis. An affliction that hit some women after the age of seventy with the belief they could be as rude as they pleased. "How old are you? If you don't mind my asking?"

Of course she minded, because she knew where this conversation was headed. "Not at all. I'll be thirty-four in a few months."

"Oh." She raised a glass of wine to her lips but paused as if a thought had just occurred to her. "You'd better hurry, then, hadn't you? You don't want your eggs to wither. That happened to Patricia Beideman's daughter Linda. By the time she found a man, she couldn't conceive outside a petri dish." She took a drink, then added, "I have a grandson you might be interested in."

And have Berni for a grandmother? Hell, no. "I'm not dating right now," Clare said, and grabbed a tray of canapés. "Excuse me." She left the dining room before she gave into the urge to tell Berni that her eggs were none of the older lady's damn business.

Clare didn't believe the biological clock started counting down until a woman was over the age of thirty-five. She was safe for a year, but her stomach twisted into a knot anyway. She figured it was from the stress of forcing herself to be polite *Not* withering eggs. But . . . the twisting knot was kind of low for a stomachache. Maybe . . . ? *Damn that Berni.* As if she didn't have enough pressure in her life. She had a book deadline looming over her head, and instead of working, she was passing out hors d'oeuvres to her mother's friends.

She carried the tray into the parlor. "Canapés?"

"Thank you, dear," her mother said as she looked over the tray. "These are lovely." She straightened the holly berries in Clare's pocket, then said, "You remember Mrs. Hillard, don't you?"

"Of course." Clare held the tray to one side and kissed the air above Ava Hillard's cheek. "How are you?"

"I'm well." Ava reached for a canapé. "Your mother tells me you have a new book out this month." She took a bite, then washed it down with chardonnay.

"Yes."

"I think that's wonderful. I can't imagine writing a whole book." She looked at Clare through a pair of thin tortoiseshell glasses. "You must be very creative."

"I try."

"Clare always was a very creative child," her mother said as she rearranged the canapés as if they hadn't been placed at exactly the right angles. The old passive-aggressive Clare would have accidently tilted the tray so they slid to one side. The new Clare simply smiled and let her mother do her thing. Canapé placement wasn't something to get upset about.

"I love to read." Ava was the latest wife of Norris Hillard, the richest man in the state and the third richest in the country. "Your mother suggested that I ask you for a copy of your latest book."

But her mother promising free giveaways was a little irksome. "I don't give away copies of my books, but you can buy them at any area bookstore." She looked at her mother and smiled. "I'm going to warm these up," she said, holding up the tray. "Excuse me."

She wove her way through her mother's friends, dispensed a few canapés, and made it to the kitchen without losing her cool or her smile. She expected to see Leo puttering about. Instead, Sebastian stood at the counter, his back to the room as he looked out into the backyard. He wore a white T-shirt beneath a bulky gray sweater and his usual cargo pants. His hair appeared wet against the back of his head and bare neck. At the sound of her shoes on the tile floor, he turned and looked at her. His green gaze caught and held hers, and she came to an abrupt halt.

"Where's Leo?" she asked as several hors d'oeuvres shifted precariously close to the edge of the tray.

Sebastian, being Sebastian, had made himself at home with Joyce's red wine and held a glass near his hip. "He said he's taking a break."

"At the carriage house?"

"Yeah." Sebastian's gaze lowered from her eyes to her mouth, then slid slowly to her holly berries. He pointed at her with his glass. "You look good in red."

"Thank you." She took a few steps forward and set the tray on the island in the middle of the room. He looked good too, in a totally edible way, and she purposely kept her distance. Her stomach felt light and heavy all at the same time, and she made an attempt at polite conversation. "What have you been doing since yesterday?"

"I was up all night reading." He took a drink of his wine.

The distance between them allowed her stomach to settle, and she took a relieved breath. "What about this time?"

He looked at her over his glass, then said, "Pirates."

"Internet pirates?"

"Internet?" He shook his head and one corner

of his mouth slid up into a smile. "No. High seas. The real swashbuckling kind."

Her first two books had been about pirates. The first featured Captain Jonathan Blackwell, bastard son of the Duke of Stanhope, while the second had starred William Dewhurst, whose love of plundering the South Pacific was second only to his love of plundering Lady Lydia. During her research for those books, she'd learned that piracy was still a problem. It certainly wasn't as prevalent as it had been several hundred years ago, but was as brutal as ever. "Are you writing an article about piracy?"

"No. No article." He walked toward her and set his glass next to the silver tray, effectively removing the nice safe distance between them. "How's the party going?"

Clare shrugged a shoulder. "Berni Lang told me that my eggs are withering."

He simply looked at her through his deep green eyes, clueless as to what she was talking about. But of course he was. Men didn't have to worry about ticking clocks or aging eggs.

"She's concerned that if I don't get to it, I won't be able to conceive outside of a petri dish."

"Ah." He tilted his head back and lowered his gaze to her abdomen. "Are you worried about that?"

"No." She placed a hand on her stomach as if to shield herself from his sexually potent gaze. If there was one man who could impregnate with just a look, it was Sebastian Vaughan. "Or at least I wasn't until today. Now, I'm a little freaked."

"I wouldn't worry about it if I were you." He glanced into her face. "You're still young and beautiful, and you'll find someone to make a baby with you."

He'd said she was beautiful, and for some stupid reason, that left her light-headed and feeling a little warm and fuzzy. It touched the little girl in her that used to follow him around. She tore her gaze from his and looked down at the hors d'oeuvres. She'd come into the kitchen to do something. What?

"If not, then you can adopt or find a sperm donor."

She grabbed the silver tray and moved toward the sink. "No. That may be fine for some women, but I want a father for my child. A full-time dad." Talk of sperm and donors made her think of making babies the old-fashioned way. And that made her think of Sebastian standing before her in just a towel. "I want more than one child, and I want a husband to help me raise them." She pulled out the garbage from beneath the sink. "I'm sure you know the importance of a father in a boy's life."

"I do, but you know that life isn't perfect. You

know that even with the best of intentions, fifty percent of all marriages end in divorce."

Thinking of him in that towel made her think of him without the towel. "But fifty percent don't," she uttered, not thinking about what she was doing as she dumped the hors d'oeuvres. As she watched them slide into the trash, she remembered that she'd come into the kitchen to warm them up, not dump them out.

"You want the fairy tale."

"I want a chance at it." Damn. She'd spent hours making those mushroom rolls. For a split second she thought about picking them out of the trash. This was Sebastian's fault. He just seemed to suck the air from the room and leave her brain deprived of oxygen. She shoved the garbage back beneath the sink and shut the door. Now what?

"Do you really believe in the happily ever after?"

Clare turned and looked at him. He didn't appear mocking, just curious. Did she still believe? Despite everything? "Yes," she answered truthfully. Perhaps she no longer believed in a perfect love, or love at first sight, but did she still believe in lasting love? "I do believe that two people can be happy and make a great life together." She set the tray on the counter next to a plate of butter mints pressed into the shape of little Christmas trees. She popped one into her mouth and leaned her behind against the counter. She'd cooked all the hors d'oeuvres and set them out already. She looked down at her red toenails as she recalled some frozen fish in her mother's freezer, but there wasn't anything she could do with that.

"Our parents never did."

She glanced up at Sebastian. He'd turned toward her and his arms were folded across the chest of his bulky sweater. "That's true, but my mother and your father jumped into marriage for the wrong reasons. Mine because she thought she could change a charming womanizer, and yours because . . . well, because . . ."

"My mother was pregnant," he finished for her. "And we know how that turned out. It was a disaster. They made each other miserable."

"It doesn't have to be like that."

"What's to stop it? Hearts and flowers and grandiose declarations of undying love? Don't tell me you actually believe in that?"

She shrugged. "I just want someone who loves me as honestly and as passionately as I love him." She pushed away from the counter and moved toward the refrigerator. She pulled open the freezer and looked in at an old gallon of ice cream, packages of chicken, and the trout Leo had given Joyce the last time he and Sebastian had gone fishing.

She closed the freezer and asked, "How about you?" She was tired of talking about herself. "Do you want children?"

"Lately I've been thinking that I'd like to have a kid someday." Clare glanced back at him as she opened the refrigerator. He took a drink of his wine, then added, "But the wife is a different matter. I can't see myself married."

She couldn't see him married either. She bent forward and placed her hands on her knees to peer into the refrigerator. "You're one of those guys."

"One of what guys?"

Milk. Grapefruit juice. Jars of salsa. "Those guys who can't see themselves tied down with one woman for the rest of their lives, because there are so many woman out there just waiting to be conquered. The 'why have oatmeal every day for the rest of our lives when we can eat Cap'n Crunch, Lucky Charms, and Tasty O's kind of guys." Cottage cheese. A piece of something shaped like a pizza slice. "Do you know what happens to those guys?"

"Tell me."

"Those guys turn fifty and are alone and suddenly decide it's time to settle down. So they get some Viagra and find a twenty-year-old to marry and pop out a few children." Cheese. Pickles. Eggs. "Only they're too old to enjoy the kids, and when they're sixty, the twenty-year-old leaves them for someone her own age and cleans out the bank account. They're sad and broke and can't understand why they're alone." She reached for a jar of Kalamata olives. "The kids don't want them to come to school programs because they're nearing retirement and all the other fourth graders think their dad is their grandpa."

Wow, she thought as she straightened, that sounded cynical. She'd obviously been listening to Maddie too much. She read the pull date on the olive jar. "Not that I'm bitter or anything," she said through a smile as she glanced over her shoulder. "Not all men are immature jerks," she added, and caught Sebastian staring at her behind. "But I could be wrong about that."

He raised his gaze up her back. "What?"

"Did you hear one word I said?" She shut the door and set the olives on the counter. She didn't have a plan for them, but they looked better than anything else in the refrigerator.

"Yeah. You assume I don't see myself married because I want to 'conquer' lots of different women and eat their Lucky Charms and Tasty O's." He grinned. "But that's not the case. I don't see myself married because I'm gone a lot and, in my experience, distance does not make the heart grow fonder.

While I'm gone, either she's moved on or I've moved on. If not, she suddenly sees my work as her competition and wants me to cut my schedule to spend time with her."

Clare couldn't fault him for the last. She knew what it was like to have to work while your boyfriend wanted to play. She felt an affinity with Sebastian until he said, "And women just can't leave anything alone. If everything is going along just fine, they have to pick at it and torture it and talk it to death. They always want to discuss *feelings* and talk about a relationship and make a commitment. Women can never just lighten up about that shit."

"My God, you should come with a warning sign."

"I've never lied to any woman I've been in any sort of relationship with."

Maybe not in so many words, but Sebastian had a way of looking at a woman that made her feel as if she were special to him. When in reality she was only special until he moved on. And she herself, who knew Sebastian for a silver-tongued snake, was not immune. Not immune to the way he looked at her and kissed her and touched her and drew her in even as she knew she should run screaming in the opposite direction. "Define relationship."

"Jesus." He sighed. "You're such a girl." He held

up one hand, then dropped it to his side. "A relationship . . . as in dating and having sex with the same person on a regular basis."

"And you're such a guy." She shook her head and moved to the other side of the kitchen island. "Relationships should be about more than dinner, a movie, and hitting the sack." She could have said more on the subject but didn't believe it would do any good. "What's been your longest relationship?"

He thought a moment, then answered, "About eight months."

She placed her hands on the white tiles and drummed her fingers as she looked across the safe distance into his eyes. "So, you probably only saw each other half that time."

"More or less."

"So in all, total, it was more like four months." She shook her head again and walked across the room to the pantry, the sound of her high heels making little *click-click* sounds. "I'm shocked."

"What? That it didn't last longer?"

"No," she answered as she opened the door. "That it lasted *that* long. Four months is a long time not to bother you with talk of commitment and *feelings*." She frowned at him, then walked into the pantry. "That poor woman must have been mentally exhausted." She moved passed the stepstool and looked for a box of this or a tin of that. Anything to whip up for her mother's friends.

"Don't feel too bad for her," Sebastian said from the doorway. "She was a yoga and Pilates instructor and I let her work out on me in bed. If I recall, her favorite position was dog down."

Which proved, yet again, woman did all the work in a relationship. "You mean downward-facing dog."

"Yeah. You know that one?"

Clare ignored the question. "So, the yoga instructor had to bend herself all around to please you. I imagine she had to rock your world in and out of bed, but what did she get out of the relationship? Besides toned abs and buns of steel?"

He grinned like a natural-born sinner. "Out of bed, she got dinner and a movie. In bed she got multiple orgasms."

Oh. Okay. That was good. She had never had a multiple orgasm. Although she thought she may have come close once.

He shoved one shoulder into the door frame. "What? You don't have anything to say?"

Really, though, she wasn't greedy. It had been so long, she wouldn't mind just having one. "Like?"

"Like a relationship is not just about sex and a woman needs more than multiple orgasms."

"Yes. They do." She closed her eyes and shook

her head. "We do, yes. And a relationship is more than sex." She looked back at him standing there like a hunk of the month. She was allowing him to get her sidetracked with thoughts of orgasms. She'd come into the pantry to find crackers or something. . . .

He pushed away from the frame and closed the door with his foot.

"What are you doing?" she asked.

He moved forward a few steps until she had to tilt her head up to look up into his face. "Apparently, I'm stalking you."

"Why?" He was doing that thing again. The thing where he sucked out all the air in the room and made her feel light-headed. "Are you bored?"

"Bored?" He took several moments to consider the question before he answered, "No. I'm not bored."

Thirteen

Sebastian was far from bored. He was intrigued and interested and very turned on. It wasn't his fault, though. It was hers. He'd read her second book, *The Pirate's Captive,* and was shocked by how much he'd enjoyed it. It was a real swashbuckler filled with high seas drama and lots of "wenching." Any woman who could write hot wenching like that had to be hot in bed.

Clare. Clare Wingate. The girl with the thick glasses who used to follow him around and annoy him a lot had turned out to be as interesting and intriguing a woman as she was beautiful.

Who would have thought?

After his cold shower, he'd sought her out to ask

her if she wanted to escape the party and have a late lunch with him downtown somewhere. Somewhere public where he wouldn't be tempted to kiss her as he had the day before. But she'd started talking about men eating women like Lucky Charms and Tasty O's, and that had started him wondering if she was magically delicious, and here they were. Shut inside the pantry.

"Then why are you stalking me here?" she asked.

He slid his hands up her arms to the shoulders of her fuzzy sweater. The height of her shoes brought her mouth just below his. "Remember when we hid in here and gorged on Girl Scout cookies? I think I ate a whole box of Thin Mints."

She swallowed hard as her amazing blue eyes stared up into his. She blinked. "You followed me in here to talk about when we used to eat cookies?"

He brushed his hands across her shoulders to the sides of her warm neck. Her pulse quickened beneath his thumbs. "No." He tilted her chin up and lowered his face just above hers. "I want to talk about eating you like a Tasty O." He continued to look into her eyes as he said, "I want to talk about all the things I want to do to you. Then we can talk about all the things I want you to do to me." All the things he'd already thought of her doing to him.

She raised her hands to his chest and he thought

she might push him away. Instead she said, "We can't do this. Someone will walk in here."

He wondered if she realized that her only objection was that they might get caught. He smiled. Her red lipstick had been driving him crazy, and he brushed his mouth across hers. "Not if we're very quiet." He pressed a quick kiss to her lips. "You don't want Joyce to walk in on us. She'd be horrified to find you in here kissing the gardener's son."

"But *I'm* not kissing you."

He chuckled silently. "Not yet."

She sucked in a breath and held it. "Your father could find us."

He brushed his thumb across the soft skin of her jaw as he continued to tease her mouth. "He's taking one of his twenty-minute naps that usually last an hour. He won't ever know."

"Why do I let you do this to me?" she asked through a sigh.

"Because it feels good."

She swallowed and her throat moved beneath his hands. "Lots of things feel good."

"Not this good." Her fingers curled into his sweater. "Admit it, Clare. You like how this feels as much as I do."

"It's only because . . . it's been a while."

"A while since?"

"I've felt this good."

It had been a while for him too. A while since he'd thought about a woman as much as he did Clare. Especially since he wasn't even having sex with her. He tilted her face up a little more, and while his mouth lightly touched hers, he waited. Waited for the last sweet moment of hesitation. The moment right before she lost the battle with herself and melted into him. When she was no longer the perfect Clare. No longer hiding behind bland smiles and rigid control. The moment right before she turned soft and passionate all at the same time.

He felt the hitch in her breathing and the press of her fingertips into the weave of his sweater the second before her hands slid up his chest, leaving a trail of fire to the back of his neck. Her lips parted with a barely perceptible *ahh,* and she was his. Her acquiescence excited him almost as much as her fingers combing through the back of his hair. It raised the flesh on his back and chest and turned the interest in his pants as hard as rock.

He kept the kiss light, taking his time to taste a hint of mint on her breath and feel the soft warmth of her mouth. He let her set the pace and settled into a hot, wet kiss that was as excruciating as it was sweet. He felt her passion grow and build. He felt it in her touch and heard it in the little moan in her throat.

She pulled back, her breathing rapid, her eyes wide and dilated. Her hands gripped his shoulders and she said just above a whisper, "Why do I always let this happen?"

Frustration clawed at his chest and between his legs. His breathing was only slightly calmer than hers. "We already covered that."

"I know, but why with you?" She licked her wet lips. "There are lots of other men in the world."

He pulled her against his chest until her breasts were pressed into the front of his sweater. "I guess I make it feel better than those other men." Talk time was over, and he lowered his mouth once again. There was no hesitation in her this time. Only passion, hot and fluid and every bit as needy as his own.

He placed a hand on her round behind and shoved one knee between hers. He settled her against the hard ridge of his erection, turning his desire for her into a hot greedy thing he could barely control. Her kiss turned wetter and hungrier, and he gave her what she needed.

She'd been wrong about him. He didn't want a woman to bend herself around for him. Although there was nothing wrong with rocking his world in bed. Or out of bed. Or in the pantry. At the moment Clare was doing a really good job of it. He slid his hand from her behind to her waist and slipped his fingers beneath the bottom edge of her sweater. Her skin was soft, and he drew a circle on her belly with his thumb. She moved against his erection and he fought the urge to push down her pants and have sex with her right there. On the floor of the pantry where anyone could walk in, satisfying his lust between her soft thighs and easing the razor edge of desire that twisted and turned low in his belly and added a slice of pain to the pleasure.

He raised a hand to the top button of her sweater and pulled. The sweater parted, and he continued to kiss her senseless as he lowered his hand to the next button. The last thing he wanted was for her to stop him. There would be time to stop, later. Right now he wanted just a bit more. Five more buttons and his hand slipped between the edges of her sweater and he cupped her breast. Through the lace of her bra, her hard nipple poked the center of his palm.

She pulled back and lowered her startled gaze to his hand. "You unbuttoned my sweater."

He brushed her nipple with his thumb, and she closed her eyes and her breathing caught in her chest. "I want you," he whispered.

She looked up at him, desire and control conflicting in her blue eyes. "We can't."

"I know." Through the tiny wholes in the lace,

he felt tantalizing hints of her warm flesh. "We'll stop."

She shook her head but didn't remove his hand. "We should probably stop now. The door doesn't lock. Someone could walk in."

True. Normally that might have given him pause. Not today. With both hands, he pushed the edges of her sweater farther apart and lowered his gaze. "Ever since that night at the Double Tree," he said, "I've thought of this. Of undressing you and touching you." He looked at her cleavage and her hard nipples pressing against the red lace of her bra. "Of having another look at little Clare."

"I'm not little anymore," she whispered.

"Yes. I know," he said, and slid three fingers beneath the shoulder strap. "I like this. You should always wear red." Beneath the satin and lace, he slipped his fingers to the red bow nestled between her deep cleavage. He bent forward and kissed the side of her neck while his hands opened the little closure hidden beneath the bow. The bra released and he pushed it, along with her sweater, down her arms.

"But you look better naked these days." Her full white breasts were perfectly round and topped with small dark pink nipples, puckered and ready and offered up like dessert. He lowered his head and kissed the hollow of her throat, her cleavage, and the side of her breast. He looked up into her face as he opened his mouth and touched his tongue to the tip of her pebbled nipple. He rolled it beneath his tongue, and she brought her hands to the sides of his face and arched her back. Her nostrils flared, and she watched him through blue eyes turned liquid and shining with passion.

Sebastian moved his hands to her back and held her while he opened his slick mouth and sucked her inside. His tongue played with the hard and soft textures of her flesh as the sharp edge of lust tugged and twisted and tortured him.

"Stop!" she whispered, and pushed him away.

He looked up at her, dazed and drugged with the taste of her skin lingering in his mouth. Stop, he'd just gotten started.

Outside the closed door, someone turned on the sink faucet. "I think it's Leo," she whispered.

His grasp on her back tightened as he heard the muffled voice of his father through the door. The last thing he wanted was to stop, but he didn't want his father to walk in on him and Clare either. "Come to the carriage house with me," he said next to her ear.

She shook her head and pulled out of his embrace. The sound of the water stopped and he recognized his father's footsteps, fading in the direction of the dining room.

He ran his fingers through his hair as sexual frustration smashed into him. "You have a big house. I'm sure there are plenty of rooms to finish this."

Again she shook her head as she reached for the cups of her bra and closed the red lace over her breasts. Her dark ponytail brushed her shoulders. "I should have known you'd take things too far."

His frustration beat at his brain and pounded his groin and he wanted to damn well finish what they'd started. In the carriage house. Her house. The back of a car. He didn't give a shit. "Less than a minute ago you weren't complaining."

She glanced up, then back down, as she hooked the bow between her breasts. "Who had time? You move too fast."

Now she was making him angry. Just as she had the morning at the Double Tree. "You were into everything I was doing to you, and if Leo hadn't walked into the kitchen, you'd still be moaning and holding onto my ears. In another few minutes I would have had you completely naked."

"I wasn't moaning." She pulled the edges of her sweater together. "And don't fool yourself. I wouldn't have let you take off any more of my clothing."

"And don't lie to yourself. You would have let me do anything I wanted." He fought the urge to grab her and kiss her until she begged him for more. "The next time you let me undress you, I'm going all the way."

"There won't be a next time." Her hands shook as she buttoned her sweater. "This got out of control before I could stop it."

"Right. You're not a girl with only a vague idea where this was leading. The next time, I'm going to finish the job that your old fiancé couldn't quite get done."

She sucked in a breath and looked up at him. Her eyes narrowed and she was once again the old Clare. Perfectly groomed and in control. "That was cruel."

He felt cruel.

"You don't know anything about my life with Lonny."

No, but he could guess. The sound of footsteps returned to the kitchen once more, and he leaned forward and said just above a whisper, "I'm giving you fair warning right now. If I ever have my face buried in your breasts again, I'm going to give you what you need so damn bad."

"You have no idea what I need. Stay away from me," she said, and stormed out of the room, shutting the door behind her.

He would have loved to storm out too, but he

had a painful problem residing in his pants and pressing against his zipper.

Through the door he heard his father's voice. "Have you seen Sebastian?" Leo asked.

Sebastian waited for her to rat him out. Just as she had years ago when she'd been angry with him. He looked around for something to shield his obvious erection.

"No," Clare answered. "No, I haven't seen him. Have you checked the carriage house?"

"Yes. He's not there."

"Well, I'm sure he's around somewhere."

Fourteen

Fiona Winters was quite positive she was not the sort of woman to attract the notice of a man such as Vashion Elliot, Duke of Rathstone. She was his daughter's governess. A nobody. An orphan with a few farthings to her name. She liked to think she was a good governess to Annabella, but she was hardly pretty. Or at least not in the fashion of opera singers or ballerinas, as was the Duke's well-known preference.

"I beg your pardon, your grace?"

He took a step back and tilted his head to one side. His gaze moved across her face. "I think the fresh air of the Italian countryside has added a nice glow to your cheeks." He raised a hand and captured a stray wisp of her hair dancing on

*the breeze before her eye. His fingers brushed her
face as he tucked it behind her ear. "You look
much improved in the past three months."*

*She held her breath and managed a strangled,
"Thank you." She was sure a steady diet had
more to do with her health than fresh air. Just as
she was sure the Duke of Rathstone meant nothing by his comment on her appearance. "If you'll
excuse me, your grace," she said. "I must get
Annabella ready for the Earl and Countess
Diberto's visit."*

Clare reached for a research book on peerage
and cracked it open. She was about to introduce two new characters and had to make sure
she knew the correct titles of the Italian aristoc-
racy. Just as she'd flipped to a page in the middle
of the book, the doorbell rang and "Paperback
Writer" played throughout the house. It was Saturday morning and she wasn't expecting anyone.

Clare rose from her chair and moved to one of
the dormer windows that overlooked the driveway
in front. Leo's Lincoln was parked below, but she
had a feeling Leo wasn't the driver. She pushed
open the window and a blast of cold December air
hit her face and seeped through the tight cotton
weave of her black turtleneck.

"Leo?"

"Nope." Sebastian stepped out from beneath her porch and looked up at her. He wore his black parka and a pair of black-rimmed sunglasses.

She hadn't seen him since the day before, when she'd run out of her mother's pantry. She could feel her cheeks heat up despite the cold. She'd hoped that she wouldn't have to see him for a while. Maybe a year. "Why are you here?"

"This is where you live."

Looking down at him made her stomach feel a little light. The kind of light that had nothing to do with any sort of deep emotion and everything to do with desire. The kind of desire any woman would feel for a man whose looks combined with his smile were an overkill. "Why?"

"Let me in and I'll tell you why."

Let him in her house? Was he crazy? Just yesterday he'd warned her that he was going to give her what he thought she needed. Of course, that had all been predicated on her finding herself half naked with him again. And she wasn't altogether sure she could swear—

"Come on, Clare. Open the door."

—it wouldn't happen again. And while she'd love to blame the whole thing on him, he'd been right. She was old enough to know where an unbuttoned sweater would lead.

"I'm freezing my ass off out here," he called up

to her, interrupting her thoughts, not that they were cohesive anyway.

Clare stuck her head farther out the window and looked at the neighbors on both sides. Thank goodness no one heard him. "Quit yelling."

"If you're worried I'm going to try and jump your bones again, don't," he yelled louder. "I can't take another rejection so soon after the last. I had to stay in that damn pantry for a good half hour."

"Shhh." She shut the windows with a snap and moved from her office. If she hadn't been afraid of what he might holler next, she wouldn't let him in, but she suspected he knew that. She moved down the stairs and through the kitchen to the entry. "What?" she said as she stuck her head out the front door.

He shoved his hands in his pockets and grinned. "Is that how you greet all your guests? No wonder everyone thinks you're such a nice sweet girl."

"You're not a guest." He laughed, and she sighed with resignation. "Fine." She swung the door open and he stepped inside. "Five minutes."

"Why?" He stopped in front of her and pushed his sunglasses to the top of his head. "Are you having one of your prayer circles?"

"No." She shut the door and leaned her back against it. "I'm working."

"Can you take an hour's break?"

She could, but she didn't want to spend any of her breaks with Sebastian. He smelled like crisp cold air and one of those man soaps like Irish Spring or Calvin Klein. He was acting more chipper than normal and he'd turned down his mojo, but she didn't trust him. Now it was her turn to ask, "Why?"

"So you can come help me pick out a Christmas present for my father."

She didn't trust him not to try something, and she didn't trust herself not to let him. "Wouldn't it be easier to buy a gift in Seattle?"

"Dad's not coming to Seattle for Christmas, and I finally found a buyer for my mother's house. I don't know if it'll close in time for me to make it back here to spend it with him, so I was hoping to find something before I have to leave. You'll help me out with this. Right?"

"Not a chance."

He rocked back on his heels and looked down at her. "I helped you with the outdoor lights, and you said you'd help me out with Leo."

She didn't think that was exactly how it had happened. "Can't it wait until tomorrow?" Tomorrow. A whole twenty-four more hours to forget about the things he'd done with his mouth. Things besides talking. Things he was really good at doing.

"I'm leaving tomorrow." As if he read her mind, he held up his hands and said, "I won't touch you. Believe me, I don't want to spend another day with blue balls."

She couldn't believe he'd just said that to her. Wait, this was Sebastian. Of course she could believe it. He must have mistaken her astonishment for confusion because he tipped his head back and raised a brow.

"You have heard of blue balls?"

"Yes, Sebastian. I've heard of . . ." She paused and raised a hand in the air. ". . . of that." She didn't want to talk about his testicles. That seemed highly . . . personal. Something he'd discuss with a girlfriend.

He unzipped the front of his coat. "Don't tell me you can't say blue balls."

"I can, but I prefer not to have those words in my mouth." Lord, she hadn't meant to sound like her mother.

Beneath his coat he wore a chambray shirt tucked into his jeans. "This, from the woman who called me a dickhead. You didn't seem to have a problem with that in your mouth."

"I was provoked."

"So was I."

Maybe, but he'd been the worst offender. Lying about them sleeping together had been worse than her accusing him of taking advantage of her. Way worse.

"Get your coat. Believe me, after yesterday, I learned my lesson. I don't want to touch you any more than you want to touch me."

Which was the problem. She wasn't all that sure she didn't want him to touch her or her to touch him. She was sure, though, that it was probably a bad idea. She frowned and looked down at herself. At the bottom of her ribbed turtleneck that didn't quite touch the black leather belt looped in the waistband of her jeans. "I'm not really dressed for shopping."

"Why not? You look relaxed. Not so uptight. I like you this way."

She glanced up at him. He didn't appear to be joking. Her hair was down and she was only wearing mascara. Sometimes her friends teased her because she put on a little makeup every day, even when she didn't have plans to leave the house. Maddie and Lucy and Adele didn't care if they scared the UPS man. She did. "One hour?"

"Yep."

"I know I'm going to regret this," she said through a sigh as she moved to the closet and reached for her coat.

"No, you won't." He gave her one of the lopsided

smiles that creased the corners of his green eyes. "I'll behave even if you beg me to throw you down and climb on top of you." He stepped behind her and helped her into her black peacoat. "Well, maybe not if you beg."

She turned her head and looked up at him as she pulled her hair from the wool collar. The ends of her hair brushed his hands before he removed them from her shoulders. "I won't beg."

He lowered his gaze to her mouth. "I've heard that one before."

"Not from me. I mean it."

He looked back up into her eyes. "Clare, women say a lot of things they don't really mean. Especially you." He stepped back and stuck his hands in his coat pockets. "Gotta purse you need to take?"

She reached for her crocodile hobo bag and hung it on one shoulder. Sebastian followed her outside, and she locked the door behind them.

"I saw a print shop downtown," he said as he walked to the passenger side of the Town Car and opened the door. "I'd like to start there."

The print shop was actually more of an art gallery and frame shop, and Clare had bought several pieces from the shop in the past. Today, as she and Sebastian walked through the gallery, she noticed the way he studied the paintings.

He'd stop, turn his head to one side, and dip one shoulder lower than the other. She also noticed he stopped most often in front of nudes.

"I don't think Leo would hang that one in his living room," she said as he studied a beautiful woman laying on her stomach amidst rumpled white sheets, the sunlight caressing her bare behind.

"Probably not. Did you see anything you like in here?" he asked.

Clare pointed to a woman wearing a sheer white dress, standing on the beach and holding a baby. "I like the expression on her face. It's blissful."

"Hmm." He turned his head to the side. "I'd say it's more peaceful." He moved in front of a chalk drawing of a nude man and woman locked in an embrace. "Now that woman's expression is blissful."

She would have said it was more orgasmic, if she were the kind of woman to say such things out loud in public.

In the end Sebastian chose a signed lithograph of a man and a boy standing on a big rock at the edge of the Payette River, fishing. While they looked at matte and frame samples, he asked her opinion about each and took her suggestions. He paid extra to have it finished by Christmas. Delivery was going to be a problem, considering the time crunch, and before Clare could stop herself, she volunteered to pick it up on Christmas Eve.

He looked at her out of the corners of his eyes and frowned. "No thanks."

She smiled up at him. "I won't wrap it in pink ribbon. I swear."

He thought about her offer as he reached into his back pocket and pulled out his wallet. "If you're sure it won't be a problem."

She had a signing that day and would be out and about anyway. "It won't."

"Okay, thanks. That's a load off." He handed over a platinum Visa, and when the shop owner walked away, Sebastian added, "If I could kiss you, I would."

She turned and held up her hand as if she were a queen. Instead of kissing her knuckles, he turned her hand over, pushed back the sleeve of her coat, and placed his mouth on the inside of her wrist. "Thank you, Clare."

Her skin actually tingled all the way up her arm, and she pulled her hand away. "You're welcome."

The hour he'd promised turned into three with a stop at P.F. Chang's in the old warehouse district. They were given a table near the back of the Chinese restaurant, and Clare couldn't help but notice the female attention that tracked them across the room. It wasn't the first time she'd noticed it that day, the furtive glances and blatant stares as they walked down the street or through the gallery. She wondered if Sebastian noticed the way women looked at him. He didn't seem to, but perhaps he was just used to it.

They started off the meal with chicken lettuce wraps, and if Clare had been with her friends, she would have ordered the appetizer as an entrée and considered that lunch. Not Sebastian. He also ordered orange peel chicken, moo goo gai pan, pork fried rice, and Sichuan asparagus.

"Are we meeting someone else?" she asked after the entrées arrived.

"I'm so hungry, I could eat a horse." He shook his head and put orange chicken on his plate. "I take that back. Horse is too tough."

Clare spooned a portion of rice on her plate, then they traded entrées across the table. "And you know this because you've eaten a horse?"

"Eaten?" He looked up from the rice. "More like I've chewed on horse."

She felt her nose crinkle. "Where?"

He served himself moo goo gai pan, then handed it to Clare. "I was in Manchuria."

She held up her hand and declined any more food. "Are you serious?"

"Yeah. In northern China you can buy packages of dog and monkey meat in the markets."

Clare looked at the orange peel chicken on her plate. "You're lying."

"No, I'm not. I saw it when I was there in '96. It's the honest to God's truth." He picked up his fork and stabbed some asparagus. "There are quite a few cultures that consider dog a delicacy. I try not to judge."

Clare didn't like to judge either, but she couldn't help but think of poor Cindy. She looked up as far as the hollow of his throat, visible between the collar of his shirt. "Did you eat dog?"

He glanced up, then returned his attention to his lunch. "Nah, but the guys and I did eat the monkey."

"You ate a monkey?" She took a drink of her cabernet sauvignon.

"Yeah. It tasted just like chicken," he said through a laugh. "Believe me, after a diet of mostly congee, the monkey was damn good."

Clare had never heard of congee and was too afraid he'd tell her if she asked. She watched him dig into his meal and set her glass back on the table. "Where's your next assignment?" she inquired, purposely moving the subject away from canines and primates.

He shrugged one shoulder. "I'm not sure. I decided not to sign a new contract with *Newsweek*. Or with anyone. I think I'll take some time off."

"To do what?" She took a bite of rice.

"I haven't figured that out yet."

She knew if she wasn't under contract, she'd be freaking out. "Doesn't that scare you?"

He looked across the table and his green eyes met hers. "Not as much as it did a few months ago. I've worked really long and hard to get where I am in my job, and at first it was scary as hell to think I might be losing my drive for it. But I had to accept the fact that I don't enjoy the travel as much as I used to. Plain and simple. So, I'm backing off a little before I burn out completely. I'm sure I'll always freelance, but I want a new challenge. Something different."

She suspected that's how he was with women too. Once the challenge was over, he'd be ready to move on to the next different and exciting thing. But whether or not she was right didn't matter. There was no way she'd ever get involved with Sebastian. Not only had she sworn off men until she sorted out her own life, he'd said himself he had problems with relationships, and his love life was not her concern.

"How about you?" he asked, and took a drink of his wine.

"No. There are no men in my life."

His brows lowered. "I thought we were talking about our work. At least I was."

"Oh." She pushed a little smile on her lips to cover her embarrassment. "What about me?"

"When is your next book out?" He set his wine back on the table and picked up his fork.

"It's out. I have a signing next Saturday at Walden's in the mall."

"What's it about?"

"It's a romance."

"Yes. I know. What is it about?" He sat back in his chair and waited for her to answer.

Surely he didn't care. "It's the second book in my governess series. The heroine is, obviously, a governess—to a reclusive duke and his three small daughters. It's kind of a *Jane Eyre* meets *Mary Poppins*."

"Interesting. So, it's not a pirate book?"

Pirate? She shook her head.

"Is the book you're working on now a pirate book?"

"No. It's the third and final book in my series about governesses."

"Good-looking governesses?"

"Of course." And why was he asking?

The waiter interrupted and asked if everything was all right, and when he went away again, Clare got her answer. "I saw your books at my dad's."

Ahh. "Yes. Bless him. He buys every one, although he won't read them because he says they make him blush."

"They must be really hot."

"I imagine that would depend on what you're used to reading."

He looked at her and one corner of his mouth slid up into an easy smile. "I can't believe little Clare Wingate grew up to write steamy romance novels."

"And I can't believe you grew up and ate a monkey. Worse, I can't believe I let a guy who ate a monkey kiss my mouth."

He reached across the table and placed his hand on her forearm. "Honey," he said, and looked deep into her eyes, "I kissed more than your mouth."

Fifteen

On the twenty-fourth of December the Boise Towne Square Mall was packed with last-minute shoppers. Christmas Muzak kept time with the ringing of cash registers. Groups of teenagers hung over the second-floor railings, calling to friends below, while mothers maneuvered strollers through the melee.

At the entrance of Walden's Books, Clare sat surrounded by a stack of her latest, *Surrender to Love,* and was partially hidden by a big easel-backed poster of a busty heroine and her shirtless hero. For the signing, she had dressed in her black double-breasted suit and emerald silk blouse. She wore black hose and four-inch pumps, and her hair was curled about her shoulders. She looked successful and sophisticated, and in one hand she held her gold Tiffany signing pen. There were ten minutes left of her two-hour signing, and she'd sold fifteen of her books. Not bad for December. It was time to sit back, relax. A slight smile tilted her red lips as she gazed down at the open book hidden in her lap: *Redneck Haiku, Double-Wide Edition.*

"Hey there, Cinderella."

Clare glanced up from a haiku about Bubba's wedding and her gaze landed on the faded button fly of a pair of well-worn Levi's. She recognized those jeans and that voice and knew who both belonged to even before she looked up past an open fleece jacket and blue shirt, past that familiar smile and dark green eyes.

"What are you doing here?" She'd heard Sebastian was back in town for Christmas. He was expected with Leo at her mother's house for dinner tomorrow night, but it was a shock to see him standing across her small table. His answer was a bigger shock.

"Buying your book for my dad for Christmas."

Seeing him, a familiar little sensation lifted her stomach. She didn't love Sebastian, but she did like him. How could she not like a man who braved holiday shopping to buy a romance novel for his father? "You could have called and I would have brought you one."

Inside his black fleece, he shrugged. "It's not a big deal."

Which was a blatant lie. No sane person was at the mall unless they absolutely had to be. "I picked up Leo's lithograph this morning." Just as much as she liked him, she was physically attracted to him. Much in the same way she was attracted to Godiva truffles. They weren't good for her and had an addictive quality. If she reached for one, she'd have to have the whole box. Afterward she'd regret it, but there was no denying how much she wanted to dive in and pig out.

His smile creased the corners of his eyes. "Did you get crazy with ribbon?"

She chuckled and sat back. "Not this time." And there was no denying to herself how much she wanted to binge on Sebastian. "I haven't wrapped it yet." Perhaps start at the top of his golden head and work her way south past the hard abs she knew were hiding beneath that flannel.

"Well?"

"Well what?"

"Are you going to invite me to your house to see it? Or do I have to invite myself again?"

She closed the book in her lap and looked at her watch. It was almost six. "Do you have Christmas Eve plans?"

"No."

She reached for a copy of *Surrender to Love* and opened it to the title page. "I'm done here, so why don't you come over and see it before I wrap it up." She wrote Leo a nice Merry Christmas message and signed her name. "Or you can wrap it." She handed him the book, and the tips of her fingers touched his over the busty heroine on the cover.

"Uh, I suck at wrapping. You can go ahead and handle that."

She placed the book of haiku on the table and stood. "I knew you were going to say that."

He chuckled, pointed at the bright yellow and red book and raised a dubious brow. "Japanese poetry?"

"Well, redneck Japanese poetry, at any rate." She stuck her pen in her small black purse. "A girl can never have too much culture," she said.

"Ah." He reached for the book and thumbed through it. "I did hear somewhere that the pursuit of intellectual and artistic endeavors are necessary for a healthy mind."

"And a sign of an enlightened society. Even a redneck society," she added as they moved deeper into Walden's.

Clare said a quick good-bye to the bookstore manager and left Sebastian standing in the long line at the registers. In one hand he held the book she'd signed for Leo, and in the other he skimmed *Redneck Haiku*.

Getting out of the mall parking lot was a nightmare. The drive across town, which normally took her twenty minutes, stretched over an hour. By the time she walked in the door, she was more than ready to be home. She kicked off her shoes and nylons and hung her blazer in her closet. As she unbuttoned her sleeves, the doorbell rang and she moved out of her bedroom to the front of the house. She opened the front door, and Sebastian was standing there, a tall, wide-shouldered outline in the darkness. She felt his gaze on her even before she flipped on the porch light and his green eyes met hers.

"How did you get here so fast?" she asked, and opened the door wider for him to enter.

Instead, he looked at her for several more heartbeats before lowering his attention to her mouth, the front of her blouse and skirt, and all the way to her bare feet. White puffs of his breath hung on the cold air in front of his face.

She shivered and folded her arms beneath her breasts. "Would you like to come in?" she said, finding it odd that he just stood as if his feet were frozen to her porch.

He glanced back up into her face, seemed to hesitate a moment, then stepped inside. He shut the door behind him and leaned back against it. The chandelier overhead showered his blond hair and shoulders in golden light.

"Are you hungry? Would you like me to order a pizza?"

"Yes," he said, finally speaking. "And no, I don't want a pizza." He leaned forward, slid his hand around her waist and pulled her against his chest. "You know what I want."

Her hands slid up the soft fleece of his jacket. The way he looked at her, his meaning was clear. He explained it anyway.

"Ever since that night when I saw you strip down to your little thong, I've thought of making love to you a dozen or so different ways. When I went to your signing tonight, I told myself I was there just to get your book for Leo. That's thirty percent true. Seventy percent a lie. On the way over here I thought of all the ways I could try and get you out of your clothes, but when you opened the door just now, I realized I don't want to *try* and get you out of anything. We're no longer kids. Playing games. I want your full participation while I strip you naked."

A part of her wanted that too. Really wanted it. The way he looked at her twisted a heated knot deep in the pit of her stomach. They were both fully clothed and Sebastian still wore his jacket, yet he turned her on with nothing more than the press of his body and the sound of desire in his voice.

"Just in case you're confused about what I mean," he added, "if you don't kick me out right now, we're going to have sex."

What about tomorrow? her inner voice asked. The twisting knot, deep in the pit of her belly, answered, *Who cares!* Her rational voice slightly edged out the desire spreading warm tingles across her flesh. "I'm obviously attracted to you, but I can't help but think we'll both regret it. Is a few hours of sex worth it?"

"I'm not going to regret it, and I'm going to make damn sure you don't either. And it doesn't matter now, we're beyond that particular bullet point." He lowered his face and kissed her throat just beneath her ear. "We need to have crazy hot sex and get it out of our systems. I've thought about it, and there's no other way."

His breath warmed the side of her neck, and she closed her eyes. She'd never made love with someone with whom she didn't have a romantic relationship. At least none that she could recall. "Has that worked for you in the past?"

"For me?" He kissed the shell of her ear. "Yes."

Maybe he was right. Maybe she needed to do it and get it out of her system. Falling in love first had clearly not worked for her. She was in the mood for sex. Not love.

"When was the last time you got laid, Clare?" he whispered.

When? Jeez . . . ahh . . ."April?"

"Nine months? Before your breakup with Lonny, then."

"Yes. When was the last time for you?"

"I'm assuming you mean with someone else in the room." His quiet laughter brushed her cheek.

"Of course."

"I've had sex twice since I was tested in August for anything and everything from malaria to HIV. Both those times I used a condom." He brushed his mouth across hers and said, "Does getting off in my shower, thinking of you, count?"

"No." She might have fantasized about him once or twice. "Was I good?"

"Not as good as you're going to be."

Her hands slid up the front of his jacket and she grasped both sides of the open zipper in her fists. Her lips parted and he fed her a slick, wet, devouring kiss that slammed into her and raised her to the balls of her feet.

Within the chandelier's soft glow, his tongue touched and teased. His hand moved through her hair and down her back, drawing her close, until the hard bulge of his erection pressed into her stomach.

Somewhere in the house the furnace clicked on

and forced air through the vents. She wanted Sebastian. All of him. She wanted the way he touched her and kissed her and made her feel, like he couldn't get enough, and she would worry about the repercussions and regret later. An acquiescent moan came from her throat as she kissed him back and surrendered to the desire bigger than her ability to hold it back. Not that she wanted to even try.

The sound of her moan triggered a sudden response, as if he'd been waiting for it. Within seconds his hands were everywhere, touching her anywhere within reach. Somehow she ended up with her back against the door and her blouse on the floor. She pushed Sebastian's jacket from his shoulders, and he shook it from his arms. Their lips parted long enough for her to pull his shirt over his head. Then he was against the door once again with his hand on her breasts and his fingers brushing her nipples through the satin of her bra. It was crazy and hot, like nothing she'd ever experienced before. Two people giving in to a purely physical and consuming need. A carnal drive for sex, and she didn't have to worry about what he'd think of her the morning after. There would be no morning after, and she could give in to it completely for the first time in her life.

He groaned deep in his throat and pulled back.

His breathing was heavy when he said, "Clare." The desire burning in his green eyes told her exactly what he was thinking. His hands slid to her behind and he ground his incredibly hard penis against her. "One time might not be enough."

Her body ached with response and she swayed into him. Her breasts brushed against his chest. "Two times?"

He shook his head as he slid his hand down her left thigh and lifted her leg to his waist. "All night."

She leaned forward and kissed his throat as her hands slid up and down his bare sides. "Mmm, well, I should probably tell you that I don't really have a kinky sex room."

"That works out because I prefer sex in a bedroom." He moved his other hand to her thigh and lifted. Her skirt bunched around her waist and she wrapped her legs around his waist. "I'm hoping to get there eventually." Through the soft fabric of his jeans his erection pressed into the crotch of her black lace panties. He kissed her as they moved into the living room. Light from the entry hall cut a white rectangular pattern into the darkness. His hands held her behind as he carried her to the medallion-back sofa, covered with her great-grandmother's doilies. Within the dim light of the room she lowered her feet to the floor and slid her mouth to the side of his throat.

"Turn on the light," he said, and she felt the heavy vibration of his voice against her lips. "We're not going to do this in the dark."

Clare pushed her hair out of her face as she moved first to an end table, then across the room to switch on two lamps. "Is that enough light for you?" She reached behind her and unbuttoned the back of her skirt as she walked toward him. The lined wool fabric slid down her legs, and she kicked it aside, leaving only her black nylon bra and lace panties. Time for modesty had long since passed. The night at the Double Tree, she'd already stripped down to nothing but a thong. While she didn't remember it, he clearly did, and he obviously liked what he'd seen. "Or do you want more?"

He watched her walk toward him from beneath his heavy lids, his hot gaze touching her all over as he stepped out of his shoes. "More? What do you got?"

One brow rose up her forehead as she let her own gaze slip from the hollow of his throat to the defined chest muscles covered in light brown skin. A dark-blond happy trail led her gaze down his hard six-pack abs and tanned stomach, past his navel, and to the waistband of his jeans. "I don't think I've got anything that you haven't already done before." She placed her hands on his shoulders, then ran her fingers lightly across his chest. His muscles bunched beneath her touch, and she slipped her hands down his flat belly. "I don't do yoga. No downward-facing dog." She slid her hand to his button fly and brushed the long, hard length of him though his pants. "Sorry. With me, you get straight-up sex."

"I've been so turned on for months, you don't have to do anything but lie there and breathe." His head dipped and he kissed her shoulder. He unhooked her bra and it fell to her feet. "I'm happy to do the rest."

She pulled the five metal buttons of his fly, then slid her hand beneath his white boxer briefs. "You don't want me to do this?" She wrapped her hand around his hot, thick shaft. As she'd suspected the first night he kissed her, Sebastian had grown into a big boy.

His response was a strangled, "No! Yes!"

"Which is it?" With her free hand she shoved his pants and underwear down his thighs. "No?" Her thumb slid up and down the thick cord of his penis. "Yes?"

"Yes," he hissed between his teeth. Then his mouth sought hers and the warm male scent of him filled her nose and she breathed him deep into her lungs. He smelled like clean skin and he tasted like sex. There was no future with Sebastian. There was only tonight. That was enough.

He grabbed her wrists and pinned them behind her back, smashing her breasts against his chest. Damn," he said, his voice strained, his breathing rapid. "Slow down or I'll beat you to the finish line. As it is, I'll probably only last five seconds."

She'd take it. Five seconds of Sebastian sounded better than anything else she'd had in a very long time.

He let go of her and removed his pants, underwear, and the socks from his feet. Naked, he was beautiful. Perfect except for the scar on his knee that he'd gotten from falling out of a tree on her mother's property. When he bent to grab his wallet from the back pocket of his jeans, she had an urge to lean forward and bite him. "I assume that patch on your hip isn't nicotine," he said as he straightened.

"No. It's Ortho Evra."

"Is it about ninety-five percent effective?"

"Ninety-nine."

He took her hand and placed the condom in her palm. "I'm leaving the choice up to you."

While she might find him completely edible, for Clare there was no choice. She ripped open the plastic pouch and took out the lubed ring of latex.

She positioned it over the plump head of his penis and slowly rolled it down to the base of his shaft. "Sit down, Sebastian," she said. When he obeyed, she pushed her panties down her hips. He watched them slide down her legs, then his gaze slid back up to her crotch.

"You're beautiful, Clare." He reached for her, and she knelt, straddling his lap. He kissed her stomach. "All over." He cupped her crotch and brushed between her legs with his fingers. "Especially here." He held his erection with one hand and pushed her down with the other. She moaned as she felt the head of his penis, smooth and hard and hot. He slid partway into her, and her body resisted the intrusion. She was so ready for him that there was only intense pleasure. She placed her hand on the sides of his neck and lowered herself until she was seated to the hilt. Sensation slashed through her body, from the top of her head to her toes. Her eyes closed and she squeezed her muscles around every solid inch of him. It had been so long, she was content to glory in the length of Sebastian buried deep within her.

Evidently, he was not as content. One second she was squeezing him, taking her time, and in the next she was on her back on the sofa, staring up into his face. He had one foot planted on the floor and was still deeply embedded inside her.

"This is the part where all you have to do is breathe." He pulled out almost completely, only to thrust so deep she felt him against her cervix. "Is this enough for you?" A deep groan tore through his chest and echoed her own pleasure. "Or do you want more?"

She wrapped one leg around his back. "I want more," she whispered as he began to move, setting a perfect rhythm of pleasure. "That feels so good." She licked her dry lips. "What happens if I stop breathing and pass out?"

With his face just above hers, he said, "I'll wake you when it's over."

Her chuckle turned into a long moan as he moved faster and every cell in her body focused on the shaft pounding into her. Faster, harder, and more intense. Over and over. His harsh breath brushed her cheek as he drove into her. Caressing and building sensation. Stroking her inside all at once. She moved with him, matching thrust for thrust. In and out again and again. Caught up in the hot pleasure she never wanted to end, she didn't know how long they'd been going at it until he said, "Clare." His voice was harsh, ravaged. "Honey, are you just about there?"

Before she could answer, she cried out as an exquisite climax crashed over her, flushing her body with heat. She saw and heard nothing over the pounding in her chest and head. Her inner muscles clenched and drew him deeper. Milking him with hot liquid tugs. He drove into her harder and harder, pushing her up her great-aunt's sofa until he too climaxed. An explosion of curses were forced from his throat and collided with the sound of intense male pleasure, primal and possessive. With one last thrust he slid his arms beneath her shoulders and crushed her tight against his chest.

"Clare," he whispered between ragged, rough breaths. "If I'd known you were so good, I would have thrown you in the bushes and done this the first night I kissed you back in September."

"If I'd known it would be this good . . ." She swallowed and licked her dry lips. ". . . I probably would have let you."

He was silent for several more moments as he kissed the side of her head, basking in the sweet warmth of afterglow. "Clare?"

"Hmm."

"The condom broke."

Her afterglow popped like a soap bubble. She pushed at his shoulders as she felt the blood drain from her head. "When?"

He looked down into her face. "About five seconds before I came."

"And you didn't stop?"

He chuckled and pushed her hair from her forehead. "I have some control, but not at that point. Not when I'm feeling your orgasm grabbing my cock like that." He kissed the end of her nose and smiled. "I swear to God, Clare, I don't think I've ever come that hard."

"How can you smile?" She shoved his shoulders, but his arms around her tightened.

"Because you're wearing that little birth control patch that's ninety-nine percent effective." His smile grew bigger. "Because you feel good, and because you're clean, and I know I'm clean."

"How do I know that for sure?"

"Because I would never lie to you about something so important. Trust me, Clare. I'm not going to hurt you."

Trust Sebastian? She looked into his eyes. There was no teasing or laughter or trickery. Just the honest truth. He pulled out a little, then slowly thrust inward again.

"If I thought there was a remote possibility of anything bad, I'd tell you. Believe me."

Believe him while he was still buried deep inside her? "If you're lying to me, I'll kill you. I swear I will." He continued with slow thrusts, and despite herself, she moved with him.

He grinned as if he'd just won the lottery.

"Coming from the author of *Surrender to Love,* that's not very romantic."

"Love and romance are overrated." She ran her hands over his shoulders to the sides of his neck. "Crazy hot sex is so much better."

Sixteen

"Merry Christmas." Clare wrapped her arms around Leo and gave him a big hug. She glanced over his shoulder at Sebastian standing a few feet behind his father, wearing black wool trousers and a deep caramel-colored sweater, which was about the exact color of his short hair. He also wore a hint of a smile as his gaze held hers, and she recalled with perfect clarity the previous night. She felt a flush spread across her chest and looked away.

"I loved the picture," Leo said as Clare dropped her arms and stepped back. "Sebastian told me you helped him pick it out."

She focused her attention on Leo and tried to ignore the butterflies in her stomach. "I'm glad you like it." Several months ago, she, Leo, and her mother had decided not to exchange gifts. Instead, they agreed to donate the money they would have spent to the Salvation Army.

"And he got me your book, but you know that."

"Yes, and I know you'll put it on your mantel with the others." She held out her hand toward Sebastian, hiding behind the cool, collected facade she'd developed long ago. "Merry Christmas."

He took her hand in his and his smile turned knowing. Last night and until late that morning he'd touched her all over with those big warm hands. After the first time on the couch, they'd taken a short break to eat a pizza before starting over in the bedroom and ending up around two-thirty in her shower, soaping their bodies and sliding their mouths across their clean wet skin. "Merry Christmas, Clare." His thumb brushed hers and the tone of his voice suggested he was reading her mind.

Clare suppressed the urge to flip her hair or fiddle with the neckline of her black satin halter. She hadn't dressed in anything new or different this year. She wore the ankle-length red velvet skirt and fringy belt she always wore on Christmas with knee-high black leather boots. Nothing special to attract extra attention. At least that's what she told herself, but she didn't bother believing it. She looked good and she knew it.

"What would you gentlemen like to drink?" Joyce asked. Sebastian dropped her hand and turned his attention to her mother. He and Leo had Glenlivet on the rocks, and while Joyce poured, she said she thought scotch sounded like such an excellent choice that she'd join them. Clare stuck with wine.

After a half hour's discussions of the weather and the latest world events, they moved to the formal dining room. There, among the holly and tapered candles, they feasted on the Wingate traditional dinner of glazed ham, potatoes grandmere, candied sweet potatoes, and green beans with cashews and tarragon. In Clare's great-great-grandmother's individual crystal compotes, Roman punch was served next to each plate.

As the oldest male, Leo had been given the chair at the head of the table, with Sebastian to his right and Joyce on the left. Ever the etiquette stickler, Joyce had insisted that Clare sit next to Sebastian. It would not be right to have both females on the same side of the table. Normally it would not have been a problem and Clare would have exerted herself to engage the guests in conversation. But tonight she couldn't think of anything to say to the man who'd given her three orgasms the night before, nor to Leo, who had always been a father figure to her. She felt sure she had a big neon Had Crazy Hot Sex Last Night sign above her head, and was afraid that if she did or said the wrong thing, everyone would notice.

She was so new at sex without commitment—or at least without a nice dinner and a movie date first. She wasn't exactly embarrassed—or not as much as she probably should be, especially given the oral aspect of their shower—but just didn't know what to say or do. She felt completely out of her element. Thank God no one seemed to notice.

Sebastian didn't appear to labor under such uncertainty. He relaxed in the chair beside her, charming her mother with little stories about all the places he'd traveled and asking questions about her various clubs and charities. He was used to no-strings sex, and Clare had to admit that she was somewhat irritated by his composure. It seemed only right that he be as rattled as she was.

"I've been trying for years to convince Claresta that she needs to become involved in my Ladies of Le Bois club," Joyce said as she tipped back her Glenlivet. "Through various benefits, we raised more than thirteen thousand dollars this year. We were especially excited to have Galvin Armstrong and his orchestra play for us at the Grove. I know Clare would enjoy herself if she'd just get involved."

Galvin Armstrong was older than Laurence Welk, and Clare needed to change the subject before she suddenly found herself involved in next year's benefit. "Sebastian ate a monkey." Leo and Joyce abruptly turned their attention to Sebastian, who stared at her with the fork halfway to his mouth. "And a horse," she added for good measure.

"Really, son?"

"Oh." Joyce set her glass on the table. "I don't think I could manage a horse. I had a pony as a child. Her name was Lady Clip Clop."

Slowly, Sebastian turned his head and looked at Clare. "I've eaten a lot of different things. Some were good. Some not so good." He smiled. "Some I wouldn't mind trying again."

The memory of him feathering her navel with warm kisses popped into her head. *I think you're going to like this,* he'd said last night as he worked his way south. *It's a little something I learned from a French lady in Costa Rica.* And she had liked it. A lot.

"But at the moment I'm hungry for Christmas ham." Sebastian turned his gaze across the table as he placed his hand on Clare's thigh. "This is wonderful, Mrs. Wingate."

Clare glanced at him out of the corner of her eye as he slowly pulled up her skirt.

"Please call me Joyce."

"Thank you for inviting me tonight, Joyce," he said, the poster child of choirboy politeness as his fingers gathered her skirt.

Clare wasn't wearing nylons, and she reached beneath the table before he could touch bare skin. She carefully grabbed his wrist and removed his hand.

"I received a Christmas card from your father's sister," Joyce announced, looking across the table at Clare.

"How is Eleanor?" Clare sank her spoon into her punch. As she placed the rum slush in her mouth, Sebastian flipped her skirt above her knees and replaced his hand on her now bare thigh. Startled by the warm contact, she jumped a little.

"You okay?" Sebastian asked, as if inquiring about the weather.

Clare pasted a strained smile on her face. "Fine."

Oblivious, Joyce continued, "Apparently, Eleanor has discovered religion."

" 'Tis the season." She placed her hand over

Sebastian's, but his grasp tightened. Short of wrestling his hand off her and drawing attention to what was taking place under the table, there was nothing she could do.

"Eleanor always was a trial," her mother continued. "She was somewhat of an embarrassment, which is quite an accomplishment in that family."

"How old is Eleanor?" Sebastian asked, his tone polite and curious as his hand crept higher. Skin on skin, heat spread warmth up Clare's thigh, his touch calling forth physical memories of the night before. In her bed and shower, and of course on the antique sofa.

"I believe she is seventy-eight." Joyce paused to spear her remaining green beans. "She's been married and divorced eight times."

"Once was enough for me," Leo added with a shake of his head. "Some people never learn."

"That's the truth. My great-great-uncle Alton was wounded in a marital dispute," Joyce confessed, uncharacteristically forthcoming regarding Wingate skeletons, thanks to her third glass of Glenlivet. "Unfortunately, he had a fondness for other men's wives. Neglected his own, though. Typical."

"Where was he wounded?" Sebastian slid his fingers to the front of Clare's panties. Her gaze got a little fuzzy and she about melted off her chair.

"Bullet in the left buttock. He was running away with his pants down."

Sebastian chuckled and his fingers brushed her through the spandex cotton blend. She squeezed her thighs and stifled a moan as the conversation continued without her. Leo made a comment about . . . something, and Joyce responded with . . . something, and Sebastian tugged at the elastic around the top of her leg and asked something. . . .

"Isn't that right, Clare?" Joyce asked.

Her eyes refocused on her mother. "Yes. Absolutely!" She shoved his hand from her crotch and stood, careful to make sure her skirt stayed down. "Dessert?"

"I don't think so right now." Her mother placed her linen napkin on the table.

"Leo?" Clare asked as she gathered her plate and flatware.

"None for me. Give me half an hour."

"Can I take your plate, Sebastian?"

He stood. "I'll take it."

"That's okay." The last thing she needed was for him to follow and finish what he'd started. "You just sit and relax with my mother and Leo."

"After a big meal, I need to walk around," he insisted.

Joyce handed Clare her plate. "You should show Sebastian the house."

"Oh, I don't think he cares about—"

"I'd love to see it," he interrupted her.

He followed her into the kitchen and they set the plates in the sink. He leaned a hip into the counter and ran the backs of his fingers up her arm. "Since I walked in the house tonight, I've been wondering if you had on some sort of bra under that thing. Guess not."

She looked down at the two very distinct points in the front of her black satin halter. "I'm cold."

"Uh-huh." He brushed his knuckles across her left breast. Her lips parted and she sucked in a breath. "You're turned on."

She bit her top lip and shook her head, but they both knew she lied.

He sighed and dropped his hand. "Show me the damn house."

She turned on the heels of her boots and left him to follow behind. Yes, the last thing she needed was for Sebastian to work his moves on her in her mother's house. But there was another part of her, the new part that had just discovered the pleasure of meaningless sex, that wanted him to do that and more.

She showed him the parlor her mother used for an office, the main living room, and the library. He kept his hands to himself, which was almost as frustrating as when he'd touched her. "I used to spend a lot of time in here as a kid," she said, pointing to the floor-to-ceiling rows of leather-bound books. The room was furnished with old leather chairs and several Tiffany lamps.

"I remember." He walked along the built-in mahogany shelves. "Where are your books?"

"Oh. Well, my books are paperbacks."

He looked across his shoulder at her. "And?"

"And my mother doesn't think paperbacks belong with leather-bound books."

"What? That's ridiculous. You're a member of her family. Much more important than depressed Russian authors and dead poets. Your mother should be thrilled to put your books in here."

Well, she'd always thought so, or at least thought she should be given equal shelf space in her own mother's house. To hear Sebastian say it stirred unwanted feelings in her chest. "Thank you."

"For what? Does your mother know how hard it is to get a book published?"

But this was Sebastian. She could not allow herself to feeling anything for him but a mild friendship and a raging physical attraction. "Probably not, but it wouldn't matter if she did. Nothing I ever do will be good enough, or exactly right, or perfect. She's never going to change, so I've had to.

I don't kill myself to please her nor purposely irritate her anymore."

"No." He laughed quietly. "You just deflect attention off yourself and onto me."

She smiled. "That's true, but you really should suffer a little for eating poor Mr. Bananas." She nodded toward the doorway. "I'll show you upstairs."

He followed close behind as she moved up the curved staircase. She showed him three guest rooms, her mother's bedroom, and finally the room she'd occupied growing up. It still held her queen bed with heavy wooden pineapples on the posts, the same armoire, dressers, and five-drawer vanity. The only thing that had changed was the bedding.

"I remember this room," Sebastian said as he moved farther inside. "But everything was pink."

"Yes."

He turned to her and said, "Close the door, Clare."

"Why?"

"Because you don't want your mother to see what I'm going to do to her little girl."

"We can't do anything in here."

"You almost sound like you mean that." He walked across the room and shut the door himself. "Almost." He walked back, ran his hands up her arms to her shoulders and the back of her neck. He kissed her, and before she realized what he was about, his fingers were at the bow at the back of her neck and he lowered her halter to her waist.

She pulled back and covered her bare breasts with her hands. "What if someone walks in?"

"They won't." He grasped her wrist and placed her palms on his shoulders. "Your nipples are hard and your panties are wet, so I know you want this too." He cupped her breasts and brushed the stiff tips with his thumbs. "I've been thinking about doing this since I walked into the house. All through your mother's charity event stories, I wondered if anyone would notice if I disappeared beneath the table and kissed the insides of your thighs. I wondered if you were as turned on as I was. Then I felt your panties and I knew I was going to be inside you at some point tonight." He kissed the side of her throat, and she slid her hands beneath his sweater and the T-shirt he wore beneath.

"I thought that after last night, you weren't supposed to want to have sex anymore," she said, and slipped one hand to the button on his trousers. "That it would be out of your system."

"Yeah. I underestimated you. I predict it's going to take at least one more time."

He grasped the back of her thighs and lifted. Clare wrapped her legs around his waist, bringing her crotch against his bulging penis as he carried her the short distance to the heavy oak vanity.

"Tell me how bad you want it." He set her on the vanity and worked her skirt up around her waist.

"So bad I'm letting you undress me with my mother downstairs."

He pushed her thighs apart and touched her through her panties. "Walking around this house, knowing you're this wet, has about killed me."

She unzipped his pants and slid her hand inside his boxer briefs. Within her palm she felt his pulse beating and squeezed. "You're hard."

"I'm going to make you come."

"I'm counting on it."

Instead of pulling her panties from her legs, he slid the thin strip of fabric to one side. Then he pushed into her, thick and enormous, and she wrapped her calves around his behind until he was buried deep inside. His flesh felt hot and she tightened her muscles around him. The kiss he gave her was soft and sweet as he began to move, withdrawing slightly and easing himself back inside. "You feel as good as I remember," he whispered just above her lips. "So slick and tight."

Clare's head fell back against the mirror, and he kissed the side of her throat just below her ear.

"I want you so much," he said. "I want to kiss all the good parts like I did last night." He ground his hips against her and groaned deep in his throat. He pulled out, then thrust hard. If there'd been anything in the drawers of the vanity, it would have made a lot of noise. Thankfully, it was empty, and the only sound in the room was that of heavy breathing.

Steadily he pumped into her, stroking the inside of Clare's wet walls and massaging her g spot. It didn't take long for the first wave of orgasm to crash into her and wash her body in intense white heat. It stole her breath and curled her toes inside her black boots. Just as it eased, it started all over again.

"Oh my God!" she gasped as a second orgasm grabbed hold. In the midst of her own amazing pleasure, she felt his powerful ejaculation inside. He groaned deep in his chest, his knees buckled a little, and his grasp on her thighs tightened to keep him from falling.

"Christ Almighty," he managed through a rough, hoarse whisper.

When it was over and the last pulsation subsided, she dropped one leg from around his waist as he struggled to find breath. She'd never experienced anything like it in her life. When she could finally speak, she looked up into his green eyes and said, "That was amazing."

"I thought so."

She blinked several times. "I had a multiple orgasm."

"I could tell."

"I've never had one before."

One corner of his mouth slid up. "Merry Christmas."

A few days after Christmas, Clare met her friends for lunch at their favorite Mexican restaurant. Over a huge combo platter they discussed books and brainstormed plots. Lucy was deep into deadline, as was Clare, and Adele had just finished a book. Maddie's books didn't come out as often as the three genre writers, and she was taking several months off to relax and get her head right after her last true crime novel. Well, as right as was possible with Maddie, Clare thought.

They chatted and laughed as they always did. Shared bits and pieces of their lives. Dwayne was still harassing Adele, leaving random stuff on her doorstep; Lucy was thinking about starting a family; and Maddie had just purchased a summer home in Truly, a small town a hundred miles north of Boise. The one thing that Clare did not share with her friends was her relationship with Sebastian. Primarily because there was no relationship, just sex, and she wasn't the type of person to talk about her sex life. Not like Maddie—if she'd had one to talk about. Another reason was because it was still all so new that she didn't know what to think about it herself.

Sebastian had left town the day after Christmas, but not before driving to her house and waking her up one last time. She'd never met a man who wanted sex as much as he did. No. Strike that. It had been a while since she'd been with a man who wanted sex as much as he did, but she'd never met a man who was as good at it as he was. A man who said, "This is what I'm going to do to you," and then not only did it, but exceeded all expectations.

When she got home from lunch with her friends, there was a message on her answering machine from Sebastian.

"Hey there," he began as she took off her coat, "I have a big New Year's Eve party here in Seattle that I need to go to. I was thinking that if you didn't have plans, you could be my date. Give me a call back and let me know."

New Year's Eve? In Seattle? Was he insane? She poured herself a Diet Coke and phoned him back to ask him that exact question.

"It's an hour's flight," he said. "Do you have plans?"

If Sebastian were actually her boyfriend, she might play harder to get. Pretend she did have plans but was willing to break them just for him. "No."

"I'll pay for the ticket," he said.

"That won't be cheap." She grabbed her Coke and walked upstairs to her office. "What's your ulterior motive?"

"I get to spend time with a beautiful woman."

Just a few days ago she'd been thrilled when he said she was beautiful. The little part of her that still resided down deep. The part that had followed him around as a child. Now, she wasn't so sure how she felt about the compliment. Now, it seemed like something a man would say to his girlfriend, and Clare felt she could not afford to let the tiniest hint of a relationship past the wall she'd built to protect her heart. She dismissed it as meaningless. Something men always said to women. It meant nothing. "Don't tell me there aren't any women in Seattle you could ask." She waited for the first jealousy pinch. The gnawing on her heart. When she felt nothing, she smiled. She liked him as a friend. A woman couldn't be jealous of a boy friend who wasn't a boyfriend. Especially when he lived in another state.

"A few, but they're not as interesting as you. Not as much fun."

"Meaning they won't have sex with you?"

"Oh sure, they'll have sex with me." His laughter carried across her phone line. "But since you brought it up, bring something sexy because I think we need to make love a few more times to get it out of our system."

Make love. What they did together was not making love. They had sex. Hot, wild, unbelievably good sex, but it was different from making love. It was purely physical. The earth did shake, and her heart didn't feel as if it might burst. That was making love, and she knew the difference. "Ah. Like ipecac."

"More like sex therapy. I think we could use the workout. I know I could."

Which she had to admit sounded good. After feeling undesirable for several years, having a man want her as much as Sebastian did was addictive. And right now in her life, hot, wild, unbelievably good sex was better than love. In the future, she would once again look for a soul mate. Someone to spend her life with. She wanted a husband and a family. She wanted a "happily ever after" with a "happily ever after" man. It was in her DNA to want those things, but for now she just wanted to have fun with a "good time" guy like Sebastian.

Who could never, ever be confused with "happily ever after" man.

"Okay," she agreed. "But I have to shop for something to wear when I get there. Are you up for that?"

There was a long pause, and then, "I might need extra therapy to get over the trauma."

She laughed and began to tick off the stores in her head. Beside the regular list of suspects like Nordstrom, Nieman's, and Saks, she'd hit Club Monaco, BCBG, and Bebe.

Wow, a shopping *and* sex binge. Just a few months ago her life had sucked, but what a way to start the new year.

Seventeen

Sebastian picked up the knife and cut several turkey sandwiches in half. He placed them on a plate and grabbed a tube of Pringles. He'd never flown a woman in just so he could spend the day in bed with her. But then he didn't think he'd ever been with a woman quite like Clare before.

Wearing only his underwear, he grabbed lunch and walked from the kitchen. He'd picked Clare up that morning from Sea-Tac, and it wasn't until he'd watched her come down the escalator toward him, looking gorgeous in her black coat and red scarf, that he realized how much he liked being with her. They had a lot in common. She was smart and beautiful and didn't make demands. More important, she was just easy to be with. In his experience, once a man had sex with a woman more than twice, they always brought up the R word—relationship—which was always followed closely by the C word—commitment. Women just couldn't seem to relax. They always had to complicate things.

He walked into his bedroom and his gaze went to Clare, sitting in the center of his bed, a tangle of white sheets pulled up beneath her armpits. "There's nothing to watch but football," she said with disgust as she flipped through television channels with the remote. "I hate to watch football. I dated a guy once who taped all the games."

Her hair was a mess and there was a pink sucker bite on her shoulder. "I watch football if there's nothing better to do." He set the plate on the edge of the bed and crawled toward her. He handed her half a sandwich and kissed the mark. He liked the way her skin smelled and the taste of her in his mouth.

"I broke up with him when I caught him watching football while we were having sex." She took a bite, then swallowed. "He'd turned on the television but kept the sound on mute so I wouldn't know."

"Sneaky bastard." Sebastian popped the top of the Pringles can and ate a few.

"Yeah. I'm a sneaky bastard magnet." She turned off the television and tossed the remote on the bed. "Which is why I'm taking a break from men."

He paused mid-chew. "What am I?"

"You're just a friend with benefits. And believe me, after Lonny, I need the benefit of benefits." She laughed and took another bite.

Which was one more reason he liked her. He handed her some chips and grabbed half a sandwich for himself. "Tell me something. If you're a girl who likes lots of benefits, and we both know that you are, how did you end up engaged to a gay man? Wanting to please your mother only explains it to a point."

She thought a moment as she scarfed several Pringles. "It happened little by little. At first the relationship was fairly typical. He was less sexual than other boyfriends, but I told myself it wasn't a big deal. I loved him. And if you love someone, you have to be accepting. Then once you're that deep in denial, you really don't see anything. Actually, you probably don't want to see it." She shrugged. "And other than sex, there really wasn't one huge sign. Just lots of little signs that I ignored."

"Like that lacy, girly girl crap hanging over your bed. A heterosexual guy wouldn't have put up with sleeping under that."

She looked at him and pushed her hair behind one ear. "You did."

He shook his head. "I have sex under it. I don't sleep under lace." Which reminded him of the sex they'd just had. It started by his front door and ended in a naked tangle on his bed. She'd been as hot for him as he had been for her, and for a man to know a woman wanted him as much as he wanted her was a powerful aphrodisiac. The sex would have been even better if it hadn't been for the condom she'd asked him to wear.

"I thought you trusted me without a condom," he said and ate a chip.

"I did trust you." She tilted her head to one side and looked at him. "But I assume you are seeing other women now and I have to be careful."

"Seeing other women? Since last weekend? Thanks for the compliment, but I don't move that fast." He'd *assumed* she hadn't seen anyone, and the thought that she might have bothered him more than he wanted to admit. "Have you been with another man?"

She recoiled. "No."

"Then why don't we keep it that way?" He

reached for a bottle of water and unscrewed the cap.

"Are you saying you want to be sexually exclusive? Both of us?"

He took a drink of water, then handed to her. He liked the idea of Clare only having sex with him, and he didn't want to have sex with another woman. "Sure."

"Can you do that?"

He scowled at her. "Yeah. Can you?"

"I just meant that you live in a different state."

"That's not a problem. I'll be visiting my father a lot, and believe me, I've gone without sex before. I didn't like it but I survived."

She took a drink and seemed deep in thought before she handed him back the bottle. "Okay, but Sebastian, if and when you find someone, you have to tell me."

"Find someone? Find someone to what?"

She simply stared at him.

"Okay." He leaned forward and kissed her bare shoulder. "If I get tired of you, I'll tell you."

She slid her hand up his chest and scattered goose bumps across his skin. "I noticed you didn't mention what happens if I get tired of you first."

He laughed and pushed her down on the bed. That wasn't likely to happen.

After they finished lunch, they showered and left the apartment for what Sebastian had thought would be a quick trip to Pacific Place Mall. He wasn't big on shopping and he didn't own a lot of clothing. He had a few Hugo Boss suits and some dress shirts, but he much preferred cargo pants, where he could stash gear, and comfy cotton T-shirts from Eddie Bauer. In fact, shopping was one of his least favorite things to do, but for some reason he allowed himself to be dragged around downtown Seattle while Clare tried on racks of clothing, inspected numerous handbags, and got a crazed look in her eyes when she discovered silver shoes in Nordstrom.

After the fifth store and numerous bags, Sebastian relaxed and just took it all in. He couldn't say he had fun, but it was interesting. Clare had a definite style and knew what she wanted when she saw it. By the time they walked into Club Monaco, he could predict what would draw her attention.

That morning when he picked her up from the airport, he'd wondered why she'd brought two big suitcases for such a short trip. Now he knew.

Clare was a classic shopaholic.

Later that evening Sebastian took her to the New Year's Eve party of his former college friend, Jane Alcot-Martineau. He'd known Jane long before she'd gotten herself hyphenated. They'd attended the same journalism classes at the University of Washington, and while Sebastian had taken off after graduation to freelance across the country and eventually the globe, Jane had stuck around Seattle. She'd eventually landed a job at the *Seattle Times*, where she'd met and married hockey goalie Luc Martineau. They'd been married for a few years and lived in an apartment not far from Sebastian's. They had a one-year-old son, James, and Luc's sister Marie lived with them while she attended school.

"Are you sure Clare's just a friend?" Jane asked as she handed him a Pyramid ale.

Sebastian stared down at the five-foot-one woman beside him, then turned his gaze to Clare, who was talking to a tall thin blond woman, her red-haired boyfriend, and a beefy Russian defenseman. "Yeah, I'm sure." Clare wore a shiny silver tube of a dress that looked like she'd been wrapped up in tinfoil, then had someone take their hands and press it against her body. The dress wasn't exactly scandalous, but several times during the evening, Sebastian noticed a few muscle-necked hockey players unwrapping her with their eyes. When they found out she was a romance writer, their interest intensified. He knew what the bastards were thinking.

" 'Cause you look like you're ready to cross-check Vlad," Jane said.

Sebastian carefully unfolded his arms from across the chest of his blue dress shirt and took a drink of his beer. "Do you think I can take him?"

"Heck no. He'd kick your sissy reporter butt." Jane had always been *almost* as smart as she was a smartass. "He's 'Vlad the Impaler' for a reason. Once you get to know him, he's a nice enough guy." She shook her head and her short black hair brushed her cheek. "If you didn't want these guys to hit on her, you shouldn't have introduced her as your 'friend.' "

Jane was probably right, but introducing her as his girlfriend seemed too soon. And Clare probably wouldn't have appreciated it if he'd said, "This girl is mine so back the hell off!" Clare might not be his girlfriend, but she was his date, and he didn't like watching other men move in on her. "You do know that I was kidding, don't you?"

"About taking on Vlad? Yeah. About Clare being 'just a friend,' I think you're kidding yourself."

He opened his mouth to argue but Jane walked away to join her husband. Later that night as he watched Clare sleep, he wondered what it was about her that drew him in and refused to let go. It wasn't just the sex. It was something else. All that shopping she'd subjected him to should have cooled his interest. But it hadn't. Perhaps it was that she had no expectations. She didn't seem to want anything from him, and the more she kept her distance, the more he wanted to pull her closer.

At six the next morning Sebastian woke, restless, and yanked on a T-shirt and a pair of cargo pants. While Clare slept, he started a pot of coffee, and as it brewed he called his dad. It was seven o'clock in Boise, but he knew Leo was an early riser. His relationship with his father was improving slowly with each visit. They weren't exactly close, but both of them were making a real effort to repair the damage of the past.

He hadn't spoken with his father since Christmas, but he was fairly certain Leo didn't know about his guest asleep in his bed. He hadn't mentioned it, and he didn't know how the old man would feel about what he had going on with Clare. Okay, that was a lie. Leo wouldn't be thrilled, but of course, he'd known that going in. He knew it the first time he kissed her, and he knew it the last time he made love to her the night before. He'd come to the conclusion that he and Clare were consenting adults and what they consented to do was between them and no one else.

After he got off the phone with Leo, he moved into his office. The last few months he'd been toying with the idea of writing fiction. A series of thriller/mystery novels with a recurring central character much in the vein of Cussler's Dirk Pitt or Clancy's Jack Ryan. Only his main protagonist would be an investigative journalist.

Sebastian sat down at his desk and booted up his computer. He had a sketchy plot outline and a vague notion of character, but after two hours of solid writing, it became more concrete in his mind.

A noise from the kitchen drew his attention from the drama taking place in his head, and he glanced up from his computer screen as Clare walked into the room wearing a plain blue nightgown that matched her eyes. It was short and had little straps and was sexy as all hell simply by virtue of not trying too hard. A lot like Clare herself.

"Oh, sorry," she said, and stopped in the doorway. I didn't know you had to work."

"I don't." He stood and stretched. "I'm not really working. Mostly just playing around."

"Solitaire?" She moved farther into the room and took a drink of coffee from the mug in her hand.

"No. I have an idea for a book." It was the first time he'd been this excited about writing anything in a while. Probably since before his mother had died.

"On a story you've covered recently?"

"No. Fiction." It was also the first time he'd mentioned what he was doing. He hadn't even told his agent yet. "I was thinking more along the lines of an investigative journalist who uncovers government secrets."

Her brows rose up her forehead. "Like Ken Follett or Frederick Forsyth, maybe?"

"Maybe." He came out from behind his desk and smiled. "Or maybe I'll become a male romance novelist."

Behind her mug her eyes got wide and she started to laugh.

"What are you laughing at? I'm a romantic guy."

She set the mug on his desk, and somehow her laugher turned into a choking jag that lasted until he threw her over his shoulder and carried her back to bed like Valmont Drake from her latest book, *Surrender to Love*.

On the third day of March, Clare turned thirty-four with real ambivalence about becoming another year older. On one hand, she liked the wisdom that came with age and the confidence that came with that wisdom. On the other, she didn't like the ticking time clock in her body. The one that kept track of every day and every year and reminded her that she was still alone.

A few weeks ago she'd made plans to celebrate the day with her friends. Lucy made dinner reservations for the four of them at The Milky Way in the old Empire building downtown, but they were expected to meet at Clare's house first for a glass of wine and to give Clare her birthday gifts.

As Clare dressed for the evening in a Michael Kors jersey dress she'd picked up on sale at Nieman Marcus, she thought of Sebastian. As far as she knew, he was in Florida. She hadn't spoken to him in a week, when he told her he'd decided to write a piece on the most recent wave of Cuban immigrants to hit Little Havana. In the past two months she'd seen him at least every other week when he'd drive or fly into Boise to see his father.

Clare hooked a pair of silver hoops in her ears and sprayed Escada on the insides of her wrists. For now, her nonrelationship with Sebastian was working. They had fun together and there was no pressure to try and impress him. She could talk to him about anything, because she didn't have to worry about whether he was Mr. Right. He clearly wasn't. Mr. Right would come along. Until that time, she was happily spending time with Mr. Right Now.

When he came into town, she was glad to see him, but her heart didn't race or pinch, and her stomach did not get light and queasy. Well, perhaps a little, but that had more to do with the way he looked at her than what she felt for him. She did not lose her ability to breathe or think rationally. He was just easy to be around. The day it no longer worked was the day she would end it—or he would. No hard feelings. That was the deal. They might be exclusive for now, but she knew that it wouldn't last forever, and she didn't let herself think too far ahead.

She reached for a tube of red lipstick and leaned toward the dresser mirror. She wasn't ready for a serious relationship. Not yet. Just last week she'd decided to test the waters and had met Adele at Montego Bay for the restaurant's eight-minute date night, in which a person spent eight minutes getting to know someone before moving on to the next table. Most of the men she'd met that evening had seemed perfectly fine. There'd been nothing really wrong with them, but two minutes into her first "date," she'd opened her mouth and said, "I have four children." When that hadn't totally turned him off, she'd added, "All under the age of six." By the end of the evening she'd somehow become a single mother who collected stray cats. When that hadn't totally turned off one stalwart dater, she'd alluded to "female troubles," and he'd practically knocked over the table in his haste to get away from her.

The doorbell rang as Clare finished with her lipstick, and she moved through the house to the front door. Adele and Maddie stood on her porch, gifts in hand.

"I told you two not to get me anything," she said, knowing full well that they totally would.

"What's this?" Maddie asked as she pointed to an express mail box at her feet.

Clare wasn't expecting any mail orders or anything from her publisher. When she knelt to pick it up, she recognized the Seattle return address. It had a Florida postmark. "I think it's probably a birthday present." Sebastian had remembered her birthday, and she tried to tamp down the pleasure of it before it reached her heart. When she heard footsteps walking up the drive, she half expected to see Sebastian. It was Lucy, of course, and she was carrying a bouquet of pink roses and a small gold box.

"I thought I'd beat you girls here," she said as Clare let her friends into the house.

Clare took the roses from Lucy and went in search of a vase while her friends hung up their coats. In the kitchen, she cut the bottoms off the stems, and her gaze drifted to the white box on the counter. She was surprised that Sebastian had re-membered her birthday. Especially on assignment, and the pleasure she'd tried to suppress brushed across her skin. She told herself it probably wasn't a thoughtful gift. More than likely the box held the usual self-serving man present. Something crotchless with nipple tassels.

"Lord, I've had enough of the cold," Maddie complained as the other three women moved into the kitchen.

"Could one of you pour the wine?" Clare asked as she arranged the flowers in some deceased rel-ative's Portmeirion vase. Lucy poured, and when she was finished, the four friends moved into the living room. Clare set the vase on an end table next to the sofa, and when she turned around, Adele was setting the gifts on the coffee table. Including the white box.

As the four women talked about getting older, Clare opened the presents her friends had bought for her. Lucy gave her a monogrammed business card holder, and Adele a bracelet with little purple crystals. Maddie, being Maddie, gifted Clare with a personal safety device in the form of a red stun pen to replace the faulty one she'd given her the year before. "Thanks, guys. I loved all the gifts," she said as she sat back with her glass.

"Are you going to open that one?" Adele asked.

"Is it from your mother again?" Lucy wanted to know. A few years ago when she'd been avoiding Joyce, her mother had sent her beautiful bed linens for her birthday. Picking up the phone and calling Clare would not have been passive aggressive enough.

"No. My mother and I are speaking this year."

"Who's it from?"

"A friend of mine." The three women stared at her, brows raised as they waited for more information. "Sebastian Vaughan."

"Sebastian the reporter?" Adele asked. "The guy Maddie thinks has heft?"

"Yes." Clare's face was purposely impassive when she added, "And he is just a friend."

Maddie sucked in a breath. "Just a friend, my ass. I can tell by your face you're hiding something. You always get that look when you're hiding something."

"What look?"

Lucy pointed at her. "That look." She took a drink of her wine. "So, is he a boyfriend?"

"No. He's just a friend." When her friends continued to stare at her, she sighed and confessed, "Okay. We're friends who have sex."

"Good for you!" Maddie nodded. "Adele told

you that you should use him as a rebound man."

Adele nodded. "I've had a few, and sex without strings is some of the best kind."

Lucy was quiet for a few moments, then asked, "Are you sure?"

"About what?"

"That you can handle sex without strings? I know you. You've the heart of a pure romantic. Can you really handle sex without falling in love?"

"I can handle it." She set her glass on the coffee table and reached for the white box. To prove it, she'd show them the gift from Sebastian was no big deal. None at all. "And I am handling it." She opened the white mailer and smiled. Inside was a smaller box wrapped in pink metallic paper and excessive bows and ribbon. "It's working out great. He lives in Seattle and sees me when he's here in town to visit his dad. We have a lot of fun and there are no expectations."

"Be careful," Lucy warned. "I don't want to see you hurt again."

"I won't get hurt," she said as she unwrapped the pink paper. "I don't love Sebastian and he doesn't love me." She looked down as she opened the box, and nestled in white and pink polka-dot tissue was a black leather belt. On the heavy silver buckle was the deep inscription, BOY TOY.

Clare stared down at the gift as she felt a sharp

pinch in her chest and a frightening little flutter in her stomach. At the same time, she felt like she was being thrust to the top of a roller coaster. Up, up, up, and she knew there was nowhere to go but straight down. *Boy Toy.*

"What is it?"

She held it up and her friends chuckled. "Is he marking his territory?" Adele asked.

Clare nodded, but she knew it wasn't like that at all. It was worse. He'd looked into a young, awkward girl's heart and given her what she desired most. He'd paid attention. He'd listened to her and gone to a good deal of trouble to get it for her. He'd wrapped it in pink and he'd made sure it arrived on her birthday. Her face was suddenly hot, and her pinching heart pounded frantically, beating against the wall she'd built to keep Sebastian out. The wall she hid behind to keep from falling madly and completely in love with a man so totally wrong for her. Around her, her friends talked and laughed and seemed oblivious to the struggle within her to stay on top of the roller coaster. To struggle and fight and hang on. But it was too late. She was helpless as she started the plunge. Deep emotion rushed toward her, and the overwhelming force of it threatened to rob her of breath. She told herself that she couldn't let herself love him, but it was too late. It slammed into her, and she fell madly, deeply, completely in love with Sebastian Vaughan. Splat. "Oh no," she whispered.

Lucy noticed something was wrong and asked. "Are you okay?"

"I'm fine. I think turning thirty-four has put me in a weird mood." She laughed and prayed she sounded convincing.

"I understand. When I turned thirty-five, I started getting a really panicky feeling," Lucy said, and Clare breathed a little easier. "It's normal."

Later, during dinner, Clare tried to tell herself that the burning in her chest wasn't *real* love, that it was a result of the jalapeno shrimp bites she ordered for an hors d'oeuvre. The tears threatening to sting the backs of her eyes were the result of turning another year older. It was normal. Even Lucy thought so.

But by the time the meal ended with crême brulée, Clare knew it wasn't the jalapeno nor the day. She was in love with Sebastian, and she didn't think she'd ever been so scared. Sure, there had been other scary times in her life, but she'd always known what to do. This time she had absolutely no idea. Somehow while she'd been convincing herself that all she felt was friendship, her love for him had snuck up on her quietly. It hadn't been a whap to the chest or a breath-stealing glance from across the room. No warm fuzzy tingling zaps to the heart when she thought of him. Instead, it had grown from a little seed, finding the cracks and fissures in the wall guarding her heart, entangling her without her even knowing it until she was caught good and tight.

While she and Sebastian talked about a lot of different things, they had never talked about what they felt for each other. But at least she wasn't in denial. Not anymore. Yes, he wanted to be exclusive, but she knew he didn't love her. She'd been with men who'd loved her. She might not have felt so strongly about them, but she knew how a man in love acted. And it wasn't like Sebastian.

Once again she'd fallen for Mr. Wrong. She was such a fool.

That night she went to bed thinking of Sebastian, and when she woke, he was still on her mind. She thought about the smell of his neck and the touch of his hands, but she refused to call him. She had a perfect excuse. She should call and thank him for the birthday present. In fact, etiquette demanded that she at least call him, but she refused to give in to the temptation to hear his voice. Perhaps if she just tried to ignore her feelings, they would go back into hiding. She didn't kid herself that they would go away. She was a thirty-four-year-old relationship veteran and former love junky. But perhaps, if she were very lucky, his absence would make her heart grow a little less fond.

Eighteen

Three days after Clare's birthday Sebastian called, and she discovered that she wasn't so lucky. Not at all. If anything, the sight of his name on her caller ID made her chest hurt.

"Hello," she answered, striving to sound calm and a little blasé.

"What are you wearing?"

She looked down at her robe and bare feet as she pulled a brush through her damp hair. "Where are you?"

"On your porch?"

Her hand stopped, as well as the blood flow to her head. "You're outside my house?"

"Yeah."

She tossed the brush on her bed and walked

from her bedroom toward the entryway. She
opened the door and there he stood, wearing a
white T-shirt beneath a deep green wool button-
up and looking beautiful. Smile lines creased the
corners of his green eyes, and he hooked his
phone to the brown leather belt wrapped around
the hips of his faded jeans. Oh God, she was in
trouble.

"Hello, Clare." The sound of his voice sent hot
little tingles up her spine and raised little goose
bumps on the back of her arms.

"What are you doing?" she asked into the receiver. "You didn't tell me you were coming to visit
Leo."

"Leo doesn't know I'm here." He took the phone
from her, hit the Off button, then handed it back.
"I flew in to see you."

She looked behind him at the Mustang parked in
her driveway. It had Idaho plates. "Me?" Her heart
wanted to take that as a sign that he cared for her
more than just as a friend with benefits, but her
head wouldn't let her.

"Yeah. I want to spend the night. The whole
night. Like when you came and stayed with me in
Seattle. I don't want to sneak back to Leo's like a
kid. Like we're doing something wrong."

She should send him away before she fell even

more in love with him, but the problem was, it was far too late. She opened the door wide and let him in. "You want to sleep here?"

"Eventually." He followed her inside and waited until she'd closed the door before he reached for her.

"There's lace on my bed, remember? Something bad might happen if you sleep in a girly girl bed."

He pulled her against his chest. "I'll risk it."

"Thanks for the birthday gift." She smiled and placed her hands on his shoulders. "It was very thoughtful of you to get it here on my birthday."

"Did you like it?"

"Loved it."

"Show me," he said as he swooped in and planted a kiss on her mouth. He touched her as he always did, only this time there was a difference in the way she responded. No matter how she tried to hide from it, she was in love with Sebastian. Her heart was involved, and when she took him to her bedroom, it was more than just sex. More than pleasure and gratification. For the first time, she truly made love to him. The warmth of emotion spread through her body from the inside out. From the center of her chest outward to the tips of her fingers and toes. When it was over, she pulled him close and kissed his bare shoulder.

"You must have really missed me," he said next to her ear. He'd noticed the difference in their sex but misinterpreted what was behind it.

Sebastian stayed with her for two days and talked to her about growing up with his mother and his guilt over his relationship with his father. He told her how angry he'd been when he'd been sent away as a child. She suspected he'd been more than angry. Although he might not admit it, she was sure he'd been hurt and bewildered too.

"I learned my lesson. That was the last time I told a girl how babies are made," he said.

"Good. I was terrified of sex for years after that, and it was all your fault."

He'd placed an innocent hand on his chest. "Mine?"

"Yes. You told me sperms were the same size as tadpoles."

He'd laughed. "I don't remember, but I probably did."

"You did."

They talked about their writing, and he told her he'd been hard at work on his book. He talked about the twists and turns of the plot and said he figured he was about halfway through. He also confessed he'd read all her books. She'd been so shocked she hadn't known what to say.

"If they didn't have half-naked guys on the covers, I think more men would read them," he told her over dinner at her house.

She hadn't thought it possible, but that night, looking across the table while he ate veal with sage marinade, she fell in love with him even more. "It may surprise you to know that I do have male readers. They write me all the time." She smiled. "Of course, they're all incarcerated for crimes they didn't commit."

He paused over his veal and looked up at her. "I hope you don't write them back."

"No." Perhaps he didn't love her now, but he was here, with her, and who knew how he would feel next week or next month.

The next time Sebastian drove into Boise, he was on his way home from a ski trip in Park City, Utah, where he'd met up with some of his journalism friends. It had been three weeks since his last visit, and he had plans to stay with Leo for several days and do some fishing at Strike Dam, where his father had told him people were pulling out twenty-two-inch rainbows. But within a few hours of his arrival, he called and picked Clare up at her house. Sebastian hated shopping more than any man she'd ever known, and he conned her into going to the mall with him. Leo's back had started "acting up" and they went in search of a massager. Sebastian hoped to get his father feeling good enough for the drive to the dam in the morning.

Due to the change in plans, Sebastian decided to relax with Clare that evening and watch "kick-ass movies," eat "salty popcorn," and "drink beer." At least they agreed on the popcorn. Clare was more of a wine person and preferred chick flicks, but he'd promised she would get to pick the movie next time.

"What was your favorite movie growing up?" Clare asked as they walked into Brookstone.

Without hesitation he said, "*Willie Wonka.*"

"*Willie Wonka?*" Clare stopped next to a display of ergonomic pillows. "I hated *Willie Wonka.*"

He glanced at her across his shoulder. "How can any kid hate *Willie Wonka?*"

They moved farther into the store, past a couple with twins in a double stroller, and Clare asked, "Didn't you ever wonder why Grandpa Joe wouldn't get out of bed until Willie came home with the golden ticket?"

"No."

They stopped at the display of massagers. "For years he'd just laid there with the other grand-parents while Willie's mother worked to support them." She picked up a massager the size of a pen and set it back down. "Then Willie gets the ticket, and puff, Grandpa Joe's magically cured. He starts dancing around and can go to Wonka Land all spry and energetic."

"Once again, you overthink everything," Sebastian said, and picked up a massager with a bulbous blue head. "Like *most* kids, I just thought about all that candy." He grinned and held up the massager. "What does this remind you of?"

"I wouldn't know," she lied, and took it from his hands. She replaced it with one that had a big triangular head and couldn't be mistaken for anything else.

"What was your favorite movie?" he asked as he flipped the switch and rubbed it across the back of her pink fleece jacket.

"Ahh." She shivered and her voice rattled a little as she spoke. "I have several. When I was little, my favorite movie was *Cinderella*. The old Rodgers and Hammerstein television version. When I was in junior high, I loved *Pretty in Pink* and *Sixteen Candles*."

"*Pretty in Pink?* Is that one of those Molly Ringwald movies?"

"Don't tell me you've never seen it?"

"Hell no." He flipped the Off switch and picked up a massage belt. "I'm a guy. We don't watch movies like that unless there's something in it for us."

"Sex."

He grinned. "Or at least second base."

She laughed and turned toward a massage chair. Her laughter died and shock lifted her brows as she came face-to-face with her past.

"Hello, Clare."

"Lonny." He was as handsome and as groomed as she remembered. By his side stood a blonde about his same height.

"How are you doing?" he asked.

"Fine." And she was. Seeing him again, she felt nothing. Not a racing heart nor a killing rage.

"This is my fiancée, Beth. Beth, this is Clare."

Fiancée? That was fast. She turned her attention to the other woman. "It's nice to meet you, Beth." She held out her hand to the woman who obviously believed Lonny loved her as a man could love a woman. Only he wasn't capable of that kind of love.

"You too." Her fingers barely touched Clare's before she dropped her hand. The woman was in denial. As deep as she had once been, wanting to believe in something so bad, and refusing to see the reality that was staring her in the face. She supposed the right thing to do would be to let Beth in on the secret life of her fiancé, but it really wasn't her job to disillusion the delusional.

Before Clare could introduce Sebastian, he

stepped forward and offered his hand to Lonny. "I'm Clare's friend, Sebastian Vaughan."

Clare's friend. She looked over her right shoulder at Sebastian, at the reality staring right at *her*. After all these months. She was no more than a friend to him. Her chest imploded right there in Brookstone, next to all those bulbous massagers, for Lonny and Beth and the lady with twins to see. She was no better than Beth. No different from the day she had found Lonny in that closet, literally and figuratively. She thought she'd changed. Grown. Learned. She was as delusional as ever. She wanted to crawl away. Crawl away and fold in on herself.

Through a haze, she made small talk for several more minutes before Lonny and Beth walked away. She stood beside Sebastian as he bought the massage belt for Leo. He didn't see that she was falling apart. When they left the mall, passing all those people, no one seemed to notice that she was dying inside.

On the drive home he talked about his ski trip and mentioned that he was thinking about taking Leo fishing in Alaska for salmon. It wasn't until they pulled into her mother's driveway that Clare finally looked over at the man who was no more capable of loving her than Lonny.

"What's wrong?" he asked as he stopped in front

of the garage. "You've been quiet since we ran into your old boyfriend. You're better off without him, by the way."

She looked into Sebastian's eyes. Into the eyes of the man she loved with all of her heart. The eyes of the man who did not love her. She didn't want to cry, not now, but she could feel the tears scalding the inside of her chest. "Are we friends?"

"Of course."

"Is that all?"

He turned off the ignition. "No. That's not all. I like you, and we get along really well. We have great sex."

That wasn't love. "You like me?"

He shrugged and put the keys in the pocket of his black fleece jacket. "Yeah. Of course I like you."

"That's it?"

He must have started to figure out where the conversation was headed. Weariness entered his green eyes as he looked over at her. "What more do you want?"

That he asked just proved the awful truth. "Nothing you can give," she said, and opened the car door. She shut it behind her and headed across the lawn toward the back of her mother's house. If she could just be alone, locked up by herself, before she fell apart. She made it as far as the dormant garden before Sebastian grabbed her arm.

"What's wrong with you?" he asked as he swung her around to face him. "Are you all freaked out because your old boyfriend is engaged?"

"This has nothing to do with Lonny." A cool breeze tugged at her hair, and she pushed it behind one ear. "Although seeing him again forced me to see how things are between us. How they'll always be."

"What the hell are you talking about?"

"I don't want to be your friend. That isn't enough for me anymore."

He took a step back and dropped his hand. "This is sudden."

"I want more."

His gaze narrowed. "Don't."

"Don't what? Want more?"

"Don't ruin everything by talking about relationships and commitment."

Not only was her heart devastated, now he was making her really angry. So angry she had an urge to curl up her fist and sock him. "What's wrong with wanting a relationship and a commitment? It's healthy. Natural. Normal."

He shook his head. "No. It's bullshit. Meaningless, pointless bullshit. Sooner or later someone gets pissed, then the fighting starts." He rubbed his face with his hands. "Clare, we get along great. I like being with you. Leave it at that."

"I can't."

His eyes narrowed further. "Why the fuck not?"

"Because you like me and I love you." Her throat hurt from suppressed emotion. "This is no longer just a friendship. Not for me, and it's not enough just to be *liked* by you. At one time in my life I would have settled for that, hoping for more. But not now. I deserve a man who loves me and wants a relationship. A man who loves me enough to want to spend the rest of his life with me. I don't need those things to survive, but I want them. I want it all. A husband and children and . . ." She swallowed hard. ". . . and a dog."

He set his jaw and folded his arms over his chest. "Why do women push and prod and make demands? Why can't you all just chill out about relationships?"

Lord, it was as she'd suspected. She'd made the same mistake other women had made in Sebastian's life. She'd fallen in love with him. "I'm thirty-four. My chill-out days are over. I want a man who wakes up in the morning wanting to be with me. I don't want to be with a man who blows into my life just when he wants sex."

"It's more than just sex." He pointed at her as a

cool breeze played with the open zipper of his jacket. "And you're the one who said that we're just friends with benefits. Now you want to change everything. Why can't you just leave things alone?"

"Because I love you and that changes everything."

"Love," he scoffed. "What do you expect from me? Am I supposed to change who I am and fit my life to suit yours because you suddenly think you love me?"

"No. I know you can't change who you are, which is why you're the last person I wanted to fall in love with. But I thought I could handle being just friends. I thought it would be good enough for me, but it's not." Her voice wavered as she looked up into the closed angry face of the man she loved. "I can't see you anymore, Sebastian."

He held up a hand as he if meant to reach for her, but dropped it to his side. "Don't do this, Clare. If you walk away, I won't come after you."

Yes. She knew that, and the pain of knowing was more than she could bear. "I love you, but being with you hurts too much. I'm not going to wait around hoping your feelings will change. If you don't love me now, you never will."

He laughed, bitter and harsh and without a hint of humor. "Are you psychic now?"

"Sebastian, you're thirty-five years old and you've

never had a serious relationship. I don't have to be psychic to know that I am just one in a long line of women in your life. I don't have to be psychic to know you've never really been in love. The heart-pounding, steal-your-breath, crazy for one woman kind of love."

He frowned and tilted his head back as he looked down at her. "You're starting to believe your own romance novels. You have a real distorted view of men."

Her eyes filled with stinging tears. "My view of you is quite clear. I can't commit any more of my life to a man who can't commit to where he'll be tomorrow, let alone commit to being with me. I want more." She turned and moved away while she was still able to walk.

"Good luck with that," he said, stomping on her already crushed heart.

Nineteen

Sebastian walked into the carriage house feeling as if he'd been blind-sided with a two-by-four. What the hell had just happened? One moment everything had been just fine, and then Clare had started talking about feelings and commitment and love. Where had all that come from? One moment he'd been thinking about how great everything was between them, and in the next, she said she didn't want to see him anymore.

"What the fuck?"

His father turned from where he stood looking out the window at the Wingate backyard. "What was that about?"

Sebastian set the Brookstone sack on the sofa. "I got you a massager for your back."

"Thank you. You didn't have to do that."

"I wanted to."

Leo turned from the window. "Why is Clare upset?"

He looked into his father's eyes and shrugged. "I don't know."

"I might be old, but I'm not senile. I know that you two have been seeing each other."

"Well, it's over." Even though he said it, he still couldn't wrap his brain around it.

"She's such a nice sweet girl. I hate to see her upset."

"That's bullshit! She's not a nice sweet girl," he exploded. "I'm your son, and it doesn't seem to matter to you at all that I might be 'upset.'"

Leo's bushy brows lowered. "Of course it matters. I just thought you were the one to . . . put an end to things."

"No."

"Oh."

Sebastian sat on the couch and covered his face with his hands when what he really felt like doing was ramming his head through a wall. "Everything was great, perfect, and then just like a woman, she had to fuck it up."

Leo removed the paper sack and sat beside him. "What happened?"

Sebastian dropped his hand to his lap. "I wish I knew. We were having a good time. Then she sees her old boyfriend, and the next thing I know, she's telling me she wants more." He took a deep breath and let it out. He still absolutely could not believe what had just happened. "She told me that she loves me."

"What did you say?"

"I don't know. It was a real shock and just hit me right out of nowhere." He turned and looked at his father and realized that this was only the second time the two of them were talking about something besides fishing and cars and the weather. The first time since he'd dropped the globe at his mother's house. He frowned. "I think I said that I like her." Which was true. He liked her more than any woman he could recall being with.

"Ouch." Leo winced.

"What's wrong with that? I do like her." He liked everything about her. He liked to put his hand in the small of her back when they walked into a room. He liked the smell of her neck and the sound of her laugher. He even liked that everyone thought she was a sweet girl and he alone knew her wicked thoughts. And what did he get for liking her? She'd kicked him in the chest.

"I'm afraid your mother and I weren't very good examples of love and marriage and relationships."

"That's true." But as much as he'd like to blame his life on his parents, he was almost thirty-six, and there was something pathetic about a man his age blaming his commitment problems on his mother and father. *Commitment problems?* Women in his past had told him he had commitment problems, but he'd never thought it was true. He'd never thought he had a problem committing to anything. It took a lot of dedication and commitment to chase down stories and get them in print. But of course that wasn't the same thing. Women were a hell of a lot tougher to figure out.

"I thought I made her happy," he said, and felt a weight settle in his chest. "Why couldn't she just leave it alone? Why do women have to change things?"

"Because they're women. That's what they do." Leo shrugged his shoulders. "I'm an old man and I've never figured them out."

The doorbell rang, and Leo's knee cracked as he carefully pushed himself off the couch. "I'll be right back." He moved across the living room and opened the front door. Joyce's voice filled the entry of the carriage house.

"Claresta called a cab, then ran out the front door. Did something happen that I should know about?"

Leo shook his head. "Not that I know of."

"Did something happen between Clare and Sebastian?"

Sebastian half expected his father to spill the sordid details, and that he'd once again be banished from Joyce Land.

"I wouldn't know," Leo said. "But if it did, the two kids are adults and they'll work it out."

"I just don't think I can have Sebastian upsetting her."

"Did Clare tell you Sebastian upset her?"

"No, but she never tells me what's going on in her life."

"I don't have anything to tell you either."

Joyce sighed. "Well, if you hear anything, let me know."

"Will do."

Sebastian stood as his father reentered the room. He felt restless, like he was going to come apart. He had to get out of there. He had to put distance between himself and Clare. "I'm going home," he said.

Surprise stopped Leo in his tracks. "Now?"

"Yeah."

"It's kind of late to set out for Seattle. Why don't you wait until morning?"

Sebastian shook his head. "If I get tired, I'll stop." But he sincerely doubted he'd get tired. He was too pissed off. He'd only unloaded one duffel from his car, and now he walked into his bedroom and grabbed it. Within twenty minutes he was headed north on I-84.

He drove straight through. Six and a half hours of nothing but asphalt and anger. She said she loved him. Well, that had been news to him. The last time he'd checked, she wanted to be friends. In January she'd specifically told him that if he wanted to see other women, to just let her know. Like she'd be real cool with that. The funny thing was, he hadn't even considered it. Not once. Now all of a sudden she wanted more.

She *loved* him. Love. Love came with strings. It was never just given. There were always things attached to love. Commitment. Expectations. Change.

For some six and a half hours he went around and around, over and over and every other which way in his head. Thoughts tumbled and fell, and by the time he walked into his condo, he was exhausted. He fell into bed and slept for twelve hours. When he woke, he was no longer tired, but he was still angry.

He threw on a pair of sweat pants and worked out on the weight machine in his spare bedroom. He burned off some of the angry energy but couldn't exercise Clare out of his head. After taking a shower, he went into his office and turned on his computer in an attempt to fill his mind with work. Instead he recalled the time she'd come into his office wearing that blue nightgown.

After an hour of futile typing, Sebastian called a few buddies and met them at a bar not far from his condo. They drank beer, shot pool, and talked baseball. Several women in the bar flirted with him, but he wasn't interested. He was pissed off at all women in general, and smart, attractive women on principle.

He'd been shitty company, had a shitty time, and had behaved like an overall shithead. His life was shit, and it was all the fault of a certain romance writer who believed in love and heroes and happily ever after.

Over the course of the next week, Sebastian went out very little. Just to the grocery store to buy some bread, sandwich meat, and beer. When his father called, they talked about everything but Clare. By tacit agreement, they avoided the subject of his employer's daughter. But that did not mean he wasn't thinking of her every waking moment.

Nine days after he'd jumped in his SUV and driven—insane and angry—from Boise to Seattle, he stood in his living room looking out at the ships and ferries in Elliott Bay. He didn't like personal change. Especially when he didn't see it coming and couldn't seem to do anything about it. Change felt helpless. It meant starting over.

He thought of Clare and the night he'd found her on a bar stool in a pink fluffy dress. That night he'd put her to bed, and in the morning his life had been changed. He hadn't known it at the time, but she'd come into his life and changed it forever.

Regardless of what he liked or disliked, wanted or didn't want, his life had changed. *He* was changed. He felt it in the hollow place in his chest and in the hunger in his stomach that had nothing to do with food. He felt it in the way he looked out at the city he loved, yet wanted to be somewhere else.

He loved Seattle. Except for the few first years of his life, he'd always lived in Washington. His mother was buried here. He loved the water and drama and pulse of the city. He loved taking in a Mariners or Seahawks game if he felt like it, and he loved the view of Mount Rainier from the windows of his condo. He'd worked his ass off for that view.

He had friends in Washington. Good friends he'd made over a lifetime. This was where he lived, but it no longer felt like home. He belonged four hundred miles away, with the woman who loved him. The woman he liked to spend all his free time with, who was his favorite person to talk to.

Sebastian lowered his gaze to the street below. He more than liked Clare. There was no use fighting it. It was futile, and he recognized the truth of something when it hit him over the head enough times. He loved the way she laughed and the color she painted her toenails. He didn't love all that girly girl lace she had around her house, but he loved that she was a girly girl. He loved her, and she loved him. For once in his life a woman's love didn't feel like something he needed to run from any longer.

He turned and pressed his back against the window. He loved her. He loved her, and he'd hurt her. He remembered the look on her face as she'd turned away, and he didn't think he could just pick up the phone and say, "Hey, Clare. I've been thinking about it, and I love you."

Instead he picked up the phone and called his dad. Not that Leo was an expert when it came to women and love, but he might know what to do.

Clare rummaged around in her mother's attic for a bed canopy. She'd been all over town in search of one she liked, but she hadn't found it. There had to be something suitable in the stacks of bed linens in the Wingate attic.

The day after she told Sebastian that she couldn't see him any longer, she'd taken down her Battenberg lace. He'd hated it, and it reminded her too much of him. She just couldn't look up at it every night when she went to bed.

It had been three weeks since that day in the mall when she'd run into Lonny and realized that she had once again fallen in love with a man who was incapable of loving her back. And this time she couldn't even say it was because she'd been lied to. Sebastian had never loved her, and she'd known that going in. She just hadn't known she would fall in love with him.

After the fallout in her mother's backyard, she'd gone home and crawled into bed for three days, overdosing on John Hughes and Merchant-Ivory flicks until her friends had staged an intervention.

The good news was, she hadn't reached for a bottle or a warm body to make herself feel better. She hadn't even wanted to. The bad news was that she didn't think she was ever going to get over the heartache of loving Sebastian Vaughan. It went too deep in her soul. Was too tangled around her heart.

Clare opened an old wardrobe and searched through her ancestor's linens. It was all very lacy and girly, and after an hour of looking and finding nothing, she moved out of the attic and down the old curving staircase. A voice from the kitchen stopped her at the bottom of the steps. Stopped her and shattered her all at once.

"Where's Clare?"

"Sebastian? When did you get here?" Joyce asked.

"Clare's car's outside. Where *is* she?"

"Goodness! She's in the attic looking at lace."

Heavy footfalls moved across the tile and the hardwood floors and Clare's hand shook. She'd been told he wasn't expected. As she turned, he walked into the entry and her grasp tightened on the banister. Her chest got that imploding feeling again, just as strong as the day she'd stood in Brookstone dying inside.

Sebastian walked across the foyer as if the devil were on his heels, and before she could even think to move, he was in front of her, his green gaze intense as he stared down into her face. He was so close, the open edges of her black cardigan touched the front of his blue dress shirt.

"Clare," he said. One word that sounded a lot like a caress, then he lowered his mouth and kissed her.

For several stunned seconds she let him. Let her soul remember. Let it pour through her and warm up the lonely places only he could touch. Her heart seemed to weep and rejoice at the same time, but before he could take any more from her, she lifted her hands and pushed him away.

"You look so good to me," he whispered as he ran his gaze across her face. "I feel alive for the first time in weeks."

And he was killing her. All over again. She looked away before her love for him swamped her and she started to cry. "What are you doing?" she asked.

"The last time I saw you, I told you that if you walked away, I wouldn't come after you. But here I am." With the warm fingers of one hand, he brought her gaze back to his. "I'm going to turn thirty-six in two months, and I'm in love for the first time in my life. Since you're the woman I love, I thought you should know."

She felt everything inside her go real still. "What?"

"I'm in love with you."

She shook her head. He had to be teasing her.

"It's true. The heart-pounding, steal-your-breath, crazy-for-one-woman kind of love."

She didn't trust him. "Maybe you just think you're in love and you'll get over it."

Now it was his turn to shake his head. "I've spent my life waiting to feel something bigger and stronger than myself. Something I couldn't fight or walk away from or control. I've waited all my life . . ." His voice shook, and he paused to take a breath. "I've been waiting my whole life for you, Clare. I love you, and don't tell me I don't."

Clare blinked back the sudden sting in her eyes. That was the most beautiful thing anyone had ever said to her. Better than she could make up herself. "You better not be trying to trick me."

"No tricks. I love you, Clare. I love you and I want to spend my life with you. I even watched *Pretty in Pink*."

"Really?"

"Yes, and I hated every minute of it." He took her hand. "But I love you, and if it makes you happy, I'll watch teen flicks with you."

"You don't have to watch teen flicks with me."

"Thank God." He lifted his free hand and brushed her hair behind her ear. "I got you something, but it's out in the car. I didn't think Joyce would let it in the house."

"What?"

"You said you wanted a husband and children and a dog. So, I'm here with one very carsick Yorkshire terrier puppy and a willingness to work on the kids part."

Once again he'd looked into her lonely heart and given her what she'd wanted. Plus a dog. "I don't have anything to give you."

"I just want you. For the first time in a long time, I feel like I'm exactly where I'm supposed to be."

The tears she wasn't even going to try to hide spilled over the bottom of her lashes. She rose on her toes and wrapped her arms around his neck. "I love you."

"Don't cry. I hate crying."

"I know. And shopping. And asking for directions."

He wrapped his arms around her and squeezed tight. "I sold my condo and I don't have a place to live. That's what took me so long to get here once I decided where I needed to be."

"You're homeless?" she asked into the side of his neck.

"No. My home is with you." He pressed a kiss to her temple. "I never understood when my mother used to say that she'd finally found her home. I didn't understand how one place could feel any different from another. I do now. You are my home and I don't ever want to leave."

"Okay."

"Clare." He pulled back and held up a ring. A princess-cut, four-carat diamond.

"Oh my God!" she gasped. She looked from the ring to his face.

"Marry me. Please."

Emotion clogged her throat and she nodded. She was a romance writer, but she couldn't think of one romantic thing to say besides, "I love you."

"Is that a yes?"

"Yes."

He let out a pent-up breath as if there had ever been any doubt. "There's one more thing," he said as he slid the ring onto her finger. "I have an ulterior motive for buying the dog."

The ring was the most beautiful thing she'd ever seen. She looked up into his face and amended that to the second most beautiful thing. "Of course you do." She wiped beneath her eyes. "What is it?"

"In exchange for the girly wussy dog," he said, humor lifting the corners of his mouth, "no girly wussy lace on the bed."

Since she'd already put away her lace bedding, that was an easy compromise. "Anything for you." She rose on the balls of her feet and kissed Sebastian Vaughan. He was her lover, friend, and very own romantic hero, proving that sometimes a girl's worst nightmare turned into her happily ever after.

Epilogue

Clare poured a cup of coffee and looked out the back screen door into her yard. Sebastian stood in the middle of the lawn wearing nothing but a pair of beige cargo pants. The morning sun bathed his chest and face in gold as he pointed across the yard.

"Get your job done," he said to the Yorkshire terrier sitting on his bare foot. The dog, Westley—named after the hero in *The Princess Bride*—stood and walked on short little legs to plop down on Sebastian's other foot.

Westley loved Sebastian. Followed him around and worshiped him. For his devotion, most often than not, he got called Wusstley. But when Sebastian thought no one else was around, he scratched the dog's small belly and told him he was a "little stud."

Sebastian had moved into Clare's house two months ago, and within a week antique pieces had moved out. Which was fine with Clare. His sofa and chairs were more comfortable than hers, and she didn't have a serious attachment to her great-great-grandfather's gout footstool. The cherub pedestal was staying, though.

"Come on now," Sebastian said as he looked down at Westley. "We can't go back inside until you get busy."

In May they'd stuck a For Sale sign in the front yard, and hoped to have the house sold by the time they married in September. Finding a new home was proving more difficult than planning a wedding. Melding both their tastes wasn't easy, but they were determined to compromise and work it out.

Lucy, Maddie, and Adele were happy for Clare and thrilled to be her bridesmaids, although Adele and Maddie had made her promise that there would be no tulle this time.

Sebastian walked several feet across the yard, and Westley followed close behind. He pointed to the ground. "This is a good spot." Westley looked up, barked as if he agreed, then sat on Sebastian's foot.

Clare smiled and raised the coffee mug to her

lips. She'd met her friends for lunch just the day before. Lucy was still thinking about starting a family. Dwayne was still leaving random stuff on Adele's porch, and Maddie was still planning on spending the summer at her cabin in Truly. But as they'd left the restaurant, Maddie had given a hint that perhaps something was unusual. Well, unusual for Maddie. With a strange look on her face, she said, "Digging into other people's sordid pasts is a whole lot easier than digging into your own."

There were things in Maddie's life. Dark secrets she'd never shared. If and when she did, her friends would be there to listen.

Clare opened the screen door and walked out into the sunlight. "I see you've just about gotten that dog whipped into shape," she said.

Sebastian put his hands on his hips and looked up at her. "Your mutt is worthless."

She bent and scooped up the dog. "No, he's not. He's very good at barking at the mailman."

Sebastian took the mug from her and dropped his arm around her shoulders. "And imaginary cats." He took a drink of coffee, then said, "Dad and I are fishing Saturday. Wanna come along?"

"No thanks." She'd fished with the two of them once. Once was enough. Worms and fish guts were something they would never compromise on or work out.

One of the biggest surprises about Sebastian, besides his attempts at being romantic, was his relationship with her mother. He didn't take Joyce's frosty, dictatorial nature personally, nor did he take any crap from her, and the two got along wonderfully. Better than Clare would have ever imagined.

"Once the dog does his business, let's go take a shower." Sebastian handed her back the coffee and added, "I'm in the mood to get you soapy."

She set Westley on the ground and rose. "I *am* feeling a little dirty." She pressed her lips to his bare shoulder and smiled. He was always in the mood, which worked out beautifully because she was always in the mood for him.

Take a sneak peek at Rachel Gibson's
next, newest novel . . .

———————————————————

When Maddie Jones (and Rachel!)
return to Truly, Idaho,
trouble is bound to follow.

Coming 2007 from Avon Books

The glowing, white neon above Mort's Bar pulsed and vibrated and attracted the thirsty masses of Truly, Idaho, like a bug light. But Mort's was more than a beer magnet. More than just a place to drink cold Coors and get into a fight on Friday nights. Mort's had historical significance—kind of like the Alamo. While other establishments came and went in the small town, Mort's had always stayed the same.

Until about a year ago, when the new owner had spruced the place up with gallons of Lysol and paint and instituted a strict no panty-tossing policy. Before that, women throwing their undies like a ring toss up onto the row of antlers above the bar had been encouraged as a sort of indoor sporting event. Now, if a woman felt the urge to toss, she got tossed out on her bare ass.

Ah, the good old days.

Maddie Jones stood on the sidewalk in front of Mort's and stared up at the sign, completely immune to the subliminal lure that the light sent out through the impending darkness. An indistinguishable hum of voices and music leaked through the cracks in the old building sandwiched between Ace Hardware and the Panda restaurant.

A couple in jeans and tank tops brushed past Maddie. The door opened, and the sound of voices and the unmistakable twang of country music spilled out onto Main Street. The door closed and Maddie remained standing outside. She adjusted the purse strap on her shoulder, then pulled up the zipper on her bulky blue sweater. She hadn't lived in Truly for thirty years, and she'd forgotten how cool it got at night. Even in June.

Her hand lifted toward the old door, then dropped to her side. A surprising rush of apprehension raised the hairs on her arms beneath her sweater and tilted her stomach. She'd done this dozens of times. So why the apprehension? Why now?

Because, she answered herself, it was a lot easier to dig into other people's lives than it was her own, and once she opened that door, there was no going back.

If her friends could see her, standing there as if her feet were set in the concrete, they'd be shocked. She'd interviewed serial killers and cold-blooded murderers, for God's sake. Compared to interviewing nut jobs with antisocial personality disorders, this was going to be a piece of cake. No problem. A snap.

"Get a grip, Maddie," she muttered, reaching for the door and opening it. Her stomach fluttered, then settled, and her apprehension dissolved beneath a heavy dose of her strong will. Nothing was going to happen. Nothing was going to jump out from the shadows. There were no bogeymen . . . but just in case of trouble, she always carried an arsenal of personal safety items in her handbag.

The heavy thump of the jukebox and the smells of hops and tobacco assaulted her as she stopped just inside and let her eyes adjust to the dim light. Mort's was just a bar. Like a thousand others she'd been in across the country. Nothing special. Not even the array of antlers hanging above the long mahogany bar was anything out of the ordinary.

Maddie didn't like bars. Especially cowboy bars. The smoke, the music, the steady stream of beer. She didn't particularly care for cowboys, either. As far as she was concerned, a pair of snug Wranglers on a tight cowboy butt couldn't quite make up for the boots, the buckles, and the wads of chew. She liked her men in suits and Italian leather shoes. Not that she'd had a man, or even a date, in about four years.

She studied the crowd as she wove her way to the only empty stool in the middle of the long oak bar. Her gaze took in a mix of locals and those, like herself, who were in Truly for the summer. She noticed cowboy hats and trucker caps. Ponytails, shoulder-length bobs, a few crew cuts, and a mullet or two. What she didn't see was the one person she'd come searching for, although she didn't really expect to see him sitting at one of the tables.

She wedged herself onto the stool between a man in a blue T-shirt and a woman with over-processed hair. Behind the cash register and bottles of alcohol, a mirror ran the length of the bar. Two bartenders pulled beers and blended drinks. Neither was the owner of this fine establishment.

"That little gal was AC/DC, if you know what I mean," said the man on her left. The guy in question was about sixty, sported a battered trucker's hat and a beer belly the size of a pony keg. Through the mirror Maddie watched several men down the row nod, paying rapt attention to Beer-belly Guy.

One of the bartenders set a napkin in front of her and asked what she'd like to drink. He looked to be about nineteen, although she supposed he had to be at least twenty-one. Old enough to pour liquor within the hazy layers of tobacco smoke and knee-deep bullshit.

"Sapphire martini. Extra dry, three olives," she said, calculating the carbs in the olives. She pulled her purse into her lap and watched the bartender turn and reach for the good gin and vermouth.

"I told her she could keep her girlfriend, so long as she brought her over once in a while," the guy on her left added.

"Damn right!"

"That's what I'm talking about!"

Then again, this was small-town Idaho, where things like liquor laws were sometimes overlooked and some people considered a good bullshit story a form of literature.

Maddie rolled her eyes and bit her lip to keep her comments to herself. She had a habit of saying what she thought. She didn't necessarily consider it a *bad* habit, but not everyone appreciated it.

Through the mirror, her gaze moved up and down the bar, searching for the owner, not that she thought she'd find him plopped down on a stool any more than sitting at a table.

"I pay for everything," the woman on Maddie's opposite side wailed to her friend. "I even bought my own birthday card and had J. W. sign it, thinking he'd feel bad and get the hint."

"Oh, geez," Maddie couldn't help but mutter,

and looked at the woman through the mirror. Between bottles of Absolut and Skyy vodka, she could make out big, blonde hair and a long, thin face and nose.

"He didn't feel bad at all! Just complained that he didn't like mushy cards like the one I bought." She took a drink of something with an umbrella in it. "He wants me to come over when his mother goes out of town next weekend and make him dinner." She brushed moisture from beneath her eyes and sniffed. "I'm thinking of telling him no."

Maddie's brows drew together and a stunned, "Are you shitting me?" escaped her mouth before she knew she'd uttered a word.

"Excuse me?" the bartender asked as he set the drink in front of her.

She shook her head. "Nothing." She reached into her purse and paid for her drink as a song about a Honky Tonk Badonkadonk—whatever the hell that meant—thumped from the glowing neon jukebox and coalesced with the steady hum of conversation. It was Friday night and Mort's was jumping.

So where was the man who owned the place? She pulled back the sleeve of her sweater and reached for her martini. She read the glowing hands of her watch as she raised the glass to her lips. Nine o'clock. He might be at the other bar, but he was bound to show up sooner or later. If not tonight, there was always tomorrow. She took a sip, and the gin and vermouth warmed a path all the way to her stomach.

She really hoped he'd show up sooner rather than later, before she had too many martinis and forgot why she was sitting on a barstool eavesdropping on needy passive-aggressive women and delusional men. Not that listening in on people with lives more pathetic than hers couldn't be highly entertaining at times.

She set the glass back on the bar. Eavesdropping wasn't her first choice. She much preferred the straightforward approach: digging into people's lives and plumbing their dirty little secrets without distraction. Some people gave up their secrets without protest, eager to tell all. Others forced her to reach deep, rattle them loose, or rip them out by the roots. Her work was sometimes messy, always gritty, but she loved writing about serial killers, mass murders, and your everyday run-of-the mill psychopath.

Really, a girl had to excel at something, and Maddie, writing as Madeline DuPree, was one of the best true-crime writers in the genre. She wrote blood and gore about the sick and disturbed, and there were those who thought, her friends among them, that what she wrote warped her personality. She liked to think it added to her charm.

The truth was somewhere in the middle. The things she'd seen and written about did affect her. No matter the barrier she placed between her sanity and the people she interviewed and researched, their sickness sometimes seeped through the cracks, leaving behind a black tacky film that was hard as hell to scrub clean.

Her job made her see the world a little differently than those who'd never sat across from a serial killer while he got off on the retelling of his "work." But those same things also made her a strong woman who didn't take crap from anyone. Very little intimidated her, and she didn't have any illusions about mankind. In her head, she knew that most people were decent, that given the choice, they would do the right thing. But she also knew about the others, the fifteen percent who were only interested in their own warped pleasure.

And if there was one thing she knew as surely as she knew the sun would rise in the east and set in the west, it was that everyone had secrets. She had a few of her own. She just held hers closer to the vest than most people.

She raised the glass to her lips, and her gaze was drawn to the end of the bar. A door in the back opened and a man stepped from the alley and into the dark hall.

Maddie knew him. Knew him before he walked from the ominous shadows. Before the shadows slid up the wide chest and shoulders of his black T-shirt. Knew him before the light slipped across his chin and nose and shined in hair as black as the night from which he'd come.

He moved behind the bar, tying a red bar apron around his hips. She knew he was thirty-five, the same age as herself. She knew he was six-two, one hundred and ninety pounds, and that he'd been named after his father, Lochlan Michael Hennessy. He went by Mick, and also like his father, he was an obscenely good-looking man. The kind of good-looking that turned heads, stopped hearts, and gave women bad thoughts. Thoughts of hot mouths and hands and tangled sheets.

He had an older sister, Meg, and he owned two bars in town, Mort's and Hennessy's. The latter had been in his family longer than he'd been alive. Hennessy's was the bar where Maddie's mother had worked, where she'd met Loch Hennessy, and where she'd died.

As if he felt her gaze, he glanced up from the strings of the apron. His eyes met hers and Maddie choked on the gin that refused to go down her throat. From his driver's license, she knew his eyes were blue, but they were more a deep turquoise, and seeing them looking back at her was a shock.

She lowered her glass and raised a hand to her mouth.

He finished tying the strings and moved in front of her. "You going to live?" he chuckled, his deep voice cutting through the noise around them.

She swallowed and coughed one last time. "I believe so."

"Hey, Mick," the blond on the next stool called out.

"Hey, Darla. How're things?"

"Could be better."

"Isn't that always the case," he said. "Are you planning on behaving yourself?"

"You know me." Darla laughed and flipped her dried-out hair. "I always plan on it."

"Uh-huh," he said, then turned his attention back to Maddie. "I haven't seen you in here before. You just passing through?"

"No. I bought a house out on Red Squirrel Road."

"On the lake?"

"Yes," she answered, and by the way Darla was practically melting all over the bar, she had to wonder if Mick had inherited his father's charm along with his looks. From what Maddie had been able to gather, Loch Hennessy had charmed women out of their clothes with little more than a look in their direction. He'd certainly charmed her mother.

"Ah. You're here for the summer then?"

"Yes."

He tilted his head to one side and studied her face. His gaze slid from her eyes to her mouth, and for several heartbeats Maddie wondered if he recognized her. "What's your name Brown Eyes?"

"Maddie."

"Just Maddie?" He glanced back up, and it was clear he didn't connect her with the past.

"Madeline . . . DuPree," she answered, using her pen name.

Someone down the bar called his name and he looked away for a moment before returning his attention to her. He gave her an easy smile and a dimple dented his right cheek. "Welcome to Truly, Maddie DuPree. Maybe I'll see you around."

She watched him walk away without telling him the reason she was in town and why she was sitting in Mort's. Now wasn't the best time or place, but there was no "maybe" about it. He didn't know it yet, but Mick Hennessy would be seeing a lot of her. Next time he might not be so welcoming.